About The Author

Andrea Jutson is a writer from Auckland, New Zealand. She has written two crime novels featuring reticent medium James Paxton, the first is *Senseless*, and is at work on a third. In her career, Andrea has been a bookseller, journalist, collections librarian, book buyer and journalist again, and once spent almost a year selling tickets at a heritage site in London. She now works at a public relations agency, and lives in South Auckland.

ISBN 9781911266969

Williams & Whiting (Publishers)

15 Chestnut Grove, Hurstpierpoint,

West Sussex, BN6 9SS

Also by Andrea Jutson from Williams & Whiting

Senseless

For information about this

and other books

published by Williams & Whiting

go to : www.williamsandwhiting.com

THE DARKNESS LOOKING BACK

LOOKING BACK

ANDREA JUTSON

Williams and Whiting

Prologue

IT DIDN'T MATTER how many times he did this. The smell still got him, stirring up chemical reactions in his body. Only three weeks on the job, and already he couldn't work out how many pizzas he'd delivered. His stomach made a noise like a half-clogged sink emptying. Felt like it too. The clock on the dash read a quarter past eight and he hadn't stopped yet.

Before long, they told him, he'd never look at another pizza with the eyes of desire again. In the meantime, the smell was filling the car. Nav had been the first to start with the wisecracks last time he'd given them a lift.

'Newmarket, my good man — and a large fries.'

'You using deodorant or something now, Haresh? Smells better in here . . .'

They'd almost pissed themselves. Idiots. But it was pretty potent in here. There went his stomach again. There was more of a truck engine-braking about it this time. When he got back he was damn well *insisting* he got a break.

This was the street now. He squinted into the darkness, trying to make out the letterboxes as he crept by. A sports model Honda Integra turned the corner behind him, driving right up his arse.

'Dick,' Haresh muttered, as it swerved round him on the wrong side of the road before he'd even had a chance to move over. The Integra's engine roared as it hooned off, making up for the two lost seconds. Its headlights picked out the brass numbers on a brick letterbox on the corner. At least now Haresh knew where he was. Right side of the street, about twenty houses out. He accelerated briefly past a few driveways, then did the crawl-past again. Ah, this was better. Seventy-three . . . seventy-five . . . seventy-seven . . . seventy-nine. He pulled into a drive behind a dark blue Audi and yanked up the handbrake.

He got out and dragged the delivery bags over the seat, then straightened, slamming the door with his hip. A largish house, well looked after from what he could tell in this darkness. It had those olden style windows with the dozens of tiny panes separated into sections — was that lead-lighting, or was that something else? — and mature trees spread all over the front lawn. Even the standalone garage had plastered walls and a tiled roof. Nice place, but then they mostly were in this area. Haresh would never be able to afford Epsom if he lived at home till he was forty and banked every dollar he earned. You could buy two decent houses in South Auckland for the price of one like this, and still have spare change.

Nice wheel trims on the Audi. Busy admiring them as he skirted the car, he wasn't expecting the sensor lights. He almost tripped on the uneven cobbles, startled into immobility. Mentally cursing himself, Haresh climbed the porch steps and stuck the drink down on the mat, freeing up a hand for the doorbell. Then he paused.

The door was open.

Haresh frowned. Just went to show money didn't buy sense.

He let his arm drop. Something made him uneasy. The warm light trickling through the crack of the open door,

2

hanging open as if forgotten, and the silence. They didn't always hear his car in the drive . . . but still. Haresh put his finger on the bell. He heard the chime inside the house. But no footsteps. He stood there for at least thirty seconds, but there was no response. He felt himself getting pissed off, and creeped out. What were they doing, having a shower before dinner? One of the guys at work told all the newbies about the best night of his career — the time a woman turned up at the door wearing nothing but a towel around her head. She'd asked for, and received, a sizeable discount.

But there was no sound of water running. No sound at all.

Haresh shifted uncomfortably on the step. He knew he hadn't got the wrong address. He checked very thoroughly, always. As he rapped loudly on the solid wood door, calling, it swung open a little further. The hall lights were off, but there was light coming from the front room. Still no sound.

He stepped through the door.

'Pizza!' He almost jumped at the sound of his own voice. It sounded unbelievably lame even to his own ears. *Good one, Haresh*.

He glanced quickly over his shoulder, then stared at the far end of the hall, but his eyes were dazzled by the crack of light ahead, and all he could see was darkness. He pressed the pizza box close to his chest, as if its warmth could reassure him, ready to fling it at anything that came out of that door.

He took a deep breath and yelled again, making as much noise as he could. Driving the monsters away. The time for politeness was long past.

Almost there now. Haresh stepped into the glow of light from the other room. Two steps further, that was all.

Now one.

Chapter ONE

THE DRIVEWAY WAS full when Stirling got there, so he parked on the road.

'Someone'll be pissed off about that verge,' Detective Rees said by way of greeting. A marked incident car was skewed with two wheels over the kerb. Its tyres had ploughed out deep furrows in the mud, soft from the morning's humidity showers.

'Somehow I think that'll be the least of their worries,' Stirling replied. His eyes rested on the ambulance backed up to the foot of the drive.

His passenger door slammed shut as Detective Sergeant Vicky Nielsen leapt clumsily from the kerb to the footpath, avoiding the sodden grass. 'What do you know, Tony?'

'No more than you yet,' said Rees. 'We just got here ourselves.'

Standing beside him, or more accurately, below him, were a couple more detectives. The fair, imperturbable Rees cast everyone in shadow.

'Let's take a look then,' said Nielsen. She ducked back into the car and pulled out the white paper suits they all had to wear, complete with shower caps. Kitted up, Stirling always felt like a Hazmat man going into a nuclear zone, though the suits were to protect the scene from *them*. Stirling got into line, following Nielsen up the drive with the others. He got a private buzz out of watching Rees obediently fall in behind her. Vicky Nielsen barely came halfway up his chest. Stirling didn't know her well, but, in his own private moments, he had to admit to being a bit in awe of the detective sergeant for whom anal was more than a personality type — it was probably a middle name. Her dark blonde, almost brown, head was bathed in harsh white light as she neared the porch. A silent crowd of people was already waiting. Stirling immediately picked the one who'd made the callout — a young Indian guy, or possibly Sri Lankan, standing off to one side, just beyond the circle of the light. Stirling could only see his eyes, and sympathised with what he saw.

A uniformed constable descended the steps towards them, recording their names and checking his watch.

'She's in the living room. First door on the right.'

'You been in there?' Nielsen asked.

The constable shook his head. 'Haven't touched anything. No need to, by the sounds of it.' He didn't seem sorry to stay on the porch.

St John Ambulance waited on the step above him, a man and a woman, their arms folded. As the police passed them, the male paramedic shook his head. 'All yours,' he said. The gesture told them everything.

Nielsen handed one suit to Rees, the other to Stirling. Rees led the way, unrolling a coil of plastic matting for them to walk on. Stirling's nostrils caught the metallic slaughterhouse scent of blood as soon as he stepped through the door. And something else. He sniffed, frowning.

'Smells like pizza.'

'Yep. Guy who phoned in was the deliveryman,' said the uniform behind him. At Nielsen's feet lay a black pizza

6

delivery bag, visible in the light from a room to their right. The heady smell of salami and onions and blood turned Stirling's stomach. Trying to ignore it, he automatically watched the floor, checking for signs of blood, of struggle or passage. There were none that he could see.

'What's this light doing on? Was it on when you got here?' Nielsen asked the constable.

'Yeah. Door was open too, apparently. That's what the delivery bloke said.' His eyes went back to the light like twin moths. 'Be prepared for when you go in. You can smell it from here.'

The living room had high ceilings and light-papered walls, with a forest green plush sofa and chairs, a flat-screen TV and DVD player, and a large stain spreading red from beneath the woman on the floor. Their footsteps squelched, even through the matting. *The red carpet treatment*, thought Stirling, then felt sick at himself.

All three of them took a moment, getting their senses back under control before going on. Her face was battered beyond recognition. In place of nose and lips and eyes was a mask of congealing blood, which streamed down her neck and soaked her clothes and everything around her. Were it not for that long hair, stiffening like brush bristles in hardening paint, it would have been difficult to identify the head as a woman's at all. Looking almost unnecessary and out of place, a bread knife stuck out of her chest. That was the most disturbing part of all. Whoever killed her had wanted to make extra sure she didn't get up again.

For some reason Stirling's eyes were drawn to her feet. Party shoes — silver, strappy high heels, decorated with fake crystals that were now splashed with blood. The toenails were a matching silver pink. This was a woman ready for a night out. He glanced away, seeing Rees staring too.

The big man's face showed the same revulsion, but to his credit he didn't turn away. Stirling had once heard a story, which he believed, about when Rees had arrived from South Africa at the age of eight. Staying in a hotel while his parents searched for a house, young Rees entertained himself by going from room to room, knocking and asking to be shown round to see if theirs was different. There was a natural curiosity in the man that never let up.

Stirling took several slow breaths through his mouth, trying not to inhale the unavoidable stench of death and takeaways, but he could still taste them on his tongue. He looked up as the tread of boots on the threshold signalled the arrival of the SOCOs. Nielsen glanced at him, her features sharp.

'Andy, see how the others are getting on with the witness. I want them out door knocking. Who are these people? Did anyone see anything? All right?' Her face turned to the wall, behind which a flight of stairs led up to the first floor, then she gave him a look that Stirling understood. 'And send someone to check the rest of the house, just in case.'

Nodding, Stirling went back outside with a trace of relief, squeezing through the press of newcomers in the hall. He pulled off his paper shoes, which weren't white any more. He stepped around the paramedics conferring with the pathologist on the porch, and spotted the deliveryman talking to one of the other detectives. The young man was tall and rail-thin, like a gangly adolescent. He was clutching a mobile. He turned slightly, and the penny dropped. He was all in black, the uniform of Hell Pizza. Stirling could almost hear the smart comments tomorrow morning: the deliveryman from Hell.

'What's up, Andy?'

Detective Constable Sean Coleman came up at his elbow, pulling his thoughts back into line.

'Sarge wants some door knocking. Something funny going on here. Big house, but she's the only one here. Any volunteers to check the house for next of kin?'

'I'll do it,' said Coleman, who was new and eager.

'Don't forget the fridge,' said Detective Ciaran Paynter.

Paynter was the sort of bloke who went to everyone's barbecues, fond of a drink and his own jokes. The rest of them grinned, enjoying the younger man's reaction. 'Funny places we've found some of them . . . Eh, Martin?'

'What?' The police photographer paused as he walked past them, already looking weary. 'Long as they're all in one piece, that's all I ask . . .' He disappeared into the house.

Coleman was trying to ignore the grinning detectives. Stirling broke the mood. He'd been there himself, not too long ago. 'Right,' he said, jerking his head towards the uniform. 'Get down to the end of the driveway — you'll control the scene better from there. If the deliveryman's talked to people they might be wanting to check it out.'

He glanced at the young Indian man standing off to one side, oblivious to the exchange. His head was bowed over his phone and he was talking into it in what Stirling guessed to be Hindi. The display glowed green in the darkness.

The constable nodded, a bit stiffly, then trudged off to stare at the road.

'And get your car off the verge before it's stuck there,' Stirling called after him.

An indistinct reply filtered back. 'Dave's got the keys.'

Stirling exchanged glances with Coleman, who rolled his eyes. 'Jesus . . .'

Coleman followed the man down the drive to fetch a suit. When Stirling turned back, the deliveryman was watching him. Stirling stuck out a hand.

'Hi, I'm Detective Constable Stirling.'

'My name's Haresh,' said the kid, slipping his phone into his pocket and shaking hands. 'Haresh Prasad.'

'Where are you from?' Stirling asked. 'India?'

'Yeah. Bangalore. We came out here about six years ago.'

Stirling glanced at his pocket, friendly. 'Was that your parents you were talking to?'

Prasad looked sheepish. 'My mum. She was worried. They wanted to come round here.'

'And are they?'

'No. I told her I'd be all right.'

'Well, that's good to hear. Can be a bit of a shock, something like that . . .'

The boy shook his head unhappily. 'I knew there was something wrong the moment I saw the door was open. It just . . . felt wrong,' he repeated lamely.

Stirling was halfway through a nod when it hit him. Another man from another country, dressed in black, being drawn to a body on his way home from work . . . Instead of nodding, he found himself shaking his head.

'PHEW! IS IT always this hot in Auckland?'

Paxton lay back on the deck, boneless with exhaustion, his head slumping against the cooler planks in the shade. 'This air is like breathing in soup. How can you stand it?'

'Beats the kind of damp you get back home.' Lena took another swig of her lime juice, the ice tinkling merrily in her glass.

'I'm melting like a Swiss chocolate! Look!' He held his arms aloft for inspection, spreadeagling himself in the shade. Sweat stippled his pale skin like an outbreak of hives.

'Harden up.' Lena gazed at him over her glass. 'And I'd say it's more like crisping than melting . . .'

'Shit.' The twinkle in Paxton's eye vanished. 'Are you kidding?'

Lena mutely shook her head, her own blue eyes laughing.

'But I was only out in the sun for, like, fifteen minutes.' He sat up and huffed in disgust, cautiously fingering his nose. 'I'm cursed. I can get sunburnt walking from my car to the front door.'

Lena opened her mouth to reply, then cocked her head. Then Paxton heard it too. The phone was ringing inside the house. Lena picked up her glass, retreating through the French doors. Paxton let his muscles relax again, idly watching the shadows dancing near his head, thrown by the trees beside the deck. Invisible cicadas scritched from somewhere in the garden, mingling with the faint murmur of Lena's voice on the other side of the wall.

Lena had moved back home to her father's place in September, figuring it would at least save her rent while she decided what to do with it. It couldn't be said that she lacked the space to think. The house had four bedrooms over two storeys.

It had felt strange, her moving back. Taking over a house that used to be her father's, and shouldn't have been hers for many years yet. She slept in her old room, not the master bedroom, and though she'd sold off a bit of furniture already, she couldn't bring herself to set up the lounge suite and various other pieces she'd brought from the rental in Glendowie. They wouldn't have looked right. For the time being they sat uselessly, covered in sheets, in a spare bedroom. Mark Bradley was dead, but he wasn't gone, as Paxton knew better than anyone.

'James!' The sound of his own name brought Paxton out of his reverie. A little drowsily he grabbed his empty beer bottle, and with a small grunt of effort got to his feet.

'Jesus!' He almost tripped over the comatose Labrador on the kitchen tiles. Glen, wisely keeping his black coat out of the sun, had chosen to stay inside where it was cooler. Lena held the phone out to Paxton, who looked at it in surprise. He could have counted the people who ever called him on one hand with several digits missing, let alone at Lena's place.

'Who is it?'

'Andy Stirling.'

Paxton took the phone. 'Hello?'

'Hi James, it's Andy. I tried you at your own place but you weren't there, so I took a stab. How are you?' There was a hollow, curiously official ring to Stirling's words. Foreboding fizzed up in Paxton's stomach.

'Good, thanks. You?'

There was the slightest pause. 'Oh yeah. Can't complain.'

'He's not English then,' murmured Lena from close behind Paxton's shoulder.

'Go away!' Paxton waved her off with his free hand. 'Do you mind?'

'Romance is still going strong, I see.' Stirling sounded his old self again for a moment.

'Oh yeah, it's great. Want to come over for dinner? Bring Nicola. We can both get picked on.'

The pause stretched out longer this time. 'Another time, thanks. As long as we're not having pizza . . .'

Ah, Paxton thought.

'Bit of a strange one yesterday,' said Stirling.

By the pricking of my thumbs . . .

They'd been friends of a sort ever since the winter, the four of them sharing dinner and a quiet evening every now and again. This time Stirling was wearing his *other* hat. And he wanted Paxton to wear his.

The detective constable sounded a bit apologetic, shrinking back from his own unspoken request. 'I shouldn't really trouble you. I'm just . . . offloading, I guess. It's not really the right sort of thing to discuss over dinner . . .'

'Gory?'

'A bit.'

'That's all right. It doesn't seem to stop the theatres selling popcorn.'

Stirling gave a laugh, but his voice was tired. 'It's different when it's real. You should know that. You can't just switch it off and walk away.'

Paxton glanced round at Lena, who was watching him quizzically, her eyebrows raised. 'No. But sometimes it's better not to.' He smiled, trying to read her lips as she framed a question. 'Real life's better than the movies. Good may not always triumph over evil, but you can at least try to stop them doing a sequel.'

Stirling laughed again, a real one this time.

Chapter TWO

'I'D BETTER LET you know — I'm not here officially.' Stirling looked sheepish, peeling at the label on his beer bottle. A lock of golden hair flopped down on his forehead. 'I'm not quite sure what my bosses would make of me talking to an amateur psychic.'

'Would it help if I offered to charge you?'

'Piss off. Amateur, professional, I don't think it matters. It's bad enough I'm talking to you, let alone both.' His gaze settled gently on Lena. 'You might not want to hear this.'

'I'm hard enough. Go on.'

Shrugging, Stirling gave them the facts. 'The woman's name was Charlotte Hiscocks. Found in her home, with severe head injuries. She'd been beaten to death, then stabbed through the heart.'

Paxton shot a rapid glance at Lena. Her eyes remained steadfastly on Stirling, giving no sign of having heard except the movement of her throat as she swallowed.

'A pizza deliveryman found her. There were no signs of a break-in, except that the door was slightly open. Nothing obviously missing, though we'll have to wait until the husband gets back tomorrow. He's been away on business in Australia.'

'Was it a sex crime?' Paxton asked.

'The coroner thinks not at this stage.' Stirling frowned. 'And there weren't even any traces of blood in the rest of the house, except for the golf club in the corner. Didn't need the coroner to tell us what the murder weapon was.

Unless the killer flew out the window, I'm guessing he took his shoes off to go out the door. I don't see how he could have avoided making a mess otherwise. But the neighbours didn't see anything. Their blinds were shut. And the people on the left were out.'

Paxton was silent, thinking.

Without realising it Stirling read his mind. 'Bloody weird.'

Paxton looked up to find the DC's eyes on him. Even after explaining the limits of his ability, after knowing him nearly six months, Paxton still got the impression that Stirling wanted him to know what he was thinking. Wanted him to prove his gift was real. Lena was worse. She *did* believe unequivocally, but Paxton's inability to read her thoughts was doubtless a constant disappointment.

Paxton sighed. 'What was it you were hoping I'd do?'

'I don't want you to do anything, exactly. I really can't have you prowling around inside the woman's house.' Stirling looked uncomfortable.

'So — you don't want me to *do* anything, but you told me anyway?'

Stirling put his head in his hands. A deep sigh emanated from between them. 'It's sad, isn't it? When it comes to murder, you're the first person I think of talking to.' He raised his head. 'You should have heard the guys at CIB. Making wisecracks about dying in the length of time it takes to deliver a pizza.'

'Whatever gets them through the day,' said Paxton. 'Can't be easy, your kind of job.'

16

'Nooo,' Stirling admitted, his frustration visible. 'But I mean — you know how Hell pizzas all have those gimmicky names?'

He mimicked Paynter. *'Shouldn't she have ordered the Mordor? Get it? Sounds like murder . . . Hur hur hur.'*

'Hmmm. So, are you all tossers on the force?'

'Only those of us who can find our own dicks.' Stirling frowned again. 'As a matter of fact, she asked for Trouble. Trouble and a Diet Coke . . .' Taking a long mouthful of beer, he took his time to swallow. 'Except, it wasn't a her, it was a *him*. A man placed the order.'

Lena seemed to get what Stirling was driving at. 'So he ordered Trouble? Then took off?'

'Exactly. Supremely ironic, don't you think?'

'And bloody intentional,' said Paxton. 'He was having a laugh . . .'

He met Stirling's eyes, and realised he *did* know what was behind them.

'Remind you of anyone?' Stirling said heavily.

TWO HOURS LATER, long after the DC had left, Paxton was still thinking about all he'd said. Part of him wanted nothing to do with any of it, was sure he couldn't be any help, even if he was called on. The other half of him was mentally doing star-jumps. That was what scared him most, even more than the vague recognition that there was another serial murderer on the loose . . .

He liked to play games.

The doorbell rang just as he was scraping his bowl for the last of the ice cream. He cleared it away with Lena's, slotting them in the dishwasher as she answered the door.

'Hey, Mandy. Come in.'

Though he'd been expecting her, Paxton's mood dropped several notches as he heard Mandy's voice in the hall. Her face fell too when he walked into the lounge.

'Oh. Hi, James. I thought you'd be at work.'

'Sorry, no, I work Wednesday to Sunday.' He took a seat, squarely in the middle of the sofa.

Mandy chose the sole armchair, crossing her legs.

Paxton smiled at her. 'So, how's your work going?'

'Oh, not bad. You know.' She shrugged. 'Work.'

'Well, *this* one wouldn't know what you're talking about,' Paxton said, slipping an arm around Lena.

Lena settled back into the sofa, tilting her head right back against the cushions. 'Ahhhh . . . I love school holidays. Specially the Christmas ones.'

'I don't,' said Paxton. 'People get so grumpy and depressed after Christmas.'

Lena laughed. 'Doesn't usually take *that* long. Most people start stockpiling grievances early.'

'Very true.' Paxton put on a falsetto. 'Teddy for little Zoe. Book for George. But if that fat old tart of an Aunty Shirley wants anything out of me she'd damn well better apologise for saying that about my Harry . . .' He grinned at Lena. 'But it's the reformed bingers I hate the most. I see them in the restaurant all the time. They spend December stuffing themselves with cakes and mince pies, and New Year chugging back anything short of oven cleaner, then on January third they suddenly wake up and turn into calorie Nazis! They make it hell for everyone else. *Do you know how bad cheesecake is for you? Ooh, not for me, thanks, I'm being good*. Meaning that everyone else at their table feels like Mr Blobby for even considering an after-dinner coffee.'

'I know! Poor delusional bastards . . .'

'At least they *try* to change things. It's good to have goals in life, you know.' Mandy's eyes returned Paxton's smile with interest. *Unlike you*.

Paxton had to give credit where it was due. Nearly half a conversation in nothing but monosyllables — he almost applauded the razor-faced bitch. Except that one hand felt more like ripping her throat out than clapping.

Lena's own smile had faded.

They'd met in this very room. Mandy in striped blouse and shoulder-length blonde hair had come straight from her job as a low-ranking lawyer in some inner-city firm. Paxton offered to make the drinks. Half an hour later, while hunting out an atlas to show Mandy where his home town was, he'd heard her voice coming through the wall.

. . . just using you! Your dad's just died. You're lonely and vulnerable right now.

Then something unintelligible from Lena. Paxton had stopped dead near the doorway, his index finger jammed between the pages of the British Isles.

Oh my God, you poor thing. I know that must feel like some kind of link, but it's not like he knew your father. Face it, he's a bartender. He's never even had a proper job. He's just been drifting through half the known world.

He must be jumping up and down at having scored a girl who's just inherited a house and all her dad's money . . .

But all Mandy knew was the précis, from the newspaper clipping. Paxton had discovered Mark's body, and he'd been preying on his daughter ever since. The part where Paxton had gone into the killer's house, saving Lena's life in the process, had been left out of the papers. Stirling had got the sole credit. At the time Paxton had been relieved, but now he would have given anything to drag Mandy down from that ten-foot spike she was wedged on.

He'd tried to make allowances. She did have Lena's interests at heart. On paper he'd even have agreed with her. He had no education, no prospects and apparently no stability. He was average — brown hair, brown eyes, medium height. No underwear model, though Lena said he had no idea how good-looking he was. She could talk. She was a typical Irish beauty, all dark hair, blue eyes and clear skin. And now, pots of money. She was miles too good for him. Mandy herself could have bought all Paxton's personal assets with the earrings she'd lost down her sofa. However, she also made it clear he wasn't worth the lint. Paxton's tolerance had fast run out. She made scarce effort to be polite even for Lena's sake, never mind his, and never made any attempt to see him as something other than a dribbling thug who'd crawled off the set of *EastEnders*. It seemed to be his lot to live in other people's boxes, and Paxton was sick to death of it. And she didn't even know about his gift . . .

The thought hauled him back to the present. 'Did you see the news about that woman who was killed in Epsom?'

Lena and Mandy frowned in unison, but it was Mandy who spoke. 'Yeah, that was creepy. Who beats someone to death and rings up for a pizza? I reckon it must have been the husband.'

'No, it wasn't. He's out of the country.'

Lena's frown turned into a glare of warning, while Mandy's changed to annoyance. 'They didn't say that. The news just said he was returning from a business trip tomorrow. It could have been in Hamilton — plenty of time to drive up and kill her then drive back again.'

'I just . . . don't think it could have been.' Paxton tried to recover from his mistake. 'And anyway, there are only about three businesses in Hamilton. Just give them all a ring now and ask if he got off early.'

'You're so smart, aren't you? Have you even been to Hamilton?'

'Yes. As a matter of fact I have.' Paxton met her stare for stare. 'Believe it or not, I don't try to be an expert on things I know nothing about.'

'James . . .' Lena was shifting unhappily beside him. Mandy kept her mouth shut, but Paxton could feel the effort it cost her.

He was tempted to ram it down her smug little throat, what it was really like to be him. How it really felt to hear the voices of the dead and feel wretched for every damn person who just wouldn't listen. The ones who wouldn't change, even though it would mean their own deaths, sooner or later. The ones who couldn't accept the truth about what had happened, pursuing some endless vendetta or beating themselves into the ground. Did you leave it all hanging over your own head or did you just walk away? And if you walked away, would it still follow you? The answer, Paxton knew, was *always*.

'It reminds me of *Der Proceß*, in a way. You've got absolutely no idea *why* any of this is happening . . . Eh, James?'

'Eh?' Too late Paxton spooled back through his memory and realised they had moved on to books.

'Have you heard of Kafka, James?' Mandy asked him. Paxton just stared at her.

Lena gave an incredulous laugh. 'Of course he has! He's actually a lot better read than me!'

It was Mandy's turn to look incredulous. For Paxton it was the last straw. He smacked his knee, idiot excitement lighting up his face like a torch.

'Oooh! Guess what, Lena? They're starting me on the wine labels at work now!' He turned a beam of sub-normal glee on Mandy. '*I'm* learning foreign languages!'

It didn't get a reply. Mandy rolled her eyes, and Lena's own were turned up towards him, pleading.

Paxton leaned forward and kissed her, then stood. 'I'm going home.' He gently cut off Lena's protest. 'I'll see you tomorrow.'

He didn't even look at Mandy as he collected his keys from the table beside her. He slammed the door as he got into his car. 'Fucking *robobitch*.'

He stared at Lena's front door, seething with resentment. The last thing he felt like doing was going home for a sleep. The air was like hot caramel. He stuck the key in the ignition and snapped on his seatbelt, still boiling. Then, just as he had his hand on the gearstick, inspiration hit. He cracked open the door again, making the overhead light come on. The slight breeze that furled in was welcome. He got the street directory and flipped through a few pages, until he found Epsom.

Chapter THREE

YOU COULDN'T, APPARENTLY, see death from the street. The address Stirling had given him looked like any other house on this road, except that no light escaped from behind the curtains. As he pulled in, Paxton was over-aware of the lights in other porches and windows, his mind calling up a neighbourhood of disapproving eyes. He got out of the car, walking slowly up to the foot of the drive. Aside from an Audi parked on the cobbles, there were no signs that anyone had ever lived here, let alone died. Paxton felt rather foolish. There was nothing to be gained from loitering, waiting to feel something that wasn't there. He didn't know what the hell he was doing here. He knew better than to suppose he would magically tune in to all the answers, but something in him wouldn't roll over. He'd come this far; he might as well make the best of it. He started cautiously up the drive.

A flash of lights got his back as a car slowed behind him. The guilt and self-consciousness ratcheted straight back up. He turned to see a sporty Peugeot hatchback pull into the drive opposite. The garage door went up automatically as someone tripped the remote inside the car. After a pause, however, the Peugeot backed out again, and a young woman got out. She went into the garage and moments later an almost brand-new BMW reversed out. The Peugeot then drove into the garage, followed by the Beemer. Paxton watched in idle fascination as two women and a man came out, and the man kissed the driver of the Beemer goodbye. He then walked down the drive to where a black Maserati was parked under a street lamp.

'Fucking hell,' Paxton muttered. 'They've got the entire EU in their garage.'

'Can I ask what you're doing here?'

Paxton jumped a mile. The expression on the woman's face as he turned around told him he'd been right to worry about the neighbours. And on top of everything else, she'd potted him talking to himself.

'I was just . . . taking a walk before bed,' he said lamely.

'Oh really? You drove over here to go for a walk?' She looked over his shoulder at the Nissan by the kerb.

Shit. Paxton sighed and dropped the pretence. 'I'd have thought there were better things to do on a Tuesday night than to watch your neighbour's house.'

'What about when one of them's been murdered by God knows who and you live right next door? I think it's a bloody good way of spending a Tuesday night.' She was probably in her late forties, with short dark hair. 'And I think my excuse is a whole lot better than yours. I saw you go right up the driveway.'

'You didn't worry about going out to confront a strange man hanging round the site of a murder?'

He watched that sink in. She glanced back at the lit windows of her house for a split second before she returned her attention to him, on the defensive.

Paxton sighed again. 'I'm really sorry. I know it looks bad. But I wasn't intending to be nosy. It's just . . . this whole thing brings up bad memories for me.'

25

This wasn't increasing her comfort levels. 'Bad, as in ...?'

'I had a friend who was murdered like this just six months ago.' He didn't mention that their acquaintance had only begun post mortem.

Her belligerence vanished, smoothing the wrinkles from her forehead. 'Really? That's awful.' Then the frown returned, this time of puzzlement. 'I don't quite see why you'd want to be hanging round the scene of another murder. If I were you, it's the *last* place I'd ever want to come. How can you bear to be reminded?'

'That's just it. It reminds me an awful lot of what happened to Mark.'

A flicker of alarm. 'You think it could be the same killer?'

'No. *That* bloke's dead now . . .'

'Really?' She'd said it so many times Paxton almost started a count. 'That's a relief for you, I guess. Did they get him in jail?'

'No, he killed himself. Hanged himself.'

There was a split second of silence. 'Wait a minute. Six months ago . . . That was that serial killer! The Eastern Strangler.'

Paxton felt the customary jolt of surprise. He forgot that what happened then hadn't been just part of his own life, remembered by him and Stirling and Lena. It had been national news, and transfixed the entire city. The woman was staring at him, appalled. 'Oh my God. Was your friend the man who died in the park?'

Paxton nodded, resigned. 'Yeah.'

'Oh my God.'

'So you can see why this has kind of got me worried. Like you, I guess.' He was well aware of the gaping holes in this reasoning, but she didn't appear to notice.

The woman was shaking her head. 'Yeah. It's horrible. Poor Charlotte . . .'

'Were you friends with her at all? How well did you actually know her?'

Now she hesitated, then said, 'I wasn't actually friends with her, no. And I think she hated *me*. She knew I was aware of what she got up to whenever her husband was away.'

Paxton was startled. 'You mean she was playing around?'

'Was she ever.' The woman was smiling darkly now, relishing her role as the insider. She folded her hands in front of her skirt, getting comfortable. 'Shouldn't really speak ill of the dead, but . . . it's Ian I feel sorry for. It's a horrible thing to say, but he's the loveliest guy, and he just had no idea. As soon as his back was turned — boom! Wasn't one for moping all by herself, that's for sure. She caught me glaring at her once, as she was getting out of a car with one of them . . .' She smiled again at the memory. 'There was one man in particular, drove a blue BMW. He was there just a couple of days before she died.'

She paused, thinking it over. 'I did wonder if he might have had something to do with it . . .'

'Didn't you tell this to the police? Have they interviewed you?'

'Not yet. We've just come back from visiting my daughter down in Christchurch. We went down on Friday night — that's when I saw his car at her place — and we flew back this afternoon. We weren't even here when it happened. We got back to hear the news. Carol from number eighty-one came and told us. She was *horrified* — she was right next door when it happened.'

'This has to go to the police. This could be exactly the information they're looking for. Do you have any idea who this bloke is?'

'I wondered if he was a colleague. He was always very well dressed, looked like a banking type. He might have been her boss . . .' A front door closed nearby, and she turned. 'Oh, here comes my husband.'

A shape was descending the steps of their house, coming to join them.

'I wondered what was taking you so long.' Now that Paxton could see him better he saw a thinning-haired man in short sleeves.

'Ron! This man here's just been saying the same thing you were telling me. We really should ring the police about that boyfriend of Charlotte's.'

'If that's what you want to call it . . . Well, it might come to nothing, but you never know. Might teach the bugger to keep it in his pants, if nothing else.'

'Are you still on holiday tomorrow?' asked Paxton.

They both stared at him. 'Yes. Why?' the woman asked.

'The police will be wanting a formal statement, first thing.' He made to go, then paused. 'And don't tell them I sent you.'

'I JUST CAN'T understand it. Why would anyone want to kill her? For Christ's sake, she always went out of her way to help people!' Ian Hiscocks gave a bitter laugh. 'It was her job!'

He was just barely holding it together. Stirling watched Hiscocks's hands on the kitchen table as he spoke, flapping about like dying fish. They weren't conducting the interview in the living room for obvious reasons. Stirling wondered if Hiscocks had even set foot in there. If he'd ever set foot in there again.

'Your wife was a mobile mortgage broker with ASB?' Vicky Nielsen kept things easy, made him focus on one simple thing at a time.

'Yes.'

'And there's no one who might have been jealous? Did she mention having problems with anyone?'

'No! There's no one. She always had plenty of time for everyone . . .'

Hiscocks's voice finally broke, and Stirling had to look away as the man started to cry. He was neither a good-looking man, nor an ugly one. He had sandy hair and an average build, and eyes an olive green, though these were by now turning red.

Nielsen took a packet of tissues from her pocket and held them out to him. Hiscocks took them, unable to thank her, and blew his nose. It was a wasted effort. The tears were still coming down hard.

'She was the only woman . . . I ever loved. We'd been together fourteen years.' Neither Nielsen nor Stirling said anything, knowing he wasn't actually talking to them. Grief was an individual thing. Despite the common guff about sharing one's grief, it was something no one else could take away for you. In the end it was yours alone, to hold close or let go.

Instead of remembering Charlotte Hiscocks's face on that blood-soaked floor, Stirling saw Nicola's. He felt the other man's anguish, understood it completely. Strongest of all was the fervent relief that he wasn't the one in his chair.

Hiscocks was shaken by a fresh bout of sobs. 'Why *her*? What did Charlie ever do to anyone?'

Nielsen rose from her seat. She went over and crouched beside Hiscocks, placing a hand on his shoulder. 'That's what we're going to find out. All right? We're going to find out who did this — that's *our* job. What *you* have to do is just keep on putting one foot in front of the other. Okay? Take it slowly, I know it's not easy, and just do one day at a time.' She rubbed his arm soothingly, her face as sombre and calm as her voice. 'You can do this.'

Already Hiscocks's sobs were quieting. This was why Nielsen was such a damn good detective, thought Stirling. And such a damn good mother. She put all the monsters to bed.

Hiscocks turned anguished eyes on them. 'I shouldn't have been away from her so often. If I'd been here, this wouldn't have happened.'

'You don't know that. You can't —'

A mobile phone started up, cutting off whatever she was about to say. The ring tone was 'The Pink Panther'. It was almost painfully jaunty under the circumstances.

Frowning, Nielsen pulled the phone out of her pocket and skated it across the table to Stirling. 'Detective?'

Recognising the wisdom of leaving her to it, Stirling took the phone into the hall, shutting the door behind him. 'Hello, this is Detective Constable Stirling.'

'Andy? Is the sergeant busy?'

'She's comforting the victim's husband at the moment. Who's this?'

'Sorry, it's Graeme Kirkpatrick here. How are you?'

Kirkpatrick was a detective senior sergeant, next up the ladder from DS Nielsen. He was overseeing the investigation, for which Stirling was grateful. At least with *him* Stirling didn't need a flak jacket just for round the office. Not like some he could have named.

'Good thanks, Senior. Given the situation. Obviously it's a bit more than I can say for the husband . . .'

'He's taking it hard, is he?' There was what sounded like resignation in Kirkpatrick's voice.

'It's cut him up pretty bad. Almost a relief when you rang to be quite honest.'

'Well, I'm sorry to do this to you, Andy. I'm afraid there are a few more questions you're going to have to ask him. I was rather hoping I'd get a chance to talk to you, actually.'

At his tone Stirling felt dread stir in his gut.

'Are you still in touch with that psychic bloke, James Paxton?'

That was a question Stirling hadn't been expecting. He tried to work it out as he answered. 'Yes, I am. Why do you ask?'

'We've just had a statement from the neighbours. The ones from number seventy-seven.'

Stirling involuntarily glanced to his right, as if he could see through several solid walls, then stared blankly at the damask wallpaper as Kirkpatrick laid it all out.

'They came just now to report seeing a man visiting the late Mrs Hiscocks. Repeatedly. And always while her husband was away.'

'*What?* Are they sure about this?' Stirling heard the pathetic cliché before it dropped from his lips. 'He could have just been a client.'

'What, with his hand up her skirt?'

'Oh Christ.' Stirling's morning was suddenly blacker than charcoal.

'You'd better ask your husband about it.'

'Look Senior, Hiscocks has absolutely no idea. He's sitting in the next room crying his eyes out. He's devastated. This is hardly the time.'

Kirkpatrick sighed. 'I know it's hard, Andy.'

There just weren't any excuses to make. Stirling was going to have to tell a newly bereaved husband that his wife had been shagging at least one other man on a regular basis as soon as the wheels of his plane lifted off the runway. His past would be blown away, just like his future.

At that moment, Stirling hated his job. He looked round for something else to latch onto. 'So why did you bring up James Paxton? What's *he* got to do with all this?'

'Well, apparently he was the one who made them get in touch with us. That's why I wondered if you had anything to do with it. He seemed to know exactly where to go.'

'He was around here?' Stirling couldn't believe his ears. 'When?'

'Last night. Just before nine?'

'Unbelievable.' Stirling was squeezing the phone so hard his fingers started to ache.

'So you did talk to him then?'

Stirling hesitated a fraction of a second before muttering, 'Yeah. I'm sorry to say I did.'

'I hope you're not doing this too often, Andy. Or is it because he's a psychic?'

'I just thought . . .' Stirling didn't know what he thought. Only that he was angry as hell. 'I'm really sorry, Senior. I told him this was *strictly* off the record.'

There was no response from the other end for a moment. Then Kirkpatrick said, 'He told them not to tell us he was there. But I gather the woman was quite fond of talking. I think she just mentioned talking to a young English bloke who'd been friends with the man who was murdered by the serial killer last July. Which gave the game away for *me*.'

'I should never have told him anything. I'm really sorry about this.'

'He seems to like playing detective, doesn't he?' Kirkpatrick's tone was thoughtful. Another couple of seconds passed before he said, 'Right, well, I'll let you get on with it. I know it's not going to be pleasant, but we have to do it. The price of justice is bloody steep these days.' He sighed. 'Like everything else. Good luck.'

Kirkpatrick clicked off. Stirling jabbed the end button with his thumb and slowly walked back to the kitchen. Hiscocks and Nielsen both looked up when he opened the door. Hiscocks was looking much better. He was chatting softly to Nielsen about his wife, looking beaten but finally calm. Stirling cursed all the few stars he could name.

'Excuse me, sir, I wondered if I might ask you something.'

Watching Ian Hiscocks' expression change to shock, then denial and anger, seeing the tears come back to the surface, he also cursed James Paxton.

Chapter FOUR

'SO THAT'S WHY you joined the force, Andy, is it? You just can't resist consorting with freaks and lowlifes.'

Stirling stopped as a familiar voice nailed him between the shoulder blades. 'Oh sorry, Ray. Did I miss our lunch date?'

He checked his watch, turning in time to see the smirk segue into a scowl on DS Gardner's pasty face.

Gardner's retort was hamstrung by the entrance of Nielsen, fresh from parking the car. He limited himself to: 'You'll wise up one day, Andy. And that'll be a lesson you'll never forget.'

'Stirling? Wise? That'll be the day.' It was Nielsen's first attempt at a smile since they'd left Hiscocks. It wasn't a very good one.

'You hear what Andy's been up to?'

Nielsen looked between the two of them, out of the loop and not liking it. 'Andy's been out with me.'

'No, Vicky, this was last night. Remember our New Age friend from the stranglings last winter? I told you about him.'

'You mean that psychic guy?'

'Yeah. Well, guess who Andy's all chummy with? He went to him for a reading on your victim last night.'

'That's bullshit,' Stirling muttered. 'He's just a friend. And he's not like that — he *hates* all this psychic shit.'

'Then why the hell is he always sticking his nose in? Or was going round to her house *your* bright idea?'

'What's this?' Nielsen's face was turned towards Stirling in surprised expectation.

Stirling gritted his teeth. 'I had no idea he'd do that.'

Gardner gave a derisive laugh. 'We couldn't take a step in the last investigation without tripping over the stupid bastard. He's convinced himself he's Sherlock Holmes crossed with What's-His-Name, that moony shyster on TV who tells people their dead grandmothers say hello . . .' He put on a gormless expression that Stirling thought suited him. 'What was her name again? Was it Judy? No, Doris? Maureen? *Mary*, that's right! I knew it began with an M . . .'

'You mean Colin Fry?' asked Nielsen. 'I've watched him when I've been at home with the kids. It was okay. Better than your usual daytime television.'

'Man's had one too many sticks of incense up his nose.'

'I'm off to grab a coffee,' said Stirling. It was that or something else.

'Hurry up, Andy, you might just catch the end of it. Before he blesses everybody.'

Stirling pushed on through the building, hearing their conversation fade behind his back.

'It's on in the afternoons actually. Have you ever even seen it?'

'I don't have time for that rubbish.'

'There are quite a number of things you don't have time for, Ray . . .'

Then Stirling was out on the street, and the voices were gone. He stared at the traffic for a beat or two, then pulled out his mobile.

THAT WAS THE good thing about this house. You could get from anywhere to the phone in two seconds. Paxton picked it up on the second ring, a boot in his other hand in preparation for heading to Lena's.

'Hello?'

'Oh good. I'm glad you're home. What the hell did you think you were doing last night?'

Paxton blinked. 'They told you.'

'Yes they bloody well told us — and believe me, I heard all about it too.'

'I'm sorry, Andy. I'm really sorry, I didn't mean to —'

'I told you *not* to go sniffing around there, and what do you do? That very same night! I've had the OC on my case, as well as Gardner.'

'Oh shit, not *him*.'

'Yeah, well you've got yourself to thank for that. Do you know how *terrible* that made me feel? The guy's just finished telling the sergeant what a wonderful woman his wife was, how much in love they were — how she was such a hard-working good Samaritan, at clients' houses at all times of day or night, for Christ's sake!' Stirling's laugh would have frightened a child. 'And *I* have to go in there and tell him *that*. My sergeant looked like I'd shot her. I don't want to tell you what *he* looked like.'

Paxton tried to step back, unmuddy his thoughts. 'I'm sorry it had to be you, Andy. But that's your job. I know I shouldn't have gone round there. I wasn't trying to interfere, I was just looking. But it would all have come out sooner or later. I've only brought you the lead a bit faster. I thought time was of the essence in these sorts of cases.'

'We can't have members of the public willy nilly questioning witnesses!'

'I didn't. It was kind of the other way round, in actual fact.'

'Do you know how much damage that can cause? We've had cases thrown out of court, *months* of hard work flushed down the toilet all because of one word to the wrong person. Not to mention my job! Did you think about that?' Paxton could almost feel Stirling's breath icing up the receiver. 'I can't ever trust you again.'

Paxton felt his own anger getting the better of him. 'Then why did you tell me? You just *happened* to drop by and casually slot all the details of a murder into the conversation! Ta for the coffee, and oh — sorry, did I give you the name, street address and graphic description of this woman who's just been done in? Pardon me, but what the fuck kind of friendly conversation is that?'

There was just heavy breathing down the line. Paxton shook his head in disgust. 'Thanks for all your help on the last one, James. You can piss off now,' he said mockingly. 'You wouldn't have found him if it weren't for me.'

'They thought I was getting a reading done! You should have heard Gardner.'

A second of deadly silence ticked by. 'So that's it. I should have bloody guessed. You're ashamed of me.'

It took Stirling too long to come up with a reply. 'I —'

'*That's* your problem, really, isn't it? And I'll bet our favourite detective sergeant was laying it on with a front-end loader. But you still haven't learnt to deal with it, have you?'

'I've had enough of this conversation.'

'Sorry, what conversation?' Paxton hung up.

He sat down on the sofa with a creak of springs.

Well, that's the end of another friendship, he thought. *I'm becoming an old hand at this*.

He bent forward and started pulling on his boots, but his fingers struggled with the laces.

PERFECT NIGHT FOR Latin dancing, thought Helen McCowan. The sort romance novelists would call sultry, although the gallons of sweat dripping down her front had all the sex appeal of a packed lunch. It was well after midnight. Their dance group had chosen to celebrate in its usual style, and now that she was back on her own doorstep she had to admit she was half cut as well as half dead. She flapped her blouse to create a bit of air, wiping the droplets off her top lip. *I'd fit in well with all those spicy Latin senoritas. I've got the moustache to match.*

'What are you grinning at?' asked Rob, his habitual twinkle in his eye. It sounded more like 'Wha' are *yew* grunnin' ah?' More than two decades abroad hadn't even put a dent in the armour-plated Glasgae.

'Never you mind,' Helen retorted. 'I don't want to be giving you ideas tonight. I'm tired.'

'Oh really? You still look pretty perky to me.' He reached out and gave her left breast a squeeze. She jumped, giggling, slapping him away.

'Randy Rob, that's what I should call you. Just got into dancing so you could feel up women.'

'Och, rubbish! I got in so I could ogle 'em. *You* were the one introduced all the groping. I didnae know where to look! I'd 'a run from sheer embarrassment, except I couldn't walk!'

'Oh, that's bloody typical of you lying Scots. Making up all these stories about how the English did you over. Boo hoo! You'll be hoeing into my Johnnie Walker and whistling "Scotland the Brave" in a minute.'

Rob grinned. 'Can I take that as an invitation?'

'No.' She smiled at him cheekily from the doorstep. 'You'll have to go whistle elsewhere. You're not getting anything out of me tonight but snoring.'

'Ah, spoken like a true Scotswoman. Sounds like the name's rubbing off . . .'

'My dearly departed was as Yorkshire as I am, Scotty boy. He'd have eaten *your* haggis for breakfast.'

Rob smirked. 'Yorkshire born, Yorkshire bred, strong in the arm, thick in the —'

'Oh piss off, you porridge-eating twit.' Helen shut the door in his face.

A second later, the door reopened and two twinkling eyes peered around it. 'Come on, it's only just been Hogmanay! Can I at least come round for a drink tomorrow?'

Finally Helen shut the door, tired but almost giddy with it. Nothing like Latin dancing for putting a bit of a sparkle back into the week. It was an adrenaline rush, way better than putting her feet up alone in the flat and scoffing Tim Tams in front of the telly. The attentions of a certain charming and totally immodest Scotsman weren't entirely unpleasant either. Helen slung her handbag on the sofa, wondering if she were really all that tired after all. Lord knew, Rob knew plenty of ways to keep a woman from sleeping. He was almost as good on his feet . . . But she heard his car starting up in the drive, and saw the lights swing round as he backed onto the road. No hard feelings, she knew. Rob always liked a challenge.

Helen went into the kitchen, suddenly in need of a strong cup of coffee. A flash of something dark and a soft thud at the window stopped her heart for a moment, but it was only Morris, the cat, leaping over the sill. She left it half open for him in the summer, and for the breeze. Nothing for intruders to steal in here; not on her pension. Not unless you counted her blood, which the thieving mozzies took in pints. She pulled the window shut and put the kettle on, spooning the sugar into the mug. Her mother would have turned in her grave, but why bother with a mingy little china cup when you could damn well have a whole mug of the stuff? Left more room for the whisky too. Say something for the Scots, they were all mad as stoats, but they could do great things with grains. Helen splashed in a fair measure of Johnnie Walker. *Only half a bottle left*, she thought. *Better cut back on the coffee* . . .

A hand shot out from behind her, latching onto the bottle and ripping it from her grasp before she was even aware of it happening. Her head was still stupidly turned towards her empty hand when the bottle landed hard on the back of her skull. It didn't shatter — that time. It landed again, harder, glass and Scotch exploding over her shoulders. Helen staggered forward, her knees buckling, throwing a hand out to the bench to save herself from falling. Her mind was out of service, simply flashing up useless questions – *Who? Why? What?*

A hand grabbed her by the back of her blouse, while another pressed hard on her mouth. A voice rasped in her ear. 'Who are you thinking of now you're about to die, Helen?'

Staring ahead, Helen saw the kettle not far from her hand. She seized it, twisted round and slopped a load of boiling water on her attacker.

Through the crushing pain in her head she heard him scream. Feeling a rush of adrenaline, she spun round, arms raised, ready to fight with everything she had. Damned if she was some little old duck, wetting herself with fear in her own home. As she raised her hand to strike him, her eyes lit on his flushed face, and the blow didn't land with all the force she'd intended. Her jaw fell open, her eyes widening, as recognition hit. Then his fist hit her face.

Helen let out a gargle of pain. He used that second of distraction to wrench the kettle out of her hand, and brought it down like an anvil on her head. It was as heavy as a full tin of paint. The kettle was still half full of water, which swilled out of the nozzle, scalding her upper body. She fought him, of course she did, but she was only making it worse for herself, jogging more boiling water onto her tender skin. Adding to the pain of more and more direct hits from the kettle, until it was impossible to know where the pain stopped and she began . . .

Finally the blows stopped. She was no longer putting up a fight. Or breathing either. He watched her for a minute, feeling his own breathing slowly normalise. He gave her head a sharp kick. It flopped back, the eyes unblinking. He turned and opened her kitchen drawers, going through them until he found what he was looking for. A sharp knife. He knelt by her warm body, raised the knife high, then nailed it hard through her chest. Straight into her heart. Then he rose and stepped over her body, heading for the handbag on the sofa. He tipped it out on the cushions. A whole pile of crap — typical female. He extracted her purse from under a packet of tissues and a bottle of perfume.

She had forty dollars in there. He folded it and stuck it in his pocket, but it wasn't what he was after. Her credit card was a Visa, issued to Helen M. McCowan. He turned it in his fingers and smiled. Going to the phone, he picked up the receiver and dialled. Difficult to hit the correct numbers in these gloves. It took a while for them to pick up, time for him to get his tone right.

He looked at her while he waited. The blood on her white blouse went beautifully with the red and black flamenco skirt, rucked up to reveal her scrawny, flopping chicken legs, spotted with age marks. The skin on her face glowed like a boiled lobster where the water had got it, and patched her upper arms. He raised his sopping shirt and looked at the damage the water had done to his own stomach. It was an angry red and, now the adrenaline was leaving him, it hurt like hell. But at least it wasn't visible. He looked back at the dead body on the floor. Her mouth gaped open and gummy, oozing blood, missing the upper row of false teeth that lay near his foot. He kicked them idly, watching them skate through the pool on the floor, leaving a trail of red until they hit her outstretched hand. Even from here, she seemed to be screaming. He smiled again as they answered.

'Hi — yeah, I'd like to request a couple of titles.'

Chapter FIVE

'WHAT'S THE VERDICT on the lover?' Kirkpatrick exited his office, meeting Rees as he came down the hall. Nielsen was behind the senior, fresh from going through the forensic results, such as they were so far. It had taken about three minutes.

Rees snorted at Kirkpatrick's enquiry, walking into the squad room. 'Sebastian Acott. All I can say is: nope.'

'But he didn't deny anything? He's given us some samples?'

'Oh yeah. They're dealing with him downstairs now. And there wasn't much to deny — the best friend was all too willing to dish the dirt. *She* had to spend all day in the branch with the guy. I'll tell you this straight, he's not the sort to joke around with pizza, or anything much. You could tell the humiliation of following a cop out of work was killing him. That kind of bloke would never get his hands dirty, except with the ink off his money.'

'What did he do there exactly?' Nielsen asked.

'Business banking. What else?' Rees shook his head. 'Can't have been much chop as a lover. The only thing to get him excited would be a point two per cent rise in the Dow.'

'So no go on Acott, you reckon?' asked Kirkpatrick, looking resigned.

'I'd be very surprised. Actually, he was trying to finger one of her other lovers. In the plural. One's gone to Australia, one's a former client and God knows who the other one is.'

Nielsen heaved a sigh. 'Should have known it was too good to be true. This is going to be one of those cases. No one with a motive. Mind you, it does look like he cleaned out her purse.'

'No prints I'm guessing?' asked Rees.

'Let's just say the purse was a lot cleaner than the floor.' Kirkpatrick stuck his hands in his pockets with a wry smile, leaning back against a desk. 'Maybe someone had a bad credit rating. Got turned down for a mortgage and got nasty.'

'Ray here yet?' Stirling walked in, clutching a cup of coffee.

'Ray? No.'

'What do you want *him* for?' asked Rees.

Stirling frowned. 'He just gave me a buzz on my mobile. Said to meet him in here.'

'I'm right here, Andy.' Gardner came into the room, followed by DS John Blundell, known affectionately as Little John for obvious reasons. All of them straightened imperceptibly. There was a feeling surrounding Blundell, one they all recognised. He was an invisibly marked man, someone who had recently been in the presence of death.

'Woodward wants to see you, Graeme,' he said to Kirkpatrick.

'What's happened, John?'

'Guess.'

'Someone else has been bashed to death.' Kirkpatrick voiced what was on all their minds.

'Yep.'

They were all completely silent, staring at him.

'An older woman, bashed and stabbed through the heart in her own home, apparently while making a cup of coffee.'

'Mrs Peacock in the kitchen with the kettle,' said Gardner.

'It's not funny, Ray,' said Kirkpatrick, with unwonted sharpness. 'I thought all this had finished six months ago. What are the chances of another serial killer so soon?'

'I'm not laughing,' Gardner replied, his face dark. 'I'm just looking at the pattern. First Miss Scarlett, then Mrs Peacock. Like fucking *Cluedo*. Our psycho's a damn comedian. Guess who found her?'

'Don't tell me she ordered a pizza?' Nielsen looked aghast.

'DVDs,' said Blundell morosely. 'Four of them. They were delivered by courier.'

'It might have been a coincidence,' said Gardner. 'But I don't think so. The choices were the first season of *Six Feet Under*, *Dead Again*, *The English Patient* —'

'Did we mention she was English?' said Blundell.

'— and, here's my favourite, *The Remains of the Day*.'

'Fucker,' said Rees shortly.

There was a moment of silence, till Gardner looked at Stirling. 'Thought you might want a bit of advance notice, Andy, so you could tell your friend Paxton. I was thinking he could maybe go and tip off a few more witnesses, upset the relations.'

Stirling wasn't going to let the bastard squeeze one word out of him. He'd learnt his lesson on that one. He gave a sidelong glance at Kirkpatrick, seeing if the Senior would back him up. But Kirkpatrick was gazing a hole through the floor.

'HELLO, AM I talking to James Paxton?'

The voice didn't sound like a thirteen-year-old girl's, so Paxton ruled out telemarketing. 'Yes, you are.'

'Hello, Mr Paxton. My name's Graeme Kirkpatrick. I'm a detective senior sergeant down at Auckland CIB. I was wondering if I could have a word with you.'

All the barriers started going up immediately. If this was a rematch of last winter's round with Gardner, Paxton wasn't playing. He kept his voice noncommittal. 'Sure.'

'I understand you've been able to crack a case for us through your unique ability. You can communicate with spirits, can't you?'

'That's right.'

'Hmmm.' The detective was fishing for something, that much was obvious. 'Would you be interested in chatting about the possibility of helping us on something else?'

'Um . . . What exactly do you mean?' Paxton wasn't quite sure he was getting this in the right context. 'Helping the police with their inquiries' had typically been as enjoyable as acupuncture with scissors.

'I notice you were keen on helping with the recent murder we had in Epsom. How about turning that into a proper commission?'

Paxton couldn't have been more amazed if Donald Trump had phoned up to offer him a job.

'Are you serious about this?'

'Do you think you'd be able to help us?'

'Er — that depends on what you're asking me to do. I'm not sure I quite understand.'

'How about you pay us a visit? Are you working today?'

'Yeah, in about an hour and a half.'

'Do you think you can make it? We're not too far from where you work, are we?'

'Not really. Okay, I'll see you as soon as I can.'

'Great. Thanks, Mr Paxton. See you soon.'

Paxton hung up, his head spinning as he went to change for work early. This was the last phone call he would have expected. From Gardner's attitude, and even Stirling's, he'd always assumed the police were sceptical about anything paranormal. Stirling was polite about it, unlike Gardner, but he never asked any questions about Paxton's abilities, and let the subject drop whenever it was raised. It seemed to be one of those regrettable delusions overlooked for the sake of friendship, like a tone-deaf mate's conviction he can carry a tune without dropping it like a china football. Yeah, yeah, mate, that's great . . . Yeah, a little bit like Neil Diamond . . .

Who was this Graeme Kirkpatrick? Paxton wished he could have called Stirling for a quick appraisal, but there wasn't time.

He was thankful no one was around to give him a second glance as he fronted up at CIB in a black shirt with a Gordon's gin logo. The reception area was a bit shabby — the place resembled an old prefab with blue carpeting and a vending machine. A plaque to fallen officers on one wall only added to the sad atmosphere. The guy manning the desk looked a picture of boredom in his Perspex enclosure. It wasn't where he wanted to spend his summer's day. However, he got on the phone to Kirkpatrick smartly enough. Obviously he'd been briefed.

A rather rumpled-looking man with a belly strode through the door from the offices inside a minute. 'Hi, Mr Paxton.' He came forward and shook hands, smiling. 'I'm really grateful to you for coming in. I promise I won't keep you long. Here, come through to my office and we'll sit down.'

He walked off again as fast as he'd come in, leaving Paxton at full stretch to catch up. Past a few basic office doors, the closeness of which suggested you'd have to shift your coffee cup every time you wanted to turn a page, then Kirkpatrick pushed open another to his right.

'Here he is. In here, Mr Paxton.'

It was a ridiculously small space for four people, and the empty chair in front of the desk was right next to DS Gardner's. The detective sergeant gave him a cheery smile that was just asking to be wiped off with a knuckle-duster.

'Hello, Mr Paxton. This is becoming quite a habit for you, isn't it?'

'How's that?' Paxton asked cautiously.

'Being a person of interest in murder inquiries.'

Paxton was saved from growling a reply by the other occupant of the room, a petite woman with golden-brown hair.

'I've been dying to meet you. This is quite exciting, actually.' She stood up, her hand already out, a smile of welcome on her face. 'I'm Detective Sergeant Vicky Nielsen. I was in charge of one of those cases you cracked for us — the security guard from the university. You saved us all a massive headache.'

'Pity he couldn't have found us the actual evidence to convict the man.' Gardner's smile was gone now, but he slouched back lazily in his chair, apparently not a threat. These weren't young, low-ranking DCs listening now — he'd have to tread more carefully.

'If it hadn't been for Mr Paxton, at least one more woman would have died. That makes him *my* hero,' said Nielsen, and sat down.

Paxton wasn't sure which made him like her more — Gardner's subsequent lapse into silence, or the friendly smile she gave Paxton, with a slight touch of defiance. Paxton wondered whether *anyone* sat next to Gardner at the pub.

'I've brought Detective Sergeants Gardner and Nielsen along to brief you on their respective cases,' said Kirkpatrick, settling himself in his own chair. He started wheeling it round the desk with his feet until he was more or less beside them, not that there was really the room. As he moved, Paxton was struck anew by his somewhat dishevelled appearance. Compared with Stirling, who was always well turned out, and the neat-looking Nielsen, and

51

even Gardner, who looked like a disreputable banker, Kirkpatrick was a breath of fresh air. Unfortunately his new position prevented Paxton from checking out the messy drifts of paper on the desk, mostly bearing the police insignia.

'Now, you can agree to help us or refuse as you see fit, but before we go any further, I'll have to remind you that this is all confidential, and if you're going to stay in this room you'll have to swear that none of the details will get passed on to any third party outside this investigation.' Here he grinned. 'And as we're policemen, you'd have to be pretty stupid to break that agreement with us. Are you clear on that?'

'Yes.'

'All right then. Do you want to start, Ray?'

All of Gardner's previous good humour had vanished entirely. What he wanted to start with wasn't a plea for Paxton's help. The demon in Paxton's head told him Kirkpatrick knew that full well, and was enjoying it, though the man's demeanour was perfectly professional. Gardner got on with the facts without any preamble, his voice an offhand grumble.

'This morning the body of a woman was found in Grey Lynn. Semi-elderly, about sixty-three years old, bashed and scalded with a kettle and its contents she'd been using to boil her tea. She'd been dead some hours, since the previous night. A courier found her — he noticed the door was open a bit when he was delivering DVDs.'

Paxton shot all three of them a startled look.

'Ring any bells?' asked Kirkpatrick. 'What topped it off was the trail of footprints — cat footprints — coming out of there. It was pretty obvious it hadn't been stepping in mud.'

Paxton nodded, looking grimly into his lap. 'And there weren't any witnesses or any apparent motive.'

'Well, it's only the first day yet,' said Gardner, looking at Kirkpatrick as he spoke. 'We may be jumping the gun on this.'

Paxton chose to ignore the comment, sticking to business as he addressed Gardner. 'Did you feel anything about the house that seemed out of place? Aside from the body, I mean.'

'Well, you'd have to ask John about that.'

'What do you mean?'

'He was the one who actually went to the place — I'm just the OC.'

Paxton was confused. 'OC is officer in charge, isn't it? You mean you're in charge of the case but you haven't actually been to the scene?'

Now Gardner smiled, his superiority returning. 'There's something you have to learn about investigation processes, Mr Paxton. Just because someone attended the scene as part of Crime Squad doesn't mean they'll be assigned the case. Chances are, because they're so bloody buggered after the night shift, someone else will get the job while they go home and sleep. You just got lucky with me last time. We were overworked at the time, so the cases got doled out to whoever was handy.'

'Things haven't changed, Ray,' said Nielsen. 'That was eighteen hours, that last shift.'

'You're in charge of Charlotte Hiscocks?' Paxton couldn't refer to her as just 'the Epsom one'. The dead always had names and identities.

'That's right.'

'And I was in charge of the Gloria Tan investigation, that poor woman in the Countdown carpark last year,' said Kirkpatrick. 'You've helped us all out, one way or another.'

Paxton answered honestly. 'I'm just glad it's over, Sergeant.'

Gardner smiled.

'*Senior* Sergeant,' Nielsen corrected. 'Detective Senior Sergeant — Ray and I are the sergeants.'

'That's okay, Vicky, it can get a bit confusing if you're not used to it.'

'Sorry, that's right. You did tell me,' said Paxton, feeling stupid. 'I've just never heard of a senior sergeant before. I don't think they have those back home.'

'Oh yes,' said Kirkpatrick, smiling. 'You lot have Inspector Morse and all those fancy British sleuths who seem to be the only detectives on their entire city police force. Well, we're a law unto ourselves out here. You won't see the DIs going out to crime scenes.' His smile faded. 'But getting back to the subject, do you think you'd be willing to help us get some insights into these investigations? We couldn't afford to pay you, I'm afraid. This would be on a voluntary basis.'

It figured, thought Paxton. They paid off street-walkers, petty thugs and other seedy informants, but heaven forbid they should have the shame of a medium on the payroll. He just nodded, and Kirkpatrick continued.

'I'm not quite sure how you operate. Do you need any objects, or a visit to the location? How would you go about it?'

Paxton hesitated. 'The thing is, I can't promise anything. I could go out to these places, but there's no guarantee I'll pick anything up. I can ask the spirits to talk to me, but if they won't, they won't. And they might not be able to help either.'

'But it's worth a shot. As it stands we haven't got much else to go on, and it looks like these killings aren't one-offs. This guy's just gonna keep on going. Officially we can't really accept anything you say as evidence — the law hasn't caught up with the trends these days. But you might be able to give us a few leads. Show us where to start looking.' Kirkpatrick looked bleak. 'We need all the help we can get.'

'I'll do what I can.'

'That's fantastic. Thanks, Mr Paxton.' Kirkpatrick stood, enthusiastically shaking hands. His pleased look made it all worse. 'Well, what we could do, if you want to visit the places, is arrange a time. Would you be able to go out tomorrow at any stage?'

'Er — sure. About ten? I'll be working again from five.'

Kirkpatrick glanced at Nielsen. 'Vicky?'

'Yeah, that should be fine.' Nielsen seemed pleased. 'I'll show you round a bit, make sure you have all the information you need. And then you could go out to the other woman's place after that, if you like.'

'See if you can close the DVD case.' Gardner gave a sarcastic grin. 'Meanwhile I'll get on with some digging. Who knows, your participation might even become a total waste of time.'

Kirkpatrick got in quickly. 'One thing I will say, though. You'll have to be discreet. Even if you don't talk about this to anyone, it's especially important that the press doesn't get hold of it. Don't let anyone near the houses see what you're up to. The DI was very strict about that.'

'I've learnt my lesson,' said Paxton, with absolute truth.

Gardner was last to rise, his eyes smiling. 'See you tomorrow, Miss Marple.'

He left without a backwards glance or a handshake.

Chapter SIX

IT WAS THE first time Paxton had seen the place in the daylight. A nice house, the Hiscockses had bought, but it'd probably be a hard sell.

The woman from next door wasn't home, Paxton was sure, and yet he still had that feeling of being watched. Even with DS Nielsen beside him as they walked up the Hiscocks' drive, on official business, he still felt guilty, a trespasser on sacred ground. The house's only occupant now would be its ghost, if she was home. Ian Hiscocks had gone; he hadn't wanted to spend another night in the house where his wife and then his illusions had died. Poor man.

Paxton hadn't told Lena what he was doing. He'd kept quiet about having been round here earlier as well — he didn't think she'd take his curiosity too kindly. No doubt she'd agree with Stirling. The whole murder investigation scenario was one she wanted safely in the past. His visit on Tuesday hadn't been entirely peaceful. Lena started by apologising in one breath, then admonishing him with the next. He shouldn't feel the need to run out every time Mandy came over. He was part of her life now, and she'd told Mandy so. It had ended with her accusing him of being a coward, or immature, and Paxton defending himself for trying to spare her feelings. Added to Stirling's phone call, it put him in a foul mood all day. He'd tried calling her on Wednesday, but she wasn't home. Belatedly he remembered that Wednesday morning meant grocery shopping. He'd left a message, but by the time he'd left to meet Kirkpatrick she hadn't called back.

His toe caught on a cobblestone, instantly jerking him forward a day.

'Ooh, careful,' said Nielsen, glancing back. She waited for him to catch up a step. 'Now, how do you want to do this? Just stand inside the room for a bit and see if anything comes to you? Do you need me to bring any particular items of clothing or something like that?'

'No, just going in there should be enough.' He was feeling a familiar surge of adrenaline in the depths of his belly, making him feel queasy and excited at the same time. His mind was in a tussle with his senses — stay and sort out what was wrong, or flee from what was waiting. These days it was growing easier and easier for his mind to take over.

Nielsen used the key Hiscocks had given her and led the way inside. The house had been shut up tight for two days. The summer heat had burnt away whatever oxygen might have lingered; the hallway was so close it might as well have been hermetically sealed. But that wasn't what made Paxton lose his breath as soon as he stepped over the threshold. He felt murder press against his chest, violent death beating at him from all sides. He *felt* rather than heard a scream in his head, and his stomach twisted with fear. It was fear above all else that lived here, pouring off every surface like nerve gas. The last terrified moments of a woman's life played over and over, at full volume, never to be erased.

Although he'd been preparing himself, Paxton instinctively flinched, hunching forward, struggling to suck in breaths of the air from outside. He nearly threw up.

'You all right?' Nielsen was looking at him in concern. She would only have had five years on him, at most, but he immediately felt like her kid.

'Yeah. I'm fine,' he said, shaking his head slightly to get rid of the weight of fear.

He took a step further, and an abrupt gust of ice reversed the temperature, clearing his thinking at once. Nielsen gave a sudden violent shiver, and he saw an instant of sheer terror in her eyes. Paxton took a few more steps forward, closer to the doorway on his right. There was an onrush of anger, and a crushing pain in his head. It was Charlotte.

'I'll try to help you if I can, Charlotte,' said Paxton aloud. He ignored the sight of Nielsen stopping in her tracks just ahead of him.

The pain in his head lifted, but a cramping feeling of nausea remained. He thought he heard a sound.

'You'll need to speak up. I can hardly hear you.'

Her voice sounded as if she were speaking from the bottom of a bathtub full of water. When she next spoke, it was a fraction clearer. *Nail the bastard* . . . Her voice strengthened with anger. *Why*?

Paxton guessed this was a common complaint for murder victims, but his heart sank.

'Did you know him?'

There was silence. Paxton glanced at Nielsen, as if she too could hear. The detective was standing very still as if afraid to move, her eyes glued to his face.

'Charlotte?'

But Charlotte wasn't really in the right place to talk. Some weren't — either the shock or the newness of the situation kept them from communicating properly. It was almost impossible to understand them. Paxton began to feel frustrated, the pressure to perform. The sharp pain returned to his head. He blinked, trying not to wince.

'Could you give us a description? Can you remember? I know it's all been a horrible shock for you . . . '

The pause went on for quite some time. Nielsen had noticed the intense look of concentration on Paxton's face. She leaned forward, whispering. 'Is she —?'

Paxton held up a hand to silence her. Charlotte's words came in unintelligible strings of half-heard noise, with snatches of sense.

Dark . . . Why?

'Charlotte, please try, if you can, to tell me something about what he looked like.' He almost sent up a prayer as he listened.

Dark . . .

'The house was dark? Or he was? Did you know him?' There was no response.

Nielsen finally managed to speak. 'Does she know who killed her?'

'Not that she can tell me,' said Paxton. 'I'm not really getting anything, except the word "dark".'

All of a sudden he had the impression of a necklace. He couldn't see it exactly, so much as sense it round his neck.

'I think she's telling me about a necklace. Was she wearing one when you found her?'

'No. Only her wedding ring.'

'I think the necklace is missing. I think he took it.'

'Are you sure it's a he?'

Paxton concentrated again. 'She's not giving me that either. Just keeps on about the necklace.'

He gave it a moment or two more, then shook his head. 'Is there anything else you want to tell me, Charlotte? Any message for your husband?'

Nothing.

'Your *grieving* husband? Perhaps you'd like to tell him you loved him? Set his mind at rest?'

He could have sworn there was a faint laugh.

. . . *poor Ian.*

Paxton felt a rush of dislike. 'I'll be sure to pass on your deepest regrets, Mrs Hiscocks.' He took a couple of steps towards the door.

It came as a half-giggled whisper. *No idea . . .*

Paxton couldn't help himself. 'But he'll be going to a better place than you.' He looked over his shoulder. 'See you at Armageddon.'

He pushed open the door and stalked out.

Nielsen didn't say anything when she came out of the house, locking up while he waited for her in the drive. After testing the knob to see that it was secure, she joined him in a walk back to the car.

'Well, that was a bit unsettling, I must admit,' she said.

Paxton sighed. Whether he was more angry at Charlotte or at himself he couldn't have said. 'I'm really sorry I wasn't more help. That was a big waste of time, wasn't it?' He remembered Gardner's taunt, which didn't improve matters.

'What exactly did she say?'

Paxton told her what little there was to tell. Nielsen nodded, listening carefully and noting it all in a journal.

'She wasn't strong enough, basically,' Paxton finished. 'She didn't really want to come back. I guess when you're murdered you're in shock and you want closure, but we're not going to get it from that. I'm a medium, not a miracle worker.'

Nielsen gave him a reassuring smile. 'I wouldn't worry about it. That's the frustrating thing about this job. If you can't figure out the killer within the first twenty-four hours, you've usually got a really long slog ahead.'

Paxton was grateful to her for trying to cheer him, not to mention believing him without question. In the car she had made an effort with sensible questions, asking him how long he'd had his gift and how it actually felt. It made Paxton look forward with even less enthusiasm to the next task on the agenda — meeting up with Gardner at Helen McCowan's. He rubbed his arms. Even out here in the sunshine, he couldn't get warm. As they drove away, the feeling of nausea stayed with him, following him from the house.

Chapter SEVEN

NIELSEN ECHOED HIS thoughts as she pulled up behind Gardner's car in the driveway. 'Good luck.' From her smile, Paxton guessed she was talking about more than just the job.

'Looks like you feel the same way about him as I do.' Nielsen wrinkled her brow, no longer joking. 'Ray's a good cop. His manner can be a bit off-putting, true, but you've just got to ignore him. His bark is a lot worse than his bite — and some of the things he comes out with are downright funny.'

'Yes, he's a funny kind of man.'

'Just don't let him bother you! Gosh, I can see why you and Andy Stirling are such good mates.'

Paxton grinned. Nielsen wound down the window to let Gardner lean in.

'Gidday Vicky, how'd it go?'

'Oh, not too bad. We got a *little* bit of information. By the sounds of things, the lover is out of the equation. Seems she spent the day with him.'

Paxton turned as he glimpsed other figures moving towards him. Andy Stirling had got out of the other car.

'Wasn't expecting to see *you* here,' Paxton told Stirling.

'I'm a nosy bastard. It comes with the job.'

Paxton smiled. He hadn't seen Stirling this relaxed in a while.

'Morning, James.'

Paxton jumped a little when the voice came so close to his shoulder. He didn't return Gardner's smile. It was the first time the sergeant had called him by his first name, and it grated on Paxton's ear. Deliberate, Paxton thought. The bastard was trying to catch him out.

Gardner was looking at Stirling, clearly not best pleased. 'Care to explain what *you're* doing here?'

Stirling said equably, 'I've never seen James at work before. Senior said I could come along and watch.'

'You expecting see-through people to float out of the walls? This isn't *Ghostbusters*, Andy. I hope.' He gave Paxton a derisive smile. 'Try not to produce any ectoplasm from your nostrils — it's still a crime scene.'

When Paxton said nothing, Gardner began walking towards the front steps. Behind his back, Paxton twisted a finger up his nose, making a face at Stirling, who gave a slight snort. Gardner looked round, his hand on the doorknob, and glared at Paxton.

'If you're going to play silly buggers, there's not much point in us being here. Maybe a blow-by-blow account of the woman's murder will change your tune a bit. If you can get a word out of her, you might soon wish you hadn't.'

The back of Paxton's neck prickled as he got near the house. An indistinct wrongness was alerting him to its presence, sending out dark tendrils that triggered something inside him. It grew stronger as he approached, its force almost turning him back. The door had swung shut a little, almost closing, as if it didn't want him to enter. By the time he forced himself up the steps to touch

64

his palms to the wooden surface he was aware of nothing else. He found himself staring at the door, entranced, expecting blood to come leaching from the wood. He turned his palms over, surprised to see only pale pink skin. The house almost seemed like a live being, pushing him away, pulsing with fury, turning the sky around it dark. Whoever this Helen McCowan had been, she had a strong personality. Even with her passing, it lingered in the house like damp in the walls. And the smell . . .

'James?'

Paxton blinked, his eyes focusing on Stirling, who was looking back round the door. 'Sorry, what?'

'What is it? You getting something?' Stirling looked a bit apprehensive, as if he didn't quite know how he felt about this. 'The DS just wanted to know if you needed anything.'

'Electroshock, by the looks of it,' said Gardner.

Paxton ignored him. 'I don't need anything, thanks.'

'Coming in, or were you planning on holding your séance on the doorstep?' Gardner disappeared into the house.

Following, Paxton couldn't stop the nerves returning. He cast around a bit, soaking in the crackling atmosphere, but nothing else would come, other than that live-wire-in-water current of something deadly.

'Helen?' he called, testing. 'Helen, I'm listening.'

Stirling was holding his breath. Even, Paxton fancied, Gardner himself, standing with his arms folded. But no one responded. The event of her death was here, but the spirit had fled. Helen plainly wasn't the sort to look back. Paxton looked round at Stirling, shaking his head.

'I'm not getting much. There's a kind of record of what happened — she was surprised, I think. It was really sudden. But how often is murder expected?' Paxton sighed. 'At least it was quick. I'm not getting a whole lot of suffering. Thank God. I can sense her, but only the imprint. More what she left behind than a current presence. There's no spirit here to talk to, if that's what you were hoping. She's passed on. Sorry.'

'Well, can't you call her up or something like that?' Gardner looked as if he'd got exactly what he'd expected — a big gob of snot, dressed up as a supernatural.

Paxton rubbed a hand down his face, mashing his nose towards his chin. 'Not unless you want me to call up a whole bunch of other things by mistake. Perhaps other people are comfortable with that, but it's something I've always avoided doing.'

Your gran could do it, his mind said.

Your gran believed in God, was the reply. *She believed in her own protection.*

'What about if you picked something up?' Stirling looked surprised by his own question.

'I think it's about time we left,' said Gardner dismissively. 'We've got strong leads to follow up on.'

'No, I mean, an object that belonged to her. Wouldn't that tell you something about her — maybe why someone would have killed her? I dunno.' Stirling shook his head.

'It was a serial killer, Andy,' said Gardner. 'Pretty blood is red and shiny. There's your reason.'

'Well, seeing he's here, he might as well give it a go. See if we can get our money's worth.'

Mild though Stirling's voice was, Paxton caught the look in his eyes and recognised it at once — the innate desire to contradict anything Gardner said. Paxton felt like smiling. Nielsen had been bang on. More worryingly, however, he also sensed Stirling's desperate wish that Paxton would achieve something to give his sergeant the big finger. The weight of expectation was worse than the pressing sense of death. He didn't fancy telling them he seldom read objects. His mind went back to a game they'd made him play in the upper sixth, on the last day of term. Even his history teacher had got in on it.

Hey James, read my ring. It's really old.

Hey James, what does my watch say about me?

Here, try reading this old textbook — see if it remembers anything . . .

Or how about the chair? Or this 20p?

Yeah, brilliant!

He was at the centre of a classroom of laughing faces, eager to hear his stories, true or false, but just as eager to catch him out. *Ha, wrong! I got it on holiday. Yeah, Paxton's wrong! I got him!*

A derisive noise from Gardner broke into his thoughts. 'What money's worth? We paying $3.99 a minute for this or something?' He gave Paxton a smile of contempt.

'How about something from her room? Jewellery, that usually has a story attached.' Stirling ducked into Helen's bedroom and the others followed without protest. It was in their natures to look around. Paxton wondered how many detectives justified fingering other people's underwear in the name of a pivotal lead. Despite himself, he felt a tugging of curiosity. Who was this woman with the character so strong the house was almost alive with it? The air grew even heavier as he entered the bedroom; it felt like a warning.

'I take it she wasn't married then.'

No one said anything. Some houses were unnaturally feminine, with pink roses on every surface and dolls' eyes vapidly following you across the room. Under the circumstances Helen's house wasn't so creepy, but it was plain on walking into her room that no doting husband was willing to leave his bollocks at the door, tucked into the toes of his boots. There was no *His* half of the room, just a vague scent of perfume drowning in the odour of the rest of the house. A cold chill played deliberately across the back of Paxton's neck. She was hovering there in the background, wanting him gone.

Got something to say to me? he asked her in his head.

The answering silence seemed like a raised finger.

Stirling wandered over to the dressing table, on which there was a jewellery box. He opened it to the low-carat glint of gold and fake stones.

'You mean none of it was taken?' asked Paxton. He'd got into other people's heads before, after they were dead, but the way the criminal mind worked was well beyond his comprehension. Hard to believe someone would want just to take another person's life and leave all the stuff of greater street value.

'Blood is red and shiny . . . That's all they need,' said Gardner. His voice didn't carry its usual mocking tone. 'You can profile them, but you still can't understand them.'

Stirling was sifting the strings of jewels through his fingers, plucking free brooches and earrings that had got tangled up in the chains. He looked long and hard at a simple pendant before thrusting it towards Paxton.

'Here. See what you can get from this.'

Paxton's senses were alive too now, awake to every changing element. He sensed the DC's anticipation, and it puzzled him. Despite Stirling's attempts to remain totally the blank and hard-faced cop, there was no masking the tense hope coming off him. Paxton looked down at the necklace. It was a small silver cross, studded at the centre with a tiny clear stone that was probably real. He felt desperate for a moment, then, as they sometimes did, the words came tumbling out without stopping for his brain to connect.

'This is from a lover.'

He saw Stirling go rigid, just for a fraction of an instant. The DC's eyes whipped over to Gardner and back again.

'Who? Can you give me a name?'

Paxton was on the point of shaking his head, an automatic reaction, when a voice said: *Billy*.

He hesitated, then parroted, 'Billy'.

He saw a spark of disappointment in Stirling's eyes, and again wondered at it. Gardner made a small movement that Paxton couldn't interpret.

'Hey, if it's any help, I think I heard him,' Paxton added. 'It was a Yorkshire accent, thick as anything. He only said his name, but it was bloody obvious to me.'

Hope reignited in Stirling's face. 'Hey, Sarge, that could be her husband or something. Which part of England was she from?'

'She was from Wakefield,' said Gardner, in a voice dry as dead grass.

Paxton looked at Stirling, whose expression was blank. 'In Yorkshire,' he explained.

Stirling palpably relaxed, emitting a sense of triumph. On the other hand, if anything this small victory seemed to make Gardner even more suspicious. His eyes lingered on Paxton's face for an uncomfortably long while.

'There something you're not telling me?' Paxton asked, naturally looking to Stirling. But the DC's face was no longer showing anything.

'Keep going, James. We'll let you know if there's anything we'd like you to explore in more detail.'

Not for the first time, Paxton noted Stirling's ability to switch between open and official. Casting for inspiration, and feeling a bit like a monkey in a hunt-the-banana trial, Paxton was conscious of a faint burn of resentment. He stepped on it. It wasn't helping. The whole place put him on edge. It hardly put him in mind of grandmotherly biscuits and milk.

His eyes fell on the giant ceiling-high bookcase that took up one wall. A reader himself, the first thing Paxton tended to aim for in a strange house was the bookcase. Books told you a lot about their owners, and this collection was impressive. The bookcase was stuffed full of paperbacks. Most people would banish such a thing to their lounge, but Helen had her priorities right — pride of place next to the bed. She'd barely have needed to get up to pick out another title. Only a small bedside table lay in between, with another pile of books on top of it.

Paxton glanced at them curiously, then recoiled.

'Christ, *how* old did you say she was?'

The others looked at the books and sniggered. Romances of the worst kind. The ones that didn't even bother to pretend they were high-class drama, going instead for covers featuring bare-chested rugby types with bad haircuts and tight trousers. Paxton wanted to rail at the wasted space, but he was amused, despite himself. His own gran had read *Reader's Digest* and Catherine Cookson.

'Wish my grandma had been more like this,' said Stirling, picking up his thoughts. 'Maybe then she wouldn't have kept sending me books on native birds and the great scientists every Christmas.'

Her image still floating near the surface of his mind, Paxton flashed back to Christmas with *his* gran, going to the rest home a few streets over while Mum had the roast in the oven. Nat had grumbled almost as much as he had, reluctantly doling out tea and mince pies and slices of Christmas cake and trying not to shiver at every pat from a wrinkled hand coated in liver spots. But his sister didn't see and feel the things he did. Didn't know which ones were next . . .

Paxton quickly turned to the selection in the bookcase, and realised there was a bit more to it than there seemed. There were signs of a sense of humour. Along with the crappy romances, there was also some crime, a whole shelf of Terry Pratchetts and, to Paxton's surprise, the entire series of *Harry Potter*. He smiled. He reached out and took one, *Harry Potter and the Order of the Phoenix*, which he hadn't got round to yet.

As soon as he did so, he fumbled and almost dropped it. There was no way a children's book should be giving off vibes like this.

'Hey, *this* was from a lover too!' This time Gardner's eyebrows raised.

'There's no way this could have been from her husband — it doesn't feel like him at all.'

He was looking at Stirling again, but it was Gardner who spoke. He too was looking at Stirling, his face sharp. 'You haven't told him anything?'

'No, Sarge. I haven't.' This time the excitement was pouring out of Stirling unchecked. 'Go on, James. Can you tell us anything else? Like a name?'

Paxton cleared his mind. 'He's not dead . . . Someone's telling me it's — er, Owen? No, Warren. Billy just came in again. He's laughing for some reason.'

What's so funny? he asked. But out of the ether came — nothing. Except the sound of Gardner's voice.

'Write it down, Andy. Who knows, it may prove useful.'

Stirling looked away. The DS was plainly mocking him for something, but Paxton couldn't figure it out.

'Look, do you want me to check these ones?' he asked, gesturing at the stack of romances. 'They were probably the last things she was reading.'

'Don't worry about it,' said Gardner. 'If you've been getting those kind of signals off kids' books, God only knows what one of *those* would do. Frankly I'm not interested in finding out.' He summarily checked his watch. 'Are we about ready to go?'

'You're sure it was Warren?' Stirling was watching Paxton again, disappointment marked in the quietness of his voice.

'I'm never sure of anything I'm told, Andy. Except that I've been told.'

Stirling shrugged. 'Well, thanks for trying.' And Paxton knew that he'd lost him. Stirling would never again be so willing to believe. This was Paxton's only, shining chance to persuade the DC to trust his ability, and somehow he'd cocked up. Stirling would forgive him anything but making him look stupid, again.

'You coming, Andy?'

Stirling glanced at Gardner. 'Yeah, lock the place up. But I'm not coming back to base just yet — I've got a few things to do first.' A look over his shoulder seemed to include Paxton in his plans.

It was only when Paxton stepped outside and felt his spine lengthen that he truly realised how much the atmosphere of the house had been pressing on him. He remembered the feelings as he'd approached, and shivered.

'I know it's only midday, but after that I've got a sudden craving for a whisky.'

Stirling looked at him askance. 'I thought you weren't much of a drinker.'

'I'm not, but *she* must have been. Couldn't you smell it? The whole time we were in there, the air was just reeking of Scotch.'

Stirling had stopped walking. 'I couldn't smell anything.'

'It was her. If I hadn't known any better, I'd have thought she drank herself to death.' He said it wryly, half-joking, but Stirling was staring at him as if he'd just started gargling Old Icelandic.

'Andy, what is it? I deal with dead people all the time, and *you're* giving me the creeps.'

Stirling looked embarrassed, as if he didn't know how to start.

'Are you coming back with me, Mr Paxton?' Gardner was calling from the driver's seat.

'Just a minute!' Stirling called back. He turned back to Paxton, serious. 'What did Graeme Kirkpatrick tell you about the crime? Did he tell you Helen McCowan's manner of death?'

Paxton's confusion only increased. 'He said she was bashed with a kettle. Wasn't she?'

'Not just a kettle. We also found her in a pool of Scotch. The bottle could have dropped when she was attacked, but it looks like it was smashed over her head.'

'Shit.'

Stirling looked uncomfortable, sticking his hands in his pockets. 'Well done,' he said eventually. 'The cleaners went through the place yesterday. Either you've got a nose like a bloodhound, or . . .'

'Still haven't convinced you, have I?'

'I don't know, James. I really don't. Thing is, you got the name of the lover wrong.'

'You know who he is? You mean this was all just a test?'

Stirling's discomfort heightened at Paxton's obvious sense of betrayal. 'I was hoping you'd pass. It was Gardner's idea.'

Gardner was tapping his fingers on the steering wheel behind the windscreen. Stirling ignored him. 'John Blundell — he's the DS who came out — he ran into him. Rob, I'm talking about. Rob was supposed to meet Helen McCowan for lunch. He came round and stumbled straight into the SOCOs. He was horribly upset.'

'Oh hell. Poor guy.' Having pulled Lena away from a similar situation, Paxton knew how the man must have felt.

'Yeah, well. As you can see, he definitely wasn't called Warren. And before you ask —' Paxton had already taken a breath. 'His surname is Reid.'

'Hey, Andy, you got any work to do? Gee, I'm glad I haven't!' Gardner was leaning an arm out the window.

'All right! Better let you go.' Stirling nodded quickly at the car and moved on down the drive towards his own vehicle.

'Sorry I wasn't more help, Andy.' Paxton meant it.

'That's all right. If we were always perfect, we might turn out like *him*.' He glanced at Gardner, who was now gazing out at the street.

Paxton grinned. 'See you later.'

But as he got in the passenger's seat next to Gardner, he felt the depression return. During the drive home, he endured the other man's jibes without saying a word. Paxton didn't feel in the least like talking. Above all else, his nostrils were still burning with the sharp scent of whisky.

Chapter EIGHT

STIRLING HOPED HE hadn't shown it to Paxton, but his failure to come up with conclusive evidence was a huge kick in the teeth. He told himself the big kicker was Gardner, having yet another reason to crow over him. In his gut he knew the disappointment was also in Paxton himself. He liked the man; they were friends. Even when Paxton's tendency to overreach himself irritated the hell out of him. He'd tried to suspend disbelief and give Paxton a chance to prove him wrong, but he hadn't. Paxton was deluding himself, and it pained him. A memory from his childhood bobbed to the surface — his grandmother, the same one who sent the unwanted books when Alzheimer's started digging its claws into her mind. She'd begun calling him Harry, the name of her dead brother. But the dead didn't come back.

Stirling paused at the foot of the drive, looking back up at the house. There was nobody there. Not to be crude, but it was as silent as the grave. He just about shat his pants when a voice spoke.

'Did you know Helen?'

Stirling swung to see a man behind him, with hair well on the downward slide to grey, and an expression that suggested the news of the murder might have had something to do with it. Neatly he turned the question round.

'It seems *everybody* knew Helen. Hard to believe such a popular woman could have been murdered.'

'I read it in the papers this morning, and I still couldn't believe it. She had so much life.'

He had a soft voice and an almost scholarly manner. Stirling guessed he was one of the neighbours. It was the sort of area where the elderly lived cheek by jowl with student flats that crammed five people into three rooms, or twice that number on weekends. 'So how did you know her?' he asked.

The man looked at his feet, seeming embarrassed. However, the impression of a shared loss made it easier to talk. 'I met her at the library. She asked me for some help choosing one day, and I quite often saw her after that. We chatted a lot.'

He smiled then, a sweet smile of pleasure at the memory, though it lasted barely half a second before the pain crept back in.

'So you were friends?'

'Yes, you could say we were friends.' The man gave a rueful shake of his head at his own bad manners. 'I should introduce myself.' Shyly he held out a hand, with another sweet smile. 'Warren Lucas.'

Just for a moment Stirling's smile went to stone.

'SHE WAS AMAZING. The library was never a quiet place with her around, I can tell you that.' Warren gave a sad laugh, staring down into his coffee. 'Brought me out of my shell. She was one of a kind.'

Stirling, remembering the whisky, the library, the dead husband and the two current men friends, couldn't help but agree. They were now sitting in Helen's favourite café, a short walk from her house, where she and Warren often went together. Warren had initially been alarmed to find Stirling was a cop, but was now lost in his own world, resigned to everything but her death.

'What I can't work out is why. Why the hell would anyone want to kill Helen?'

They should have a special alphabet for homicide detectives, Stirling thought. *The Y always comes first. Then comes the X . . .*

To be fair, he couldn't see Warren giving anyone the bash. Although he wasn't, as Stirling had first assumed, a librarian himself, it was almost as bad. He'd been a quality controller for some engineering company; Stirling's eyes had glazed over after about thirty seconds and he hadn't quite caught all the details. Apparently Warren had retired about two years before, and was living a quiet and happy life on his savings devouring the Tom Clancy and Wilbur Smith shelves at the Grey Lynn library. Or had been, up till now.

'Have you found any leads so far?'

Stirling gave it a moment's thought. 'I'm not really able to discuss that, I'm afraid.'

Warren looked uncomfortable at the reminder. The thought of being a suspect hadn't occurred to him before, but it obviously had now.

'Did you ever meet a bloke called Rob?' Stirling asked him.

'No.' Warren looked puzzled.

Stirling dropped it, shrugging as if it meant nothing. He couldn't help feeling relieved. 'So, you came here often with Helen?'

'About once a week. It was our ritual on Wednesdays.'

Here was Parsifale, one of a million cafés in the Grey Lynn/Ponsonby area, more or less trendy, more or less expensive, more or less crowded. Its coffee was as good as one might expect from the suburb that boasted the highest gay, hip urban professional and pretentious wanker population in the country, and it was just a shame that Stirling was here on business, or he'd have been making the closer acquaintance of the gateaux in the glass cabinet. Sitting opposite Warren, who was listlessly stirring his coffee, he'd have felt as much of a pig as if he'd hauled up to Dunkin' Donuts with his lights flashing.

'Did you by any chance give her a *Harry Potter* book?' Stirling kept the question just as casual.

Warren looked thoroughly spooked. 'How on earth did you know that?'

Holy shit, thought Stirling numbly. *Fuck me*. He wanted to shake his head in wonder, but he shrugged again, as if the confirmation hadn't tipped his world ever so slightly sideways. 'We have ways.'

No sense in throwing the game too soon. For all he knew, he was speaking to the killer. However, he doubted it. The man jumped a mile when a figure loomed over his shoulder.

'Don't you like my coffee? That's good coffee, I made it specially for you, and you're not drinking it!' He was a wiry little Asian man, about fifty, with an expression of mock outrage. He waved his hands, eyes crinkling in good-natured exasperation as he looked at Stirling. 'Next time I'm not giving him dessert.'

Warren looked flustered. 'Oh. Sorry, it's not the coffee. It's fine. I'm just — I've had some bad news, I'm sorry.'

The man's face immediately became paternal. 'Oh, I'm very sorry to hear that.' He glanced at Stirling and back again. 'Is it your girlfriend? She's not here today.'

'Yes.' Warren's automatic reaction was to look back down at his cup.

Stirling took it for him. 'You might have read it in the paper this morning. The local woman killed in her house.' He nodded towards the folded *Herald* on a neighbouring table. The man's eyes opened as wide as his mouth.

'No! No, that's awful!' Recovering, the café owner gave Warren a look of deep sympathy. 'I'm really, really sorry to hear that,' he repeated. 'Such a horrible thing to happen. Are you okay?'

Stirling liked him for that. No questions, except for Warren's welfare.

'I'll be fine,' said Warren, with a tired smile. 'Don't you worry about me.'

The man waved over the young assistant behind the counter, who had been watching the events curiously in between making coffees.

'Nathan! Put some muffins in a bag. You like quiche?' He fired the question at Warren.

'Oh, no, there's no need . . .'

81

'And some quiche,' he told Nathan. 'On the house. This gentleman's friend was the lady who was killed — the one in the paper.'

The young man's eyes widened too. 'Oh jeez, that's awful. Coming right up.' He jumped to fill up a brown bag with muffins, then another with pastries.

'It's okay, you don't have to do that, honestly . . .'

'Are you eating properly?' the Asian man interrupted. 'Look at you, you have not been eating. You ever need some food, you come here. You promise me?'

Finally Warren gave him a grateful look. 'Thank you,' he said quietly. 'Thank you very much.'

'What's your name?' Stirling asked.

The little man looked surprised. 'Arthur.'

'Arthur who?'

'Arthur Wong.'

'Or around here, *Never* Wong . . .'

'You be quiet, young man! I'll give you a clip round the ear!'

Smiling, Nathan set two bulging bags of food in front of Warren, thoughtfully placed in a large flat box. He patted the grieving man on the shoulder, unmistakable sympathy in his eyes. 'Anything you need, just give us a call, mate.'

Warren thanked him again, clearly embarrassed. He obviously wasn't used to being the centre of attention. That had been Helen's job.

When they left, Stirling was making notes in his brain, reminding himself to follow up with Arthur Wong later. He and Nathan had obviously seen the happy couple often. Would they also have seen Rob, or had Helen been more careful? It really hadn't been a delicate question to ask in front of Warren. All too painfully he remembered Ian Hiscocks's response to a similar enquiry.

Then a thought waved a frantic hand in front of his eyes. Stirling quickly took Warren's address and contact details, and as soon as he was out of earshot reached for the phone in his pocket, flipping through his notebook for Rob Reid. He'd almost expected the voice on the end to be pre-recorded when Reid finally picked up.

'Yeah?'

The man didn't sound happy. No one did these days, thought Stirling. Least of all himself.

'Detective Constable Stirling here, Mr Reid.'

'Oh. Hello.' The Scotsman sounded more awake.

'Sorry to disturb you, but can I just ask you one quick question? Have you heard of a man called Warren?'

There was a long pause while Rob tried to sort it out. His mind was probably fuddled by something other than grief. Finally the answer came, the one Stirling had been expecting.

'Well, not since I left Scotland. There was an English fella at work for a wee while . . .'

'No, that's all right, Mr Reid.'

'Why is that?'

'Oh, no particular reason. We've just got to go through a whole list of acquaintances, eliminating whoever we can.'

'Awwww . . .' Understanding began to creep through Rob's voice. It sounded like he was grinning. 'Wait a minute. Was that another bloke she was seeing?'

'Er — what gives you that idea, Mr Reid?'

'Sly old bint! I wouldn't put it past her. She got around, she did. Should have known I wasn't her only one.'

'It doesn't bother you?'

'Nah! She'd put in the hard yards. She was entitled to her bit o' fun.' He let out another amused chuckle.

'She sounds like quite a character.'

'Och, she was, she was that. Are you making any progress then?' The man's voice sounded almost plaintive.

'I think so. I'll let you know what happens.'

'Thank you, sir, I'd appreciate that. Oh! By the way, that necklace I told you about wasn't a cross after all, it was a kind of wavy thing, like kind of a scalloped pattern, you know. I was *looking* at a cross, but she told me she already had one.'

'Thanks, Mr Reid. I wouldn't worry about it. Righto. Take care.' Stirling clicked off.

Slowly he slipped the phone back into his pocket. The picture he was getting was developing like an horrific scene-of-crime photo. And so was the terrible feeling in the root of his brain.

Chapter NINE

'SHIT! JAMES!' LENA'S voice rang through the house. 'Come and look at this!'

'I'm just cleaning my teeth. What is it?'

'You're in the *Herald*.'

Paxton went cold all over. Hastily he spat out a mouthful of toothpaste, almost missing the sink, and sucked in a handful of water to rinse. Then he yanked a towel off the rail and rubbed his face as he hurried into the dining room. Lena sat at the table in her satin pyjamas, the paper open beside the remains of her breakfast. He watched her face as she stood and moved aside to let him see it.

Paxton speed-read the first few paragraphs, although the headline told him everything. *Police enlist psychic in hunt for killer.* The truth was out. Now everyone would know what he was, and it would all begin again, just like back in England. The demands, the pleas, the condemnation, the jokes . . .

'Couldn't help yourself, could you?' Lena said.

He braced himself for the onslaught. Instead she sighed and shook her head. 'I knew it was only a matter of time . . . If you *really* want a normal life bartending, I'm Josef Stalin.'

Paxton didn't know whether to protest or laugh, but the phone got in first. Lena went into the bedroom to answer.

'Hello?' She frowned at the response. 'Who am I speaking to, please?' Someone gave the wrong answer.

Lena rolled her eyes in Paxton's direction, shaking her head. 'I don't think he wants to talk to you right now. He's not interested in publicity, thank you.'

Shit. Paxton motioned at her to hand the phone over. Reluctantly Lena let go of the receiver. Glen wandered in, alerted by the tone of her voice, and she stroked his flank as he leaned against her legs, but she was still listening.

'James Paxton speaking.'

'Hello James, it's Philippa Grant from *Cross*.'

It had just gone from bad to worse — national current affairs.

'Sorry to disturb you, but I just thought you might like to give your side of things on tonight's show. What sort of predictions have you made about the crime?'

'I'm not allowed to discuss that, I'm sorry.'

'I guess that's understandable. But there are a lot of myths about mediums and the like, and I thought you'd be interested in showing people it's not all hocus pocus. You're obviously performing a service for the police, and Simon's really keen to have you on the show.'

'Sorry, Philippa, but I'm really not interested.'

'If you're worried about being reimbursed for your time off work —'

'It's more the loss of reputation, to be frank.'

'Well that's what you'd be defending! You could show people —'

'No, I'm talking about what people'd think if they saw me with Simon Burgess.' Paxton dropped the phone back on the hook. Then took it off again, and left it lying beside the bed. Lena was incredulous.

'How the hell did they find you?'

'One of the muppets from work must have given them my number.'

'But how did they get hold of the news in the first place?'

Paxton frowned. There was only one possible answer to that, and an ugly one. 'It would have been the police. There's no way the neighbours could have guessed.'

'But why would they want the media to crawl all over them? If they don't get pilloried, they'll get laughed at.'

'Perhaps it's someone who doesn't want me helping them. One name already springs to mind.'

Lena looked into his eyes, reading his thoughts. 'You think Gardner did it?'

'Mr Friendly? Nah. We're meeting up for a drink later.'

'You'd need to find a man with two penises to meet a bigger wanker.'

Paxton cracked up, despite his anger. 'Where did you get *that* from?'

'I'm quite proud of that actually. Oh, not *again*!'

This time it was Lena's mobile. She dived over the bed to fish it from her handbag, answering it on the fourth ring. At the response her eyes iced over. 'I'm sorry, you've got the wrong number.'

Then Paxton saw her expression change abruptly, her gaze locking on his in panic.

'I beg your pardon. I thought you were the press. Just one moment please.' She held the phone out. 'The police,' she hissed.

Paxton closed his eyes. 'Fuck.'

It was an effort to lift his arm and take the phone. Foremost in his mind was the thought that they must have got Lena's number from Stirling. The DC would kill him for this. If his superiors left him any remains to dispose of.

'Hello, James Paxton speaking.'

'Hello James, Graeme Kirkpatrick here. Did you happen to see the papers this morning, by any chance?'

'I'm just thankful I got breakfast out of the way first, that's all I can say.'

'Was it a surprise to you?'

Though it was phrased carefully, Paxton caught his meaning at once. 'I didn't say a word of this to anyone, Graeme. I've got my girlfriend here wanting to kill me for leaving her out of the loop.'

'Hmm.' The detective was silent for a beat. 'We're all a bit disappointed about this. We're not sure who the leak was, but we're going to get to the bottom of it. I don't mean to accuse you personally, but you were the first port of call, being outside the force. When it's someone *on* the force, it gets one hell of a lot harder.'

Paxton felt sorry for him, but not much better for himself. 'Could you please tell Andy Stirling that I'm not the one who let him down? I don't think he's sure.'

Kirkpatrick sounded surprised. 'He's standing just outside. I'll let him know.' Paxton could feel something else coming. 'Um . . . I should probably add, we're not sure if we'll be calling on your services again just for the time being. The fellas upstairs want to monitor what happens with the media, public response, that sort of thing. You may have noticed, image is a bit of a weak spot with the police at the moment.'

'Yeah, that's all right, I understand.' But he still felt it like a heavy boot in his backside. The distancing began.

'You may or may not hear from me again. Sorry I can't be more precise than that. I'll have to ask you to keep clear of the murder locations in the meantime as well, just for the look of the thing.'

'Of course.'

'Thanks, James. I'm sorry to spoil your morning.' He sounded like he was trying to find a gentler way of ending the conversation, but realised there wasn't anything more to say. 'Goodbye.'

'Bye.' Paxton pressed the off button and let his head fall to his chest.

'The police have just canned my involvement.'

Lena looked at him.

'They don't want anything more to do with me — and I'm not sure Graeme was convinced I wasn't behind it all.'

Lena sighed. 'It's probably for the best.' She noted Paxton's silence. 'I wish I knew who was behind it. Then I could kill him for you.'

Paxton barely mustered a smile. 'The only thing that could make my morning better would be a phone call from Immigration telling me I have to go back to my parents.'

'If you're going back to England, I'm going with you.' Lena put her arms around him, pressing her cheek against his own.

When the mobile rang again, it was barely a surprise. Paxton took it himself.

'James. Better be quick. They'd have my nuts if they knew I'd called you.'

Andy Stirling — who else? Paxton braced himself.

'Hey. I just wanted to say, you were right.' Paxton's jaw fell open. This *was* a day for surprises.

'About Warren, the book. Dammit, I don't know how you did it, but I just wanted you to know. All right? And I'm getting the feeling this has got something to do with cheating. Think about it — Helen had more than one lover, and so did Charlotte. Something's going on.'

'Hmm. I think you might be onto something there. It'd make a lot of sense. But Andy, any ideas on the leak? Who the hell did this? You *know* I didn't.'

'Yeah, I know that. But you're not one of us.' Stirling sighed. 'Some of the people round here have moss growing inside their skulls. Yeah, it's — okay, bye darling, love you too!'

Abruptly a disengaged signal cut in. So Stirling wasn't allowed to talk to him. Welcome back to your childhood, James.

He sat on the edge of the bed and let himself fall back, feeling Lena crawl into his arms.

HE FELT THE itch in his feet, again, the urge to go out into the dark and become a part of it. At night he felt invisible, and unafraid, able to be himself as he couldn't during the day. Instead of looking through him, as if he were nothing, they'd stare straight at him, seeing nothing else, their eyes full of fear. He was everything to them in that one long night, and they'd never forget him again.

Not that he left them capable of telling . . .

He put on his shoes, running shoes with soft, silent soles, and went into the kitchen for a knife. She might be alone tonight, might not, but sooner or later, they'd finally meet. He felt like he knew her already.

Chapter TEN

NO ONE AT work would know, surely. Paxton wasn't sure Brent could read, and Adam . . . Adam didn't get the *Herald*, did he?

That last hope fell over the instant he walked into the room, and caught Adam's eye.

'Is it true what they say in the papers for once?' Adam's face was unusually serious. It gave Paxton a horrible jolt. This was the conversation he'd been avoiding for months.

He mumbled, 'I didn't think you ever read the papers.'

'Jade rang me.' Jade was Adam's girlfriend this summer.

Paxton had met her a few times, but he was surprised she'd been aware of his presence, let alone remembered his name. All Adam's relationships were as intense as they were short. 'She was flicking through the paper in the staffroom at her work. She was at me to ask if you do tarot readings.' The contempt in Adam's voice was subtle but obvious; whether it was directed at him or at Jade, Paxton wasn't sure.

'You can tell her I don't,' he said quietly. 'I never touch the stupid things.'

Adam gave him a long look. 'So that's what you weren't telling me. That time you ran out, and you ended up in hospital.'

'I didn't think you'd want to know.'

'You mean you didn't want to talk about it.'

'You going to be starting work anytime soon, you two, or are you just gonna stand there costing me money?'

They both turned to see Brent, the bar manager, standing over them with a glass in his hand. It would have been easy to point out that Brent wasn't actually the owner, but instead they silently took their places. It was busy till six-thirty. Being a Friday it was after-work-drinks night and, for many, the first week back after the summer break. Everyone was still trying to hang onto their holidays, swapping stories with colleagues not seen since before Christmas.

Finally the place emptied a bit. Adam grabbed a cloth, making a show of wiping down the bar, his back to Paxton. After a few seconds he glanced round to check Brent had gone.

'Why didn't you tell me? I'd have come after you.'

'Would you? If I'd said I had a psychic message that a serial killer was just outside?'

There was a long pause. Adam shifted his weight to his other foot. Then he jumped as the phone went off at his elbow. Reluctantly he answered it. 'Hello, Anubis Restaurant and Bar.'

Even from a short distance, Paxton could hear the excitement in the caller's voice. It sounded high-pitched, female.

The next second Adam's eyes shot towards him in astonishment. '*Eh?* You're joking.' He shook his head, placing his hand over the receiver. 'You're on TV, man. Change the channel.'

'*What?*' Something nasty kicked Paxton in the stomach. 'What the hell? Who's that?'

'It's Mel.'

Mel was the student who worked both the bar and the restaurant. It was her night off.

Adam was waving a hand at him. 'She says you're on *Cross*. You're up next.'

Paxton grabbed the phone. 'Mel, what the fuck?'

'James! Is that really you they're talking about? Are you psychic?'

Every muscle clenched in Paxton's body. He wanted to crawl under the bar, then punch something. 'I'm a medium,' he muttered.

'Oh my God. It really *is* you. I can't believe it. I just saw an ad. It's on after the news — some psychic woman's going to be making predictions about those women who were killed. They mentioned your name!'

Adam was already going up to the TV, flicking from Sky Sport to the news. Though his back was to it, Brent sensed the change immediately, his gleaming bald head swivelling round.

'Why didn't you tell me? I can't believe I work with a psychic — a *famous* psychic. God, you should have told us!'

'I can't talk now, Mel, sorry. It's a bit busy.'

'Okay, but you have to tell me —'

'Brent's coming. I'll see you later. Bye.' Paxton hung up and turned to face the half-empty restaurant. Brent was on the other side of the room, next to the TV mounted on the wall. Paxton caught the look Brent sent him a moment later, when Adam had finished explaining. It was the look he might have given if one of the All Blacks had been outed as a transvestite: sheer incredulity, and denial. Paxton willingly broke eye contact as a customer came up to the bar. When he'd finished pouring him a beer, Paxton risked another look at the TV. Brent was still standing there, his arms folded, gazing up at the screen. It was possibly the first time in his life he'd ever watched current affairs. Adam was heading back in Paxton's direction. He hooked a thumb over his shoulder.

'Go on, go watch it. I'll guard the fort here.'

'I'm not sure I *want* to see this. I told those bastards I *didn't* want an interview.'

His anger felt like poison in his own veins. God only knew how the police were going to react to this one. The newspapers were bad enough, but national TV . . . Paxton pushed through the flap in the bar and took up a position behind Brent, who glanced at him, but said nothing. The news was just wrapping up. Without any ad break, it cut straight to a preview for *Cross*, hosted by Simon Burgess, the man who believed in nothing.

'Just what is the world coming to? Murders in our largest city, police without leads, investigations in disarray — so much so, they're consulting a psychic! Tonight I'll be talking to Detective Inspector William Woodward of Auckland's Criminal Investigation Branch and a well-known local medium, Cristiana Austin, to get the *other side* of the story.' Burgess gave a cynical little smile.

Brent, seeing a line-up of people at the bar, went to give Adam a hand, leaving Paxton alone in front of the TV.

He stood fidgeting until the ad break finished, and Burgess's face was back on the screen. He had the silvering hair and strong features of a born statesman, except that Burgess had a healthy contempt for anyone on either side of the political line. He got involved only to stir. Paxton's hostility multiplied tenfold as soon as Burgess opened his mouth. He was smiling.

'Good evening. Just *where* are your taxpayer dollars going these days? In this day and age of the latest computer technology, when every schoolkid knows all the forensic jargon from the cop shows, when DNA tests are solving cases decades old,' Burgess paused for breath, 'the New Zealand police are resorting to fortune tellers. Sorry, *mediums*, who say they can communicate with the dead. What is going on? Two women dead, possibly thanks to the same killer. Charlotte Hiscocks, a mortgage broker from Epsom in Auckland, and Helen McCowan, a pensioner from Grey Lynn, both brutally murdered in their own homes. And, according to our sources, police are consulting one James Paxton, a local *bartender* and sometime psychic.'

Paxton felt his fingers curl at Burgess's tone.

'Who, if you remember, was first on the scene of one of last winter's murders. Does anyone else see a pattern here? Well, here to explain we have Detective Inspector William Woodward of the Auckland Central CIB, and professional medium Cristiana Austin. Thanks for coming, Inspector.'

'Evening, Simon.'

So this was Kirkpatrick's boss. The camera had shifted to a solid-looking man who radiated unruffled calm. Paxton had expected someone harried, or at the very least angry and defensive, but he was surprised. Burgess was going to have a hard road taking the piss out of him. Woodward would piss on him right back.

'So tell us, Inspector, *why* go to Mr Paxton? Is this a sign of desperation?'

Woodward smiled. 'No, Simon, it most certainly isn't. And I think you'll find that psychics have been employed by the police on a number of occasions, across the world as well as in New Zealand. It's no new phenomenon. We use animals with extra senses humans don't have, so why not people?'

'But wouldn't you say this is, well, all a bit flaky? What do you think the public will have to say about a supposedly First World police force using their money to pay a fortune-teller? It doesn't make a good impression, surely. I mean, when can we expect the voodoo dolls and the witch doctors?'

'I don't know where you get the fortune teller bit from, Simon. As I understand it, fortune tellers predict someone's future, and I'm afraid these poor women don't have one.'

'Come on, Inspector, that's a bit flippant —'

Woodward cut calmly across him. 'No, Simon, I'm not the one being flippant at all. As far as I'm concerned, this is no laughing matter, and we shouldn't be poking fun at it. If you think that this sort of thing is an imprecise science, no doubt you're right. But unfortunately, so is all police work. Even the folks in the labs at ESR, overworked as they are, will get it wrong. Samples will get contaminated or misfiled, witnesses give faulty or false statements. When you work in my job, evidence is very rarely perfect.'

Burgess opened his mouth again, but Woodward didn't let him get started. 'But the main thing is doing *something*, getting as *much* information as we can to get these criminals off the streets. Because the more we have, the more likely we are to find the truth. I have implicit faith in Mr Paxton's ability — and might I add, he is *not* being paid for his help — and I'm not going to apologise for doing everything I can to track down a very dangerous person and bring relief to the grieving families.'

He sat back, everything in his manner proclaiming he was finished. Paxton wanted to cheer. He was startled to hear such a glowing reference from a senior member of the police, someone he'd never met. Clearly a lot more went on behind the scenes than he'd ever know.

Without a word Burgess turned away, meeting the friendlier gaze of his second guest. She was probably in her forties, with black hair pinned up stylishly, understated make-up, and wore a Celtic cross around her neck, underneath a smart silver blouse. If she was indeed a medium she looked as though she charged well for it.

'Cristiana. What have you got to say about the psychic process? You've been a medium for the past twelve years, is that correct?'

'A professional one, yes, that's correct. I've been doing it for quite a bit longer than that.' She was friendly without being air-headed or sprout-eating earnest — not your average flake.

'And what are your feelings about these cases? Can you tell us who this killer is?'

Cristiana took a moment. 'Well Simon, I've been focusing on that all afternoon, and what I'm being told is that this is the work of someone who doesn't know either of the women personally, but who has a severe mental problem. He'll have been in trouble before. I'd say he's male, Maori or Pacific Island, in his late twenties. And I'm getting the name George. George or Jordan, something like that. I —'

Burgess interrupted. 'Well that's all very well and good, but how do we *find* this George? Or Jordan. How do we stop him killing again?'

'I sense he's somewhere near the water. In a white wooden house with a fireplace, and a white car in the driveway. He will be caught sometime soon, I feel.'

'Well, that's good to hear. I hope there won't be too many more murders in the meantime. Now, Inspector, how does that information tally with what you've heard from your own source, Mr Paxton? It's a pity we couldn't have him on the show tonight, but he tells us he's under a confidentiality agreement.'

'Yes, that's correct. And I'm afraid that even if this lady here had given us a phone number, there's no way I'd be letting on. There's still an investigation under way, and I don't want to make our offender go underground.'

'He's *already* underground, Inspector. No one can find him!'

Woodward smiled. 'Sorry, Simon, he's not underground yet. He's still very much on the surface, walking around with you and me. He's somebody's next-door neighbour.'

For once, Burgess didn't respond. Woodward went on, 'You can bet we have some leads, but at this stage I can't tell you what those are. I can only appeal to the public to give us any further information they might have.'

Paxton was pleased to note that Burgess looked distinctly disgruntled. He thanked Woodward and Cristiana, then ran off the contact numbers for the police. The segment was over.

That hadn't been so bad. Paxton had actually sort of enjoyed it. He was bloody impressed with that DI, wished he could have met him. He'd made mincemeat out of Burgess. And thank God they hadn't brought *him* too much into it. He pondered what the TV psychic had said. He'd be delighted if he could be even half as accurate as she was. Not only a rough age, but the ethnicity, part of a name and a description of the man's house. Jesus. Paxton was lucky if he even got past the roar of blood in his ears. Perhaps it was just sour grapes, but he'd bet everything he had she was fake.

He turned around to head back to the bar, and promptly met Brent's eye. The bar manager had come up behind him silently. How long he'd been listening was impossible to tell.

'Bit of a dark horse, aren't you, James? You mean to say you can talk to ghosts and stuff?'

'I didn't mean to say anything,' Paxton muttered.

'Didn't think you were the sort to believe in that stuff, let alone go around chatting to them.'

'Do you believe in spirits?'

'Only the ones behind that bar.' Brent looked over at the familiar ranks of bottles, all neatly, comprehensibly labelled.

'Well done. Everyone else grins like a mental patient whenever they say that.'

Brent smiled, then gave him a long, scrutinising stare. 'What other secrets are you hiding, I'd like to know?'

'Next week I'm booked in for a sex change, and then I'm converting to Islam,' said Paxton sarcastically.

Brent gave him another look. 'Shit you're weird, mate.' He walked back over to the bar. Perversely, Paxton felt better.

Chapter ELEVEN

'YOU'RE AS BAD as he is. He was all over me for shopping him to the media last time, when all the time it was the people from over the road! You're both bloody paranoid.'

Stirling gave Gardner a contemptuous look, forced to be even closer to him than he liked in the crowded office. 'Well, you tell me who else'd want to discredit him so badly. If anyone's got a stronger motive than you for getting Paxton thrown off the case, I'd like to know who.'

Gardner merely rolled his eyes. 'As far as I can see, he doesn't even need the help. What do *you* think, Tony?'

When he so desired, Rees's face could out-granite a cliff's. 'I went to a fortune teller once. As a kid. She told me I'd become a reporter, because I asked so many questions.'

Gardner and Nielsen laughed.

'Guess that answers that then,' said Gardner. 'Flipping journos. She might as well have told you you'd become a rent boy. Same difference really.'

Stirling glared at him. 'If you don't believe in psychics, then how do you explain James Paxton knowing the name of the second lover, as well as smelling the Scotch?'

'I dunno. All those years working in a bar, he could probably smell vodka from half a mile. *And* tell you if it was Smirnoff or Stolichnaya.'

'I'm telling you, there's no way he could have known. We need his help.'

Rees looked awkward. 'Listen, Andy, I know he's a friend of yours, but these people have all sorts of tricks.

He might not even realise he's doing it, but he's getting the information some other way. Maybe he *did* smell the whisky somewhere, or saw an empty bottle of it in one of the rooms.'

Stirling was hurt by Rees's disbelief. Of all his colleagues, the solid South African was probably his closest mate, the one he could always count on to sail him through rough waters. Rees was the last person he ever wanted to brawl with, even if only metaphorically. 'Then how do you explain him knowing about Warren?' Stirling asked.

Rees shrugged, shaking his head. 'I can't.' It looked as though it were killing him inside. 'But there's bound to be something. Call me a suspicious copper — the job's soaked through to my bones.'

'So you reckon Paxton's the leak then?'

Rees's tone was careful. 'I'm not saying anything, mate.'

'Says it all, I'd say,' said Gardner.

Rees gave him one of those impenetrable glances. Stirling knew he disliked the sergeant as much as he did; it was only that he kept his personal demons on a short leash.

'They're all as bad as each other,' Gardner went on. 'Did you hear that medium lady say the killer was somewhere near water? We're on a bloomin' isthmus! I read about that once in a book on English murder cases. Some idiot phoned in saying the body was within fifty miles of water. I mean, Christ.'

Frustrated, Stirling slumped back in his chair, sending it rolling into the side of the desk. 'I guess it doesn't really matter. The media's got their little burning man, and God forbid we should let him anywhere near the investigation now.'

'I don't know why Graeme thought it was such a great idea in the first place,' said Gardner.

'Well, don't forget it was Woodward's too,' Nielsen said, reminding them all of her presence. She sat on the edge of her desk, sipping a cup of coffee. For some reason, after Stirling had invaded her cubicle, Rees and then Gardner had followed, pursuing his own little vendetta. At her remark, everyone looked surprised.

'I thought Wooden Willy just okayed it when Graeme asked him,' said Gardner. 'Then had to cover Graeme's arse on TV.'

'Oh yeah, Graeme approached him about it, but Willy was all for it,' said Nielsen. 'He's had dealings with mediums and psychics before. Apparently they've been a real help in the past.'

'You mean he actually meant what he was saying last night? I never thought Willy would be the sort to go for all that mumbo-jumbo.' Rees was doubtful.

'He didn't get to the top for being closed-minded and just your average plodding copper,' said Nielsen equably.

'Yeah, well, we're not getting anywhere on this investigation if we're all just sitting round discussing the afterlife,' Gardner replied, stepping towards the door. 'We deal with enough psychos out there without having to work with one.'

Stirling took a deep breath. 'Paxton *didn't* go to the media. Which means that one of us is behind it.'

He couldn't help looking at Gardner.

An amused smile broke out on the DS's face. 'When you wake up screaming in the night, Andy, am I the one who jumps out of your wardrobe?' He leaned in closer, knowing full well how much Stirling hated having anyone in his personal space. 'Don't make me your personal bogeyman.' He smiled, making sure the insult went home, then left.

Rees had a glimmer of movement at the edge of his mouth. 'Fuck, I don't even want to think about having him in my room late at night.'

Reluctantly, Stirling got up from his chair and forced himself to follow Gardner. Behind him he heard Rees excuse himself and trail after them towards the tearoom.

'So, were you planning on following up that lead I gave you?' Stirling called. 'I think you can hardly go past the cheating lovers angle.'

Gardner shrugged, turning. 'It has as much value as any of the other clues we've got, I guess.' For Gardner, that was tantamount to a huge pat on the back and a cigar.

'Oh yeah, is that the old engineer you were talking to yesterday?' Paynter came out of the tearoom, coffee in hand. 'I heard about that. Didn't you get a tip-off from that psychic friend of yours?'

'Yes I did,' Stirling answered, not letting himself look at Gardner.

'Did he dangle one of those crystals around when he was doing his thing?' Paynter went on with a grin. 'Surprised that psychic on TV last night didn't bring a crystal ball along.'

'Piss off, Ciaran. I want a coffee.' Gardner stepped round him into the tiny kitchen.

Even Stirling had to force back a smile. Gardner's rudeness was wholesale; it spared next to no one. 'Found Charlotte Hiscocks's killer yet, Ciaran? Why don't you go and investigate your own case?'

'Not a lot to investigate at the moment,' admitted Paynter, shrugging, a defeated expression on his usually cheery features. 'Those other boyfriends of hers have both got alibis. I was hoping you'd be able to tell *me* something. Can't you get your friend to give us another clue?'

''Fraid not. He's been side-lined till further notice.'

'That's one thing the media's done for us anyway,' came a mutter. The contents of the fridge door rattled as it slammed shut.

'One of us must have *something*. Give me something to work with here.' All of them recognised the plea as one that had entered their own brains. 'Are we even dealing with the same killer?'

'Course we are,' snapped Gardner, reappearing with a mug.

'But I can't say our much-feted medium's given us much,' said Rees, speaking for the first time. 'Come and listen to this. God knows we all need a laugh . . .'

Stirling watched Rees and Paynter go, stung.

Heading past them up the corridor was Graeme Kirkpatrick, fresh from a private briefing with DI Woodward and the super, who in turn were no doubt reporting to the commissioner himself. Of course the brass were getting involved — the media were giving them a pasting. The police's badges were already tarnished enough, and now they were hiring psychics and allowing another serial killer to roam free, just six months after the first. Perhaps 'fresh from a briefing' wasn't the right description, thought Stirling, watching as the Senior got closer. As usual, Kirkpatrick had spilt coffee down the front of his shirt, and he looked old.

As for himself, he had no desire to go looking in mirrors.

THE TV WAS on, but only for the pictures. The sound came from the CD playing on the stereo. After spending all day surrounded by music, Alicia could no longer deal with silence. If music wasn't playing in her house, she was either out or asleep. Even then, she could easily fall asleep with the stereo on. It drove some of her boyfriends crazy, especially if they didn't have her taste. Brendan hated Adele, but Alicia had always admired her. The girl had talent. She made a point of playing Adele whenever Brendan was home.

He was out somewhere now with the boys. Probably pissed off his face again — odds on he would need a hand getting past the lounge when he rolled in at three, if he even managed that. Not that she minded a night alone. Alicia smiled as the phone buzzed again in her lap. The message said: 'What are you wearing?' Alicia looked down at her green T-shirt and old grey shorts. With a flirtatious grin, she typed back: 'How about you get creative?' She hit send, then stretched, yawning violently. The heat was making her even sleepier. The clock on the video read only nine-thirty, but she'd been up since half past four. She thought idly of locking up and going to bed. Serve Brendan right if the door was locked when he got home.

The man who'd just entered her kitchen was thinking the same thing. It did serve him right. Two months' worth of watching, and the boyfriend was only home one Friday out of eight. Hardly a surprise she was playing around — women like her would take every opportunity you gave them. Well, so would he.

Another text came in, just audible over the Red Hot Chili Peppers. 'Ski jacket and high-heeled boots?'

Alicia grinned widely, and bent her head over the little screen, trying to think of a smart answer. A pair of shoes stepped into her lounge, just out of her sight. She hit send. Then a tiny movement out of the corner of her eye made her look up and she jerked back in her seat. A man in a dark jacket was standing there, calmly pulling a pair of gloves tighter on his hands.

'Who are you texting?' he asked. He was smiling.

Alicia yanked her knees up beneath her, into a protective ball. 'What are you doing in here? Get out of my house.' She tried to sound commanding, though her voice shook.

'You should lock your doors.' He was coming towards her, still scarily calm.

'Get out, *now*.' Making an effort, Alicia stood, backing away towards the hall. In her panic, she wondered irrationally why he was wearing a jacket on such a hot night.

'You weren't texting your boyfriend, were you?'

For the first time she looked directly at his face. She blinked, realising she'd seen it before. The *where* danced around just beyond the edges of her mind. She opened her mouth to speak, eyes wide in astonishment, but whatever she was about to say came out as air. His hands had slid free of his jacket, bringing something shiny with them. A knife. A sharp one. Alicia met his eyes again, and, without thinking, her thumb went automatically to the keypad in her hand.

One, one —

Her scream died instantly as he clamped one hand round her throat, pressing her into the wall. With his other he thrust the knife into her stomach, and twisted. She made a choking sound, looking down to see the front of her top stained red. As her trembling hand went to touch it, the next thrust struck her chest, upwards, piercing a lung with a hiss and making her cough up blood. He held her shoulder, steadying her as the third blow went into her throat. The coughing stopped. Stab number four went through her heart, but by then she was already dead.

He watched her for a few seconds, seeing his own reflection in her dilated pupils. Catching sight of blood on his shoes, he took them off. He knew all about prints; everyone did, these days. Then he quietly let himself out the back door, and walked back to his car.

Alicia stared off into a corner. The blood had stopped gushing now. There was a moment or two of silence, then another random track came on. Adele, as it happened. "Send My Love to Your New Lover". If Alicia could have heard the opening lyrics, she would have thought it was funny.

Chapter TWELVE

LENA WAS WOKEN by the phone. Perhaps Paxton's premonitions were catching, but she was already preparing herself for bad news when she picked it up. She tried to clear her throat before she answered, vainly trying to conceal the fact she'd been sleeping at quarter to nine.

'Hello?'

'Hello, is that Lena Bradley?'

'Yes?'

'Hello, Lena, its John Merchant from the *Herald* here. Sorry, have I woken you up?'

'Yes, you have,' Lena muttered, shutting her eyes.

'Oh. I'm sorry about that. But would it be possible to chat to you for a few moments? Seeing as you're already on the phone.' He laughed.

Lena didn't smile. 'What about?'

'Just about how James Paxton helped you last year. I hear he's your partner now.'

'Look, sorry John, I'm really not interested in giving an interview. I went through a lot back then and I'm just trying to get on with my life. I've already been rung several times.'

'I'm sorry about that, but all I'm asking for is a quick word on what convinced you that your partner is genuine.'

'Sorry John. I know you're just doing your job, but you'll have to find another story to fill the space.' She put the phone down, and jerked it out of the wall. She wavered for a moment, then bent to plug it back in and dialled Paxton's number.

Paxton was still livid by the time he arrived. 'Do you know, I just had a phone call from the *Herald* myself, before I left. Then just as I was going out the door, I got the *Courier*. The reporter was one of my regulars, so I was a little bit politer about telling her to stuff off, but even so . . . I'm just glad we're not in the UK. They're bloomin' frightening.' He came over to touch Lena's shoulder, his voice softening. 'Are you okay? I'm really sorry about this.'

'Yeah,' she said, snuggling into his shoulder. 'It's just like before, isn't it? Only this time, instead of the police hounding us, it's the media.'

'Have you burned this morning's *Herald* yet? God knows what they've said about our relationship.'

Lena stared at him. 'They haven't printed anything yet, I thought. They just rang up.'

Paxton saw the look of horror on her face and felt terrible. 'Actually, the guy I spoke to said he wanted my side to flesh out what was already in there.'

Lena let him go and slipped past him to the front door, going straight down the drive to the letterbox. The *Herald* was still coiled and waiting in the slot.

The story was at the top of page three, headlined *Psychic no stranger to serial killings*.

James Paxton was first on the scene when optometrist Mark Bradley was murdered by the serial killer dubbed the Eastern Strangler in July 2003. A source

112

close to the investigation has revealed Mr Paxton was also a person of interest in that inquiry, and was questioned on numerous occasions following the deaths of Gloria Tan, Stacey Ryan and security guard Dion Mihaljevich. Mr Paxton's partner is Lena Bradley, daughter of the murdered man.

'Done their homework, haven't they?' said Paxton. It unsettled him, and made him angry. There seemed little they couldn't find out.

'That clever dick source of theirs is a cop,' said Lena. 'That's obvious. I don't see how the police can justify dropping you after this.'

Paxton looked at her with a small smile. 'And you were worried about me working with them in the first place.'

'Well, it's not fair.'

'No, but that's the law for you.' He read the rest of the article intently, wondering just how bad it was going to get. He nearly choked when he got to the sidebar. 'What the hell? Where did they get this from? There's a story here about how Helen McCowan had a jealous lesbian lover.' He cracked up, shaking his head. 'This isn't a newspaper, it's a soap.'

'So she definitely wasn't a lesbian?' Lena asked, smiling.

'Hell no! Not unless she kept it from her husband and her two boyfriends. Don't know where she'd have found the time for another one.'

'Funny how they can make up as much as they want and still have space to print the truth about us,' said Lena with a sigh.

'Are you sorry people know you're with me?'

'No, it's not that . . . I like the sympathy.' She ruffled his hair, giving the smile that killed him every time. 'I just want to be left alone. It looks like that's not going to happen now.' She sighed again.

'SHE WAS IN here every other day. It was her local café. We called each other by our first names.' The regret on Arthur Wong's face was plain. He was sitting for once, in a chair opposite Stirling.

'Did you ever see her with anyone else but Warren, the man I was with yesterday?' asked Stirling.

Arthur met his eye, and gave him a knowing look. 'I think you already know the answer to that. She was a very friendly lady. Very *young* for her age.'

They were in a secluded corner of the café, which wasn't too busy at ten o'clock on a weekday.

'Could you describe the other gentleman? If it *was* just one other gentleman?' Stirling didn't even want to think about it.

'No, there was only one. He was a Scottish man. Very strong accent. He had mostly grey hair — he would have been about the same age as Helen, I guess.'

Stirling exchanged looks with Rees, seated beside him. 'That's Rob all right.'

'You don't think *he* —' Arthur looked incredulous and worried.

Stirling put up a hand, soothing. 'I can't say too much at this stage, but we're not too concerned about Mr Reid.'

Rees took a sip of his cappuccino and plunked the cup back in its saucer. 'The question is, have you seen anyone who looked suspicious? Anyone who might have paid a bit much attention to Helen?'

At that Arthur smiled slightly. 'Everyone noticed Helen. She was always laughing — people looked at her all the time.'

'No one you noticed in particular?'

Arthur thought about it hard, then shook his head. 'No. I'd love to say there was someone who always followed them, and read a newspaper, like in the movies, but this is a café. The only excitement we get is an extra bag of coffee they forgot to charge us for. Maybe Nathan or Morgan have seen something. Nathan! Morgan! Could you come here for a moment please?'

The friendly bloke with the muffins and a young girl with red hair answered the summons, but neither had seen anything suspicious. Morgan's face, lightly sprinkled with freckles across her nose, was as upset at Nathan's.

'No! They told me all about it, it's awful. I wish I could help.' She shook her head. 'She never treated us like wallpaper, like a lot of people. Usually she'd say something, even if it was just about the weather. She was one of my favourite customers.'

'Yeah,' said Nathan. 'I wish I'd been keeping an eye out. You just don't think anything like this is going to happen.'

'It still shocks me at times, and I'm a homicide detective,' said Stirling, giving a wry laugh. 'It's a sad state of affairs when you rely on dead people to put food on the table.'

'Beautiful image there, Detective Constable,' said Rees. 'Very tasteful.' He nodded at the wall behind Stirling. 'Speaking of which, I like the artwork in here. Kind of a medieval theme or something.'

Stirling twisted in his chair to look. 'Oh yeah,' he said in surprise.

A rustic stone portico was festooned with vines and dangling grapes, while deep inside the garden a beautiful woman in a long flowing dress was attempting to charm the pants off a young man. Now that he looked, there were several other artworks like it, all with attractive scenery such as the wall of a castle or a cavern as the main focus, and small mythical figures somewhere inside the frame.

Stirling liked them. He wasn't a fan of abstract art; he preferred places and people. Things you could read.

'Ah, we have a resident artist,' said Arthur, smiling at Nathan.

'You like them?' asked Nathan, beaming. 'The paintings all fit in with the name of the café — *Parsifal*'s an opera by Wagner.'

'I just picked it because it sounded good,' said Arthur with a cheeky smile. 'And then I made it Italian because the food is better. Note how all the paintings have some kind of food in them: the grapes . . .' He pointed to the one with the castle wall. 'See the orchard beside the castle? And even in the cavern, there's a goblet and a few loaves of bread on the floor. Make the customers hungry, that's my theory. Makes them buy more. Is it working?' He gave the detectives a sly look.

Rees reluctantly pushed his chair back, getting to his feet. 'Speaking of working, we'd best be going. Thanks very much for your help on all this — we've just got to keep ploughing on.'

'But if you *do* think of anything, let us know,' said Stirling. He slid his card across the table to Arthur.

'We will.' Arthur got up too, clapping his hands together. 'Now, what would you like? You must take something when you go.'

Stirling and Rees exchanged glances again, each seeing who would give first.

'Oh, we couldn't take anything from you,' Stirling said. 'We're just doing our job.'

'Oh, no, no, no, don't be silly. You are strong, healthy men. You work hard! You need food to keep you going. You can't just live on coffee. You won't catch bad guys with no meat on your bones. Look at you!'

He had to be talking about Stirling, not Rees, who was built like a draught horse.

'No Arthur, you're the one who's been helping us, not the other way round. I've got lunch back at the office.'

'What do you have? Sandwiches?'

Actually Stirling was lying through his teeth. 'Yeah. My wife makes them. I can't disappoint her.'

'All that healthy food's not good for you. You need starch! Gives you energy. Here.' Arthur twisted his head, looking at Nathan. 'Go get them something. Better say what you want, quick, or he'll give you anything.'

The two detectives grinned, not at all minding that they were being bribed.

'I'll have a piece of that orange cake with the almonds on it if it's all right,' Stirling told Nathan. 'Thank you.'

'Mud cake, please!' called Rees to his retreating back.

'Hell, Tony, that's got to be the worst thing on the menu.'

'Is that all?' asked Arthur. 'Throw in a scone or something,' he called to Nathan, his eyes twinkling at the detectives. He shrugged. 'If you don't eat it all, you can share it.'

'Thanks very much, Arthur,' said Stirling.

Rees watched the cakes going into a bag. 'You'd make some lucky woman a wonderful husband.'

Stirling blinked. He realised that despite making friends with the little man, he'd never asked. 'Oh yeah! Where is your wife? Chained her in the kitchen?'

Arthur shook his head, and shrugged. 'She didn't like New Zealand. She stayed in Malaysia. Better for business. But at least now she doesn't nag me about wasting the sugar.'

Nathan came back over, handing them a bag each. 'I thought you should try Arthur's shortbread,' he said conspiratorially. 'He makes it himself. It's got a lemon glaze.'

Both men had to stop themselves drooling. They thanked the café staff in unison, trying hard not to walk back to the car too quickly.

'That might just be the best interview I've ever given,' said Rees, peering into his bag and giving it a sniff.

'We didn't even learn anything!'

'Are you complaining?'

They got into the car, starting on the cake without even turning on the ignition. Stirling took a look at the clock, and laughed at himself. 'It's not even eleven o'clock yet.'

Rees didn't say anything, the corner of his mouth smeared with chocolate icing.

Stirling leaned across him and turned the key with his free hand, bringing the radio to life. 'Better see what we've missed. How many Subarus have been broken into while we've been inside?' He bit into his cake, leaning back in his seat.

But there was nothing on the police radio, so he switched to the music stations instead, flicking through until he found a song he liked. He and Rees peacefully chewed their weekly allowance of fat and sugar, drifting away into the music and their own private thoughts. Stirling was listening with only half an ear when a news segment came on.

'The case of missing JaFM radio host Alicia Schofield has been filed with the police. The DJ is part of the morning show with co-hosts Joel Moorside and Curtis Webb, who raised the alarm when she failed to arrive for work this morning and could not be contacted. One of the show's producers went to search for Ms Schofield at her home, where bloodstains were found.'

By now, both Stirling and Rees had stopped eating, almost forgetting to breathe. They stared at the radio as if to look away meant certain death.

'However, there is still no sign of the young DJ, despite her friends and colleagues joining in the search. It is thought that her co-hosts will not return to work tomorrow.' There was a moment of dead air. 'God man, that's terrible. I know they're the competition, but that is just too awful for words. Our prayers are with you, my brothers. Fuck the playlist, this one's for you.'

The radio cut to 'Ain't No Sunshine' by Bill Withers. Stirling stood it for a few bars, then leaned forward and twisted it off, looking grimly at Rees, whose expression was almost identical.

'Bet you a thousand, Andy.'

Stirling shook his head. 'Bets are off.' He went for his mobile and thumbed rapidly through the menu.

'Gidday, Andy,' Kirkpatrick answered. 'How are you getting on?'

'Dick all, Senior. What's this about a DJ going missing?'

Rees signalled to him to put the phone on speaker.

'Thought you might have heard that story . . .' There was a slight grunt, as if Kirkpatrick were taking a seat. 'It's a lot worse than you think.'

'How could it be worse? He did it, didn't he? *He* did. And now he's hiding the bodies.'

'There's a hell of a lot of blood, from what I've heard. John Blundell's on it. He's notified all the hospitals, but if the unthinkable happened and she actually turned up, it'd be in the freezer section.'

'He's never hidden them before . . .'

'He hasn't bothered with the doughnuts either.'

'Eh?'

'A little surprise turned up at the scene while the guys were there. Bit creepy. The bastard sent them doughnuts.'

'Who? *Crime* squad?'

'A dozen, assorted. From Dunkin' Donuts. John said they appeared about an hour after he arrived on the scene.'

Stirling looked down at the crumpled paper bag on his lap, topped with its half-eaten shortbread.

'That's definite psycho material.'

'You're telling me. You and Tony had better get back here. Briefing's at one.'

Rees silently wiped his mouth and started the car. Stirling threw the remains of the shortbread into the bag and twisted the top. *Dunkin' Donuts*. He hurled it into the console under the radio with unnecessary force, sucking the stickiness off his fingers.

'Like he's watching,' Rees murmured.

Chapter THIRTEEN

'OUR SECOND BIG witch hunt in less than a year. It's a bit of a worry.' Kirkpatrick was leaning against Rees's desk, slapping his tie against his hand, unable to keep still. The briefing room was already full of detectives, wearing the entire spectrum of expressions from dour to asleep to excited.

'What's happening, Senior?' Stirling asked.

'You'll have to wait for William. It's over my head now.'

'You can forget sleeping from now on,' Rees said. 'Now we've got someone remotely high-profile involved, and the media are jumping up and down.' He sagged back in his chair, frowning angrily. 'What gets me is his attitude. All these deliveries, trying to be clever. What is this, *Dial M for Murder*?'

'Well, well, well. It's *The Ant and Andy Show*.' Gardner grinned at Stirling and Rees as he walked in, looking positively perky. He seemed to be relishing his chance to get stuck in. Rees glanced calmly up from his desk.

'What's yours, Ray? *Digging with Gardner?*'

Once again, Stirling had to marvel at Rees's command of his features, not to mention his quips. Gardner's face soured.

Woodward entered the room, followed by Little John Blundell, Nielsen and Paynter, who was carrying a stack of files.

'Take a seat,' Woodward told them, going to his own place beside the whiteboard. He waited for the scraping of chairs to subside. 'Hands up who *hasn't* heard the news about Alicia Schofield.'

There were a few seconds of rustling, but only of curious heads turning. Not a single hand went up.

'Good. You all got the first test right.' He nodded to Paynter, who got up and started separating the files into three piles, one for each row. 'Ciaran's just handing out all the details. You'll notice the folders contain stuff about two other homicides as well. The first one, Charlotte Hiscocks, who died in Epsom, and the second, Helen McCowan, who was found in Grey Lynn. Hence the reason for this briefing. Given the location — Ms Schofield lives in Ponsonby — and the fact that another delivery was involved, there's very little doubt we're dealing with the same bloke. Why is that, John?'

''Cause the bugger used her credit card as well, when he ordered the doughnuts.'

'Leave any for us?' someone called out from the back, to laughter.

'Yeah, if you like 'em dusted with black powder.'

'That mean they're Maori doughnuts?' called someone else. There were sniggers.

A thickset Maori detective hollered back. 'I'd shut up, boy, unless you wanna look like a doughnut, with an even bigger hole in your head than you got now.'

Woodward smiled, seeming relieved at the release of tension. 'Settle down, class.'

'But why hide the body?' asked Stirling. 'He's never done that before. He rings up delivery men. He *wants* them to be discovered.'

123

'Yeah, and who delivered the doughnuts? Dunkin' Donuts don't deliver,' Gardner spoke up from Stirling's left. The way he said it, it sounded like a slogan.

Woodward nodded. 'As John told me, the man ordered over the phone, and paid extra to get them to deliver. One of the staffers brought them down in his own car. Thought he was going to meet the real Alicia Schofield.'

'That's truly sick,' said Coleman, his face twisting.

'And it's getting top priority. Superintendent's orders. Fire any info to Graeme or myself, but all inquiries go through me.'

'Bloody media,' said Gardner.

Picking up the thread, Kirkpatrick added, 'Wish I could find out who sold us all out to *Cross*. Who on earth gave the press that lesbian story?'

Since Rees was sitting between him and Kirkpatrick, the glimmer of private amusement on his face caught Stirling's attention.

'Yeah. What a woman, eh?' Paynter was shaking his head. 'Not just an old-timer, but a two-timer. Jeez, makes you feel a bit out of it, doesn't it?'

'God, I hope they don't get hold of the doughnut story,' said Kirkpatrick. 'They'll have a field day.'

Woodward was no longer the solid, comforting figure at the head of the room.

'Whoever it is, he — or she — will soon find that putting gossip ahead of public safety is going to put them in a very, very difficult situation.' He eyeballed them all. 'I hope you're all paying close attention. Because we will find you.'

Rees caught Stirling gazing at him, and gave him a quizzical look. But it wasn't enough to undo the suspicion that had just latched its teeth into Stirling's mind.

'Don't look at us, sir,' said Gardner. 'It'll be our friend Mr Paxton, paying us back for dropping him from the investigation.'

'Or at least someone who didn't value his input,' said Nielsen, with a side glance at Gardner.

Woodward ignored both comments. 'Do you want to tell them your news, Vicky?' he asked. 'You might want to stand up.'

Nielsen smiled at him, nodding, then stood to face the rest of the group. 'It looks like we might have a suspect. For the murders, that is.'

Now there wasn't a single bored face in the room.

'Ciaran managed to get some straight facts out of a friend of Mrs Hiscocks. We all knew she played the field a bit, but it just so happens that one of her lovers wasn't quite so happy to share.'

'Remember the one who went to Australia?' asked Paynter. 'He was her first work fling, right before the richer one, Acott. Turns out she started with Acott while she was still with this man. He didn't have a clue. In fact, he left his wife for her, and got pretty upset when Mrs Hiscocks wouldn't leave *her* husband, and it all came out about Acott,' said Paynter. 'Especially when the wife cleaned him out in the divorce and he had to change jobs.

125

Imagine that, they all worked together — Mrs Hiscocks, Acott, this guy and his wife. And they all sided with her.'

'So how good does he look as a suspect?' asked Blundell, leaning forward curiously.

Paynter smiled, his eyes sparkling with glee. 'Try sending his wife *and* Charlotte Hiscocks hate mail, stalking Mrs Hiscocks for a matter of months — until about six months ago, to be exact — and threatening to kill her.'

'Bloody hell, Ciaran,' said Kirkpatrick, beaming.

'But then how do you explain the time lapse?' asked Rees. 'That was when he went to Australia,' said Nielsen. 'He was supposed to still be there. *Except* we just found out he paid a visit to his ex yesterday. Now that his lover is dead, he said he wanted to make up.'

The room was so quiet it could have been a stakeout rehearsal.

'So when did he get back?' Rees spoke for all of them.

Paynter shrugged with mock nonchalance. 'According to passenger records, two days before Charlotte Hiscocks was killed. Stayed in a motel, was out all night. Not the faintest hope of an alibi.'

'*Now* we're talking!' Kirkpatrick said, chopping his right hand into his palm.

'There's just one problem,' said Woodward, commanding the attention of the room. 'John?'

Blundell got to his feet. '*I* have a chief suspect too.' There was a general round of groaning and laughter.

'My guy is one of Ms Schofield's colleagues — namely, Curtis Webb.'

126

'Shit, the DJ? The media are gonna love that one!' said Paynter.

Again Stirling saw that private smile glance across Rees's face. 'But why?' he asked. 'I mean, that has to destroy his career.'

'Psychotic murderers aren't always the most sensible of human beings,' said Blundell. 'And as it happens he has form. Apparently he was bitter when Alicia dumped him on air for someone else, seeing as they were engaged, and he's known to be rather violent. No doubt some of you will have read about his punch-ups in a few bars around town. Plus it was kind of an unkept secret that Alicia was also having a thing with her other co-star, Joel.'

'Yeah, but that's just wishful thinking,' said Gardner. 'Where's the evidence?'

'The fact that Curtis and Joel apparently can't stand each other, and haven't ever since Alicia arrived on the scene.' Blundell started ticking them off on his fingers. 'The fact that if *anyone* hates the police enough to send us doughnuts at a murder scene, he does, because we arrested him. Some of the stuff he's apparently said about us on air . . . He won't even give us a proper statement — not even when we said it could help us find Alicia's killer. And finally, because his prints are all over Alicia's flat, his ex-fiancée publicly two-timed him and made him the laughing stock of showbiz, and he's a thoroughly unpleasant, egotistical pig with danger management issues.' He waved both hands, out of fingers. 'And he has no alibi.'

'*And* . . .' said Woodward.

127

Blundell looked at him, caught on the hop. 'Did I miss something?'

'*And* . . . at this stage, there ain't a shred of evidence to say *he* did it either.' Woodward crossed his arms. 'Read your files, fellas. Operation Othello. Let's go before he gets hold of someone else.'

Chapter FOURTEEN

WEDNESDAY NIGHT, AND the conversation in the bar was all about the murders — Alicia Schofield's in particular. Though no body had been found, no one was in any doubt she was dead. It had been three days. The kid had been just twenty-two. She'd only got her job last August, and it was freaking out everyone under the age of thirty. Even the waiting staff from the restaurant were spooked. There was no strangeness about Paxton now. They all wanted his predictions as soon as he walked in the door.

Ross the chef stuck his head out of the kitchen, calling and beckoning. 'Hey, James, do you know who did it? What happened?'

'I wouldn't tell you even if I knew.'

'I'll cook for you at your place on your next night off. I can even bring round tiramisu.'

Paxton had a sweet tooth and Ross knew it. However, his mood tonight was blacker than treacle. 'You're a sick bastard, Ross. Besides, I'm not even on the case anymore.'

'Oh, come on.'

'Piss off. Go toss a salad.'

'Fine,' said Ross, shrugging and backing off. 'Just because I can't pay you as much as the networks can . . .'

'What are you talking about?'

The small cluster of staff around him dissolved as a young man approached. He'd had a haircut in deference to the heat, and the ratty jumper had changed to an ugly checked shirt, but there was no mistaking the nose. It was

Paxton's favourite journo, John Merchant from the *Herald*. He was a good reporter, but the last place Paxton wanted him digging was in his backyard. And Merchant wasn't alone — just behind him were a reporter from the local freebie paper, a photographer and a young blonde woman with a TV camera in tow.

'Mr Paxton, could you give us some clues as to the identity of the killer? Who murdered Alicia Schofield?'

'Is Alicia Schofield dead?'

'Is it the same killer, the one who killed the women in Epsom and Grey Lynn?'

Paxton was unable even to go through to the bar — they were blocking the doorway. Merchant was squashed closest to him, dictaphone at the ready, his eyes knowing.

'How does it feel to be involved in all this again?'

'How does it feel to be served with a trespass notice?'

With unbounded relief, Paxton turned to see the restaurant manager Tanya Helms striding towards them. Tanya wasn't just the manager, she co-owned the place with her husband Regan. They'd started out running their own liquor store in Manurewa, and been robbed twice. She could sense trouble with her back turned.

'What's going on here? You can't do this on my property.'

The TV reporter stepped up to her respectfully. 'Are you the owner?'

'Yes I am,' Tanya said crisply.

'I'm really sorry about all this disturbance, but your employee here, Mr Paxton, could be of real help in reassuring the public. If you'll let us have a really quick, exclusive interview with him, you could get rid of all this crowd. We'll take him somewhere private, buy a few drinks . . .'

There was an uproar from the other two journalists, and from Paxton himself.

'I don't *want* an interview!'

'We'll be really quick, Mr Paxton, I promise.'

'I'm not even part of the investigation anymore!'

Paxton realised his mistake as soon as he'd said it. The questions rained down harder than ever.

'Have the police thrown you off the case?' Merchant asked.

'You can ask them yourself,' called another voice. 'I've just rung them.' Brent was standing nearby, with his arms casually folded.

'Trespass, harassment . . . that all, Tanya?'

'Loss of earnings. I could sue the lot of you. Customers are turning around and walking out the door. Now I suggest you all do the same, before the police get here.' She nodded at the main entrance. 'Thirty seconds. Go on. You can't treat a private restaurant like the steps of the High Court!'

Muttering, they let their notepads fall to their sides and filed out through the door like revellers who had been raided by the cops.

'You all right, James?' Tanya asked him.

'Thanks a lot, Tanya. Sorry about all that. I didn't expect —' He was both elated and embarrassed.

'It's not your fault. They should have rung for permission.'

'Yeah.'

'Come on,' said Brent. 'Maybe if you come into the bar we'll get some of *our* customers back.'

Nodding, Paxton followed. All his adrenaline was ebbing away now, leaving him tired.

'I saw them carrying cameras outside,' said Adam. 'I tried to ring you, but of course you'd already left. This is why you need a mobile.'

Paxton just nodded again. He served two customers, both of whom asked curious questions, which he fobbed off as best he could. As he looked up to give the second his change, he saw Mandy standing behind the man's shoulder. She waited her turn silently, her look turning the wine to vinegar. Paxton felt his burning anger flare back into life. As if he hadn't had enough.

As soon as the man was out of earshot Mandy stepped up to the bar. Each word was like an ice cube. 'You arsehole. You bloody arsehole.'

'Hello, Mandy.'

'What the hell do you think you're doing?'

Paxton shrugged and turned away with a sigh. 'When you work out what your point is, let me know.'

'Don't pretend you don't know, you slimy little shit.'

Paxton turned back to face her, holding a bottle of Baileys.

'Orgasm, Mandy? Looks like you could do with one.'

Her hiss had as much poison behind it as a cobra's. Despite his outward cockiness, Paxton was taken aback by her venom.

'Where do you think you get off using Lena like that? I know exactly what you're doing.'

Paxton felt his own temper slowly boiling back to the surface. 'Yeah? What's that?'

'You're just taking advantage of her, you creep. You saw a wounded, lonely girl and you went in for the kill, didn't you? As soon as her dad died and she came into some money, bang! Look who appeared.'

'Has it ever occurred to you that I might have been trying to help her? That I might actually care about her?'

'Oh, don't give me that *bullshit*. You *bastard*! You pretended to be in touch with her father just to get close to her, didn't you? You damn well *exploited* her vulnerability, and now you're sitting pretty. She thinks you're a god when really you're just some manipulative little English loser who thinks he's onto a good thing.'

Out of the corner of his eye, Paxton had seen Adam and Brent take one look at her angry posture, fingers jabbing and stiff with rage, and melt into the shadows. However, customers weren't bothering to hide their stares.

'Are you finished?'

'Like hell I am. I hope the police find out just what a fraud you are and put you in jail. You have no right to be living off Lena like you do. When are you ever at *your* house?'

'Whenever you're at Lena's.'

'Don't get smart, you prick.'

'Then how about you just shut your gob and stop being such a prissy little *bitch*? You wouldn't know what love was if it appeared on your Visa statement.'

Mandy sucked in a breath to reply, but Paxton beat her to it, with a sudden sharp look. 'Does Lena know you're so unhappy at work?'

Mandy blinked, thrown for a fraction of a second, then lashed back. 'I don't know what you're talking about. Don't try your little mind games on me.'

'He doesn't want you, does he? Your colleague. You scare him.'

'Shut up.' She was breathing faster.

'He's not the one for you. There's no point staying just for him.'

'You're just jealous because I'm so successful and you're not. You pour *drinks* for a living.'

'Your grandma says you wanted to be a nanny.'

'Look, *just shut up!*'

Everyone in the bar had gone dead quiet. Mandy had seized a glass from the counter, gripping it so hard it almost shattered in her fist. Paxton could see how badly she wanted to throw it at his head.

'You're a lawyer, Mandy. You know the consequences of breaking other people's things.'

Almost hyperventilating, Mandy glanced at the glass in her hand, then at Paxton. She looked as if she was about to cry. After a second, she slammed the glass back down on the bar. Without another word she turned and stalked from the restaurant.

Paxton should have felt triumphant, but he didn't. The voices in his head evaporated, leaving only a strong sense of guilt and not a little astonishment. He hadn't been able to do that in years. Not since he was a kid.

'Sheesh! Who was *that?*'

Paxton gave Adam a brief look. 'Lena's best friend.'

'Oooh. That's not good.'

'No.'

'What'd she want, anyway? She did not look happy with you.'

Paxton crossed his arms. 'She has so many issues I should start up a charity. Starting with getting her a boyfriend to sharpen her fangs on. No man wants to be with her. She barks in her sleep.'

Adam spluttered with laughter, but Paxton still felt the guilt sitting heavy in his stomach.

'You've been having a hell of a night, haven't you?'

'Yeah. Tell me about it . . .' He huffed out a breath, slumping on the bar. 'You know that saying, shit happens? Well, my philosophy is, it happens to me.'

A few customers drifted through from the restaurant, swapping guesses and watching him over their glasses when they thought he wouldn't notice. He was easily the most popular of the three barmen. Paxton actually saw one young woman pretend not to hear Adam calling out to her, waiting patiently behind another couple for Paxton to serve her.

However, among the staff not another word was uttered about the reporters or the murder case. It was now a banned subject at Anubis, on pain of dismissal. On balance, Paxton wasn't sure what was worse — the whispering of strangers, or the silence of his mates.

Chapter FIFTEEN

THE STREETS WERE blessedly quiet as Paxton drove home. No black dogs rushed out from the park on Patteson Avenue. Now that he'd managed to afford a new car stereo he could also listen to music on the drive, and tonight he'd chosen Linkin Park. Lena called it screaming music but it was perfect for relieving tension. Towards the end of the ride Paxton found himself drumming on the steering wheel, spitting the end of every line. In his room, he threw his clothes on the floor and crawled into bed, the lyrics running in his head until eventually he fell asleep.

A knock on the door woke him sometime around eight the next morning. He heard the door open and close before he'd managed to get out of bed, still in last night's boxers. He called out, feeling his heart speed up.

'Who's there?'

'It's me.'

Next moment, Lena appeared in his bedroom doorway.

Paxton was not a little surprised to see her. Out of habit, and because her place was nicer, they always met at her house. He half-lived there himself. He saw the tired look on her face.

'Hey, what's up?'

'Did you see this morning's paper?'

She showed him the copy in her right hand. He glared at it. 'What is it this time? I'm starting up a cult with Donald Trump."

Lena turned and walked into the lounge, dropping onto the sofa.

'They've even put where you work . . .' She unfolded it and turned to page three. Paxton took one side, reading it with her. The edges of the paper were crumpled, as if she'd been gripping them hard.

'Shit, they've taken a photo!'

The invasion of privacy was somehow worse than being discussed in the news. This was another layer of anonymity they'd just stripped away. Now anyone in the street could recognise him. They'd captured him walking into work in his black uniform. It wasn't the most flattering photo, but no one had ever managed one of those. After recapping the murders so far, and Paxton's involvement with the police, the article went on to say:

Mr Paxton is an Englishman by birth but little is known about his background. He has no known relatives in this country, and neighbours say he is extremely private.

'He keeps to himself pretty well,' said Debbie Morehu. 'Never had a word out of him in all the time he's been here. Only time I've heard him say hi is when some of the rellies were having a beer out front late at night, and called out to him as he was coming home.'

Mr Paxton has been a bartender at Anubis, an Egyptian-themed restaurant in Mission Bay, for the past twelve months.

PAXTON DROPPED THE PAPER ON THE FLOOR. Good to know you can rely on your neighbours to air your dirty laundry for you when you're laid low.'

'That's not the worst of it,' said Lena. 'Take a look at this.' She handed him another page she'd been keeping aside — the letters to the editor. Paxton read them in silence. There were several letters under the subheading 'PSYCHICS FROM VENUS, POLICE FROM MARS'. It didn't seem to matter that Woodward had said Paxton wasn't getting paid — either no one had listened, or no one had believed.

B. White from Waiuku wrote: *It beggars belief. The police complain that they can't even solve burglaries with clear camera footage and several eyewitnesses, because they're underfunded. And here they are spending taxpayer dollars on a psychic! No wonder the streets aren't safe these days. Our police aren't even on Planet Earth.*

The others were in a similar vein, calling it political correctness gone mad. Someone else got in a dig at Auckland Council, asking if a psychic could finally reach an answer to the morning traffic jams. The last letter was downright scary: *Perhaps James Paxton should go through what these poor women have gone through. He might think again about cashing in on their murders.*

'Bloody hell.' Every nerve was twitching with the urge to shiver. 'That's almost a death threat.'

He didn't want to mention the exchange with Mandy. It would only have made things worse. Lena was watching him, her face expressing nothing but deep gloom, her eyes empty.

'What's up, Lee?'

She came out of her trance. 'Oh, I just think it sucks the way they're treating you! It's like you're Rasputin, or something. Some kind of charlatan holding the country to ransom.'

'So how does it feel to be Rasputin's girlfriend?'

Lena smiled. 'That makes me an empress, doesn't it?'

'That makes you dead at the hands of the revolutionaries.'

When Lena didn't reply Paxton took her face in both hands.

'Going to stop pretending this is about me?'

She laughed softly. 'I'm never going out with another psychic. Can't I keep *anything* to myself?'

She pulled back and looked him full in the face. 'My co-ordinator said she had three phone calls yesterday. All from parents wanting to know why the school's hired a tutor who's linked to all that New Age rubbish on the news. They think you're some sick devil-worshipper or something, or at least wrong in the head, the way you keep getting involved with murders. They think I must have something wrong with me as well.' Lena gave a bitter laugh. 'They're phoning each other up, trying to gather support for a formal complaint.'

'But what about . . .? You're a great teacher! All those bouquets you got from students and their families when your dad died . . .'

' . . . don't mean anything now, apparently. It's not "respectable" to talk to spirits. At the very least, it's bad business sense. I might be giving their kids lefty ideas.'

'But you're not even a medium. I am! You haven't done anything!'

'I know. But they want me gone.' Her face grew even more pained. 'The upshot of it is, Veronique's asked me whether I'm really serious about coming back this term.'

'*What?*'

'They're not firing me, she said. She said they don't want to lose me.' Again that off-pitch laugh. 'They just want me to think very carefully about the image of the school and my responsibility to the students to set a good example.'

Paxton looked down at the top of her head. He was angrier than he had ever been in his life, even while fear stuck a knife through his chest. 'Meaning . . . what?'

She paused for a long time. 'I don't know. I just wish ...'

'You wish I'd listened to you,' Paxton said flatly.

'I didn't say that, it's just . . . You said you didn't want to get involved, then you drove straight over to that woman's house.'

'Well, what was I supposed to do? Stay here and let Mandy treat me like a rotting sardine? You weren't exactly defending me very hard.'

'That's not fair! I defend you all the time, when you're not even there.'

Paxton looked away from her, folding his arms. 'Well, that's brilliant, isn't it?' he muttered.

After a moment he heard a long sniff. 'I'm sorry, James. I just don't know what I'm going to do . . .'

Paxton turned and hugged her fiercely as she cried into his shirt. Inside he was raging, but for Lena's sake he

141

kept his cool. He contented himself by saying, 'That woman sounds like a right *bitch*.'

Lena's crying jag didn't last long — he suspected she'd wrung herself almost dry long before he came over. She sniffed, rubbing a hand across her face in an attempt to wipe off the tears.

'Veronique is a snooty cow — the kind who thinks that because she's French she's more cultured than anyone else. Truth is, she's from a tiny village in the French equivalent of the Fens. Their version of a cultural revolution is dumping bulldozers of horseshit over the town McDonald's.'

When Paxton spluttered, she gave him a small, grateful smile that almost immediately dissolved into sadness.

'Thing is, these people are really well off. They're not parents, they're customers. Whatever they want, we have to listen to.'

'What about the union? Isn't there a teachers' union you could go to?'

'The PPTA. But it's only for state schools, not private. And I'm not on a permanent contract. If they decide they don't want me this year, there's nothing I can do.'

'Can none of your work friends help you out? I mean, they have to know you're not a flake.'

She drew herself out of his arms, pulling her knees up to her chest and hugging them under her chin. 'They're all angry at me,' she said. 'They want to know why I never told them — about you being a medium, I mean. They were all so good to me after Dad died, Sylvie especially, and . . . I guess they're all really hurt.'

Once again, the familiar cloud of guilt rose up in Paxton's head. 'Did you tell them I asked you not to let anyone know about me?'

'Yeah.' But from the tone of her voice, it hadn't helped.

'Oh shit, I'm so sorry. This is all my fault.'

'No it's not. It's theirs.' She sounded so drained and hopeless that she might as well have screamed abuse at him, for all the comfort it gave. She shook her head, as if to clear it. 'I just want this all to *stop*. I feel like an outcast.'

And at that moment, Paxton realised, she'd become like him.

HE DIDN'T KNOW how long he could hold out this time. It had been too long since the last, and he could feel his instincts fighting his reason. There were more police on the streets these days; they were stupid fuckers, but they were like pit bulls after blood. He knew full well it would be fatal to act without carefully weighing up the circumstances, but it was becoming harder and harder, knowing she was waiting there, for him. He could see the light in her window from here.

Some people out there would call it wrong, he knew, would call him a monster. They didn't know what living was. Every man dreamed of this; anyone who said different was lying. Fucking hypocrites, all of them. Who wouldn't want such power, if he could get it? And the line, once crossed, could not be crossed back again. This was who he was now.

He saw a movement through the window, and his chest tightened. He moved closer, under cover of the trees and the dark. The tiny stirring among the leaves could have been the wind.

Chapter SIXTEEN

STIRLING WOKE TO the smell of baking. Even the clanging of a spoon on the side of a metal bowl was comforting, so reassuringly normal. And he wasn't due at work till one o'clock. He drifted into the kitchen, following his nose.

'Should have known you'd turn up about now. Five minutes and the coffee cake'll be ready,' said Nicola, smiling at him over her shoulder. She was rolling out something else on the bench.

'Mmm, yum.' Stirling came up behind her, wrapping his arms round her waist and giving her neck a lingering kiss. 'What's that you're making now?'

'Gingerbread men.'

'Gingerbread men? Those are kiddie biscuits.'

'I like them. And I notice they don't usually last long. Try not to pick the buttons off all of them this time. I went to eat one last time and they were all naked and missing their eyes.'

'That's your fault for putting M&Ms on them instead of icing. You know I eat any chocolate going.'

Ignoring him, Nicola gave a tremendous yawn. 'Might go back and eat breakfast in bed,' she said. 'Can't go staying up this late when I'm back at work.' She took the gingerbread cutter and started stamping out the little men. Seeing his chance, Stirling sneaked a few M&Ms from the packet.

'Oi!' She dropped the cutter and grabbed the packet from him. 'Thief. Cops are supposed to cut down on stealing.'

'Price of the job, Nics. You don't enter the criminal underworld without picking up a few tricks.'

'Yeah, well I'm in marketing, but you don't see me making you buy your own biscuits. Or anything else.'

'Oh no. That's not fair. I have nothing else to look forward to!'

Nicola laughed in his face, feeding him another M&M. She turned back to the bench, where the gingerbread cutter was still lying, half-covered in flour and dough. It was as if Stirling were seeing it for the first time. Instead of a harmless plastic man he saw a corpse outline, marked in flour instead of chalk.

Strange situation here, guys. All the limbs are stiff from rigor mortis, but the bodies were still warm when we found them . . .

He was beginning to realise the real price of the job. Normality, whatever that was, was gone for ever. The absence of Alicia's body was bothering him. And the doughnuts. If the killer had photocopied his backside and nailed it to the front door he couldn't have been more deliberately insulting. There was no doubt in Stirling's mind that the killer was losing any nervousness about his chosen career. He was just hitting his stride. Sure, that might cause him to slip up, but things were bound to get a hell of a lot nastier before he did.

Stirling didn't hold out much hope that the paper would take his mind off things. Reporters made their money from crime almost as much as the police did. He smoothed it out on the table as he sat with a cup of instant and a plate of still warm coffee cake. However, the front page was a pleasant surprise. It was all about the surfer who'd nearly drowned on Boxing Day while saving a pair of kids testing their new boogie boards in a fast-moving rip. He was now back on his board, just two days after leaving hospital, and swearing he'd do it all again. Stirling skimmed it and turned the page.

'Oh *fuck*!'

He put down his mug, grabbing the paper to read it more closely. The headline at the top of page three read: 'MURDER CASE GETS SUGAR-COATING'. Below the pictures of the three murdered women, the doughnut delivery was described in full, as was the police's current inability to find a body. To Stirling's relief, the names of the suspects weren't mentioned, but there were several quotes from people close to Alicia Schofield, expressing their outrage at the prank. Some suggested the police somehow deserved the insult. What was worse, the article went on to explain that Paxton had been given the boot after dissension in the police ranks and media scrutiny. The overall picture was of bumbling boys in blue, a force in disarray that was barely in touch with reality. Then he noticed a small advertisement for the magazine section in the weekend paper. He took a closer look, and swore again.

There was a picture of the TV psychic, Cristiana Austin, on the cover, dressed in a business suit with a crystal ball in front of her. Smaller twins of Cristiana were reflected in the ball, shrinking into nothing. Canvas's lead was 'Profiling the Profilers: Inside the world of psychic detectives'.

'What's wrong, sweetie? What are you swearing about?'

Her face flushed from bending over the hot oven, Nicola came into the room, rubbing her eyes. Stirling didn't even look up as she sat down and pulled the cake towards her, cutting a slice.

'Some *bastard* at work has been leaking to the press. They know that James was thrown off the case, and they know it was because the higher-ups were embarrassed about having him all through the papers. They think it's funny. Because he won't talk to them, they're using the predictions of this Cristiana woman, making him look like an arsehole!'

'Right.'

Nicola jerked the paper out of his hands and promptly ripped it in half. Then ripped it again.

'Give me a bit,' said Stirling. He took a piece from her and joined in the shredding, every loud tear making him feel better. He smiled at the pile of confetti on the table.

'You're cleaning that up,' said Nicola. 'I've just sat down.'

With less enthusiasm, Stirling obeyed, but no sooner had he scooped up a handful of paper than he heard his mobile in the bedroom. He dropped the scraps in the bin as he jogged to get it, taking a look at the display. New number. He pressed the button to answer.

'Hello, Andy Stirling.'

'Oh hello, Detective. It's Arthur Wong. There's something I think I should tell you.' He sounded worried.

Stirling was suddenly alert. 'What is it, Arthur?'

'I was just reading the paper this morning, and saw the article about Alicia Schofield. From the radio.'

Stirling said nothing, feeling something else coming. 'She was one of our regulars too. I recognised her.'

'You're sure?'

'Yes.'

'Sit tight, Arthur, I'll be there shortly.'

The café owner's voice cut in urgently. 'But that's not the only thing! You see, I recognised the other woman as well.'

Stirling paused, hardly daring to believe it. 'Are you talking about Helen, or Charlotte?'

'Charlotte, that's her. I knew Helen.'

'You mean all three of the women were customers of yours?' Stirling's heart was beating at twice its usual speed.

'Yes! We're all scared out of our wits.'

'Be there in twenty minutes. See you soon.'

'THEY'RE USING MY café as a stalking ground! I'm tempted to shut it down.' Arthur was throwing his arms around.

'I can see why,' said Rees. 'But that could destroy the best lead we have.'

Once again he'd accompanied Stirling to the café. Ordinarily there was no one Stirling preferred to work with more, but the tiny cracks of doubt in his mind had turned into gaping chasms of misgiving, into which all the facts were falling. Stirling cursed his detective's brain, which couldn't let a friendship stand in the way of rampant suspicion.

'Did the killer really send you doughnuts?' asked Nathan. 'I shouldn't laugh, but . . .' His smooth face cracked into a smile and he shook his head. 'Fuck, that's twisted.'

A knock sounded at the door, and they all turned. A woman had pressed her face up to the glass, shading her eyes to see in past the closed sign. Arthur shook his head at the woman, who gave him a snotty look and walked off.

'Hope we're not getting up your customers' noses too much, Arthur,' said Stirling.

'There are more important things right now,' he replied, shrugging.

'If this goes on, we could all lose our jobs,' said Nathan.

No one was naive enough to disagree with him. Nathan's eyes suddenly flashed.

'Hey, but speaking of customers, there's that one guy who always comes in and just watches people, eh, Arthur?'

'Yeah, he's *weird*!' A girl with a brown ponytail whom Stirling had never seen before was nodding. Her name was Lauren. 'It's like he has no friends. He keeps talking to me all the time.'

'Can I have a description?' asked Rees.

'Um, what would you say? Kind of wishy-washy hair, sort of blond?' said Lauren. 'He'd be in his mid-thirties, I guess.'

150

'Yeah, and if you wanna know who ate all the pies, look no further,' said Nathan. 'They're almost all he ever orders, and it shows. I call him Simon the Pieman. I reckon he'd be capable of murder if someone else got the last steak and cheese.'

'Or there's the newspaper man,' said Arthur. 'He just sits and reads the newspaper for an hour. He's in here every day.'

He too went into Rees's exercise book.

'Man, it's creepy,' said Nathan, looking unhappy. 'I know some of the customers are freaks, but . . . And you still haven't found Alicia yet?'

Stirling shook his head.

'God,' said Lauren. 'She was really cool. It's just unbelievable.'

Arthur just sighed, looking deflated. He wasn't his usual sparky self this morning. In the lull, Rees opened his folder and pulled out a series of photos. He flung them on the table with his usual blank expression.

'How about these people?'

All three of them took a good look, as did Stirling, wondering what Rees's game was. The café staff needed only three seconds. Arthur raised his head sharply, pointing at a mugshot towards the bottom of the pile, of a good-looking man in a smart shirt. He was probably in his forties, and he was smiling for the camera.

'I've seen him before!' His eyes dropped back to the picture, fascinated. 'He was the first lady's boyfriend. Charlotte What's-her-name.'

As Stirling tried not to hold his breath, the others were craning their necks. It was the same man Paynter had told them about, the one from Australia.

'Oh yeah! They were in here all the time!' Nathan was saying.

'Is he a suspect?' asked Arthur.

Stirling's eyes met Rees's. He certainly was now.

Chapter SEVENTEEN

TALL AND FAIR, Stuart Fletcher was a good-looking guy, except for the pallor of his face as soon as he opened the door to a couple of badges. It was a bit like watching a cartoon character stick a finger in a power socket — you could see the skull underneath.

'Hello. Mr Fletcher, is it?' asked Rees.

'Yes.'

'Do you know why we're here?'

'I can only guess it's about Charlotte. Ha. Good old colleagues — never forget a name, do they?'

Fletcher sounded bitter. It had been the same woman, Charlotte's best friend, who'd dished them the dirt on him. Judging by her choice of friends, and the airiness with which the information was given, Rees suspected she was very probably carrying on a few flings of her own.

'Well, I'm Detective Rees, and this is Detective Constable Stirling. Could we come in?'

Fletcher shrugged, though he plainly wasn't too happy about it. Few people ever were. 'Sure.'

Stirling followed Rees into the small living room. For someone who'd apparently been a hotshot in banking, Fletcher wasn't doing too well now. The carpet looked like it was from the original house, and the house was early seventies. The man also had about as much furniture as Paxton, and Paxton spent most of his time at Lena's. No one would want to spend long in a room like this.

There was one two-seater sofa, and that was it. Rees waved at Fletcher to sit, and the two detectives remained standing, making him even more ill at ease. Stirling let Rees go — he very seldom got the chance to see the detective interview someone. From Rees's air, he might have been at a tea party.

'So. I understand you had a bit of a falling-out with Charlotte a wee while ago.'

'She dumped me, and told me she'd never even loved me at all. Needless to say, I didn't take it particularly well.'

'Especially when your own wife found out.'

Fletcher's head dropped. 'That was the biggest mistake I ever made. The romance had gone out of things by then, but I never even tried to put it back. I just let myself get dazzled by some bitch in a skirt and thought I was in love. Poor Jane.'

'As I understood it, you sent threatening mail to your wife.'

'Yes. Look, do I have to go over this all again? Your colleague got it all out of me yesterday.'

From Rees there was nothing but silence. Fletcher glanced at Stirling, but there was no help there. He shut his eyes.

'Yes, I did threaten to kill her, and Charlotte. I did one hell of a lot of stupid things. I was drunk about twenty-three and a half hours out of every twenty-four. If I was half sober when I woke up, I hadn't drunk enough. But my wife decided not to press charges, and eventually I sobered up enough to head to Australia. Mistake number two . . .'

154

'In what way?' asked Stirling.

Fletcher made a sound that could have been a laugh or a snort. 'I thought that if I went to a new country, where no one knew my mistakes, I'd be better off. New country, new life. But your problems don't just wave goodbye from the airport.'

'Took a bit more baggage with you than you were expecting, did you?' asked Rees.

Fletcher gave him a slightly startled look then nodded. 'Wound up dead drunk on Manly Beach, with the tide coming in over my head. A couple of night clubbers found me, almost as drunk as I was. They were coming down to paddle, in the middle of winter.' He shook his head.

'What happened after that, Mr Fletcher? Did you decide to come home and confront Mrs Hiscocks?'

'No.'

'Not even to see her again?' asked Stirling. 'You were following her around quite a bit before you left.'

'I'm the world's fool, I can see that now, but I wouldn't kill anyone!'

Rees leaned forward, looking straight into his face. 'Then why are three women who ate at Parsifale dead?'

Fletcher looked startled. 'What? You mean that café in Grey Lynn?'

'You took Charlotte there, didn't you?'

'Yeah, it was one of her favourites.'

'Did you ever see Alicia Schofield there?'

'You mean that DJ who went missing? I didn't know what she looked like before I saw her on the news. I don't even listen to the radio.'

'So you didn't recognise her at all? You've never spoken to her?'

Fletcher plainly wasn't sure. 'She did look kind of familiar . . . No. Probably not. I usually didn't speak to anyone but Charlotte or the staff.'

'What about the other woman? Helen McCowan? You must have seen her. Apparently she was quite a regular.'

Now Fletcher looked even less certain, less about his facts than whether or not he should tell them. 'Her I think I *do* know. She was kinda loud. An English woman, wasn't she? She quite often came in with an equally loud Scottish bloke. You could hear almost every word of the conversation.' His face got more hostile. 'But quite how that explains why I'd want to kill her is beyond me.'

'You can't explain where you were when these women were killed?'

Fletcher sighed. 'As I've told you people before, I was home. When I get home from work, the only company I have these days is a bottle of whatever's going cheap.'

'Where *are* you working these days, Mr Fletcher?'

'Kiwibank.'

'How long have you been at this address?'

'Just moved here a couple of days ago. I was at the motel the night Charlotte was killed.' He looked away from them. 'I found out two days later, when I saw it in the paper. I can tell you, I couldn't have killed that second woman either, because I wasn't even capable of walking for about another three days.'

'Celebrating?'

Fletcher's head hung low, and his voice was even lower. 'I'm still not sure of the answer to that.'

Rees gave it another three seconds before saying, 'Can you tell us where you were on the Tuesday?'

Fletcher paused just a little too long before answering. 'I really can't remember. I was definitely drinking in my motel room, that's for sure.'

'So no one would necessarily have seen you coming and going?'

Fletcher shrugged, not seeming to care, not even looking up.

'How's the reconciliation process going with your wife?' Stirling asked suddenly.

Fletcher looked up at him. 'She hates me.'

THE RECEPTIONIST'S EYES were glued to Gardner's badge as it flashed in front of her face.

'He's actually in the studio at the moment. I'm not sure I can get him.'

'Can you find out? I'm quite happy to wait.' Gardner loosely crossed his arms and gazed at the ceiling, like someone patiently waiting for the bus.

Unhappy, the young, dark-haired receptionist patched through to the studio. 'Oh hi, Danny. Can we get Curtis out of there for a second? There's a detective here to see him. Yeah. Yeah, I know . . . He says he'll wait as long as it takes. No . . . All right, then. Thanks.'

She punched a button and pulled off her headset. 'He'll be out in a couple of minutes. They're just finishing a call-in segment.'

Gardner nodded curtly. He'd noticed the patronising tone of that 'No . . .' Bloody media again. Thought they were kings of the earth. It obviously didn't matter if Curtis had murdered his colleague, as long as the show went on.

After quarter of an hour, Gardner had glanced at the clock three times, getting more impatient each time.

'How long do these segments usually last?' he asked.

The receptionist frowned. 'I'd have expected him to be out by now. Hang on, I'll try them again. He might have forgotten.' She spoke again to the man called Danny, and the frown lines became trenches in her forehead. 'Eh? How long ago?' She looked up at Gardner, deeply worried. 'Well, he definitely hasn't turned up here. Yeah, will do. Thanks.'

Before she'd disconnected, Gardner knew what he was going to hear.

'He left the studio more than ten minutes ago.'

'He say where he was going?'

'Here. He said he was coming here to meet you.'

'Mind if I take a look round?'

She nodded readily, all her unhelpfulness gone as if by magic. 'Sure.'

Immediately Gardner ran through the door leading towards the studio. Whatever security clearance he lacked would be made up for by the gold shield in his wallet. Down a long corridor, he followed his nose to a door with a red light on the outside. He didn't even pause to reflect on how much it reminded him of another profession he regularly dealt with. He gave the door a solid rap, and seconds later, someone had the door open a crack, hissing furiously at him to leave.

'We're live on air! Don't ever do that again.'

Gardner gave her a cold stare. 'Which way did Curtis go?'

'Eh? You're the cop?' The woman stepped outside the door and shut it, with a worried glance over her shoulder.

'Is there a back door to this place?'

'Yeah, at the end of the corridor. There's a fire escape, but the alarm doesn't work.'

Cursing slipshod security and members of the public in general, Gardner sprinted for the exit. He pushed it open, and was faced with a carpark with several cars in it. There was a black hole where one reserved space sat empty.

'Shit.'

'Was it important?'

Gardner whirled round to see the woman, her thin, pointed face mystified. 'Where's Danny?'

'I'm Danny. My name's Danielle. Look, I really don't know where Curtis has gone.'

'Right, I'll need his address, phone number, and anything else you can give me.'

She looked taken aback.

Gardner huffed impatiently. 'All I want is to ask him a few questions about his relationship with Alicia, and now he's belted off. It's a bit suspicious, isn't it?'

Danielle's face suddenly went a shade or two paler. 'You think he had something to do with it?'

'I was trying to rule that out. Someone from your office told us quite an interesting story.'

From the look on Danielle's face, she was remembering exactly which story he meant. Turning his shoulder, Gardner took his radio off his belt. He almost dropped it when a loud and totally unexpected ringing sound erupted. It was his mobile, in his pocket.

'Shit, what now? . . . Ray Gardner.'

'Ray, it's Graeme.' Kirkpatrick sounded wired up.

Gardner didn't wait for an explanation. 'Curtis Webb has just done a runner from the radio station. I'm getting a squad after him.'

'Do it, then. But who knows, we might get forensics to nail him for us.'

'What?'

'We've got our body. Alicia's turned up.'

'*What*? Where?'

'Take a guess.'

'Oh Christ, what was it this time? A bunch of flowers and a card?'

'Not quite.'

THE PHOTOS STARED them all down — or rather, the corpse did. Her eyes were still open, and like the Mona Lisa's, they followed you all round the room. *Why haven't you put me to rest?* They all wanted this case solved, just so they could get that off their wall. No living flesh was that colour, and there were flecks of blood in the whites of her eyes. Most of them read horror, and pain, and fear,

160

but it was just as easy to read anger, accusation and pleading. *Why am I dead instead of you? Or your family?*

Stirling tore his eyes away as detectives filed out around him. It hadn't been the best start to the shift, for any of them. Alicia Schofield was still wearing the T-shirt she'd had on when she died, albeit with an extra hole in it. It was bright green, one of those pisstake knock-offs you could pick up at weekend markets. Just visible under the blood was a perfect rendering of the Esprit logo, except that someone had added a D. *DESPRIT.*

Should have said DECEASED, thought Stirling, before he could stop himself. He felt a moment of horror at his own thoughts, then let it go. It was better to crack up this way than the other.

'How long was she at that depot? Three days? Just think, what if no one ever found you until you started to smell?' said Paynter, staring straight at the photo.

There was an obvious comeback but Stirling missed it.

Without his even realising it, Stirling's eyes had gone back to the grisly pictures. Like any pauper from the olden days, she'd been buried in a cardboard box, but above ground. 'He's not just creepy, this guy. He's clever. Sticking a dodgy address on a box and then leaving it round the back of some shops for the courier. What the hell kind of mind is that?'

They stood in front of Alicia's scene-of-crime photos as if admiring the genius of the art. No one noticed delivery people with boxes behind shopping malls. They were just part of the urban furniture. Someone had tried to trace the courier ticket on the outside back to a certain store, hoping the courier company would keep track of which serial numbers were sent where. No go. Courier companies weren't like banks, recording every sticky label as if it were paper money. Serial numbers were only tracked once they were on parcels, not before. Making matters even more difficult, although the box had been left outside a music store, the ticket number didn't fit in the same series as the ones in their storeroom. One unfortunate constable had been sent to ask round all the shops at the mall, just in case. Stirling thought he was wasting his time, and he wasn't alone. This guy had been smart so far — he'd even used a prepaid mobile to order those doughnuts for the crime squad. Untraceable. He would have taken great care to leave that box far away from anywhere connected with him. Rees glanced over at Stirling.

'All right, Andy?'

'Yeah. Just been a long week.'

'No rest for the wicked,' said Rees. 'Which means we don't get a holiday either. Shame Curtis Webb got away this morning.'

Stirling gave him a sharp look. 'You don't think it was Fletcher, do you?'

Rees shrugged. 'I've been wrong before.'

'But you don't think it was him.'

'I'd be highly surprised. He seemed more intent on ruining his own life.'

In answer to Paynter's look Stirling pretended to swig from a bottle. He agreed with Rees. Graeme Kirkpatrick had set an unmarked outside Curtis's house, for whenever he decided to come home. He couldn't hide out for ever. Everyone at CIB was hanging out for the news. Whatever happened, Stirling reflected, he wasn't really looking forward to visiting Parsifale again. His trousers were getting harder to zip in the mornings. That café just wasn't healthy. It didn't help that the proprietor was on a first-name basis with all the dead women.

Rees's voice startled his mind away from the door it was opening. 'I'm going for lunch. Want to come?'

Paynter was already nodding a yes, as Rees met Stirling's eye. At Stirling's hesitation, he looked hurt. Shrugging, he turned for the door, while Paynter gave Stirling a puzzled glance.

'What's up? Never known you to turn down a lunch.'

'Nothing.'

Stirling forced a smile and followed, not even trusting himself to find the right answer.

Chapter EIGHTEEN

LENA HAD LEFT him at ten that morning, after Mandy rang. It felt like an omen to Paxton. He'd said something nasty, and Lena had snapped back at him. They spent a lot of their time scrapping these days, when they weren't lapsing into long silences. The honourable thing to do was walk away. *Walk away! Give her her life back!* But just as when he'd met her, he couldn't bring himself to do it.

None of them wore badges in the bar any more. It was actually Brent's idea. Too many people were coming in just to stare, making it really hard for Paxton to focus on his work. However, the ruse fooled no one. Paxton drew the line at putting on a Kiwi accent — he couldn't, anyway — and as soon as he opened his mouth, they knew at once who the English psychic was. At a quarter to seven, Paxton saw Tanya enter the bar and head for the TV.

'Sorry Brent, but there's something on those murders tonight. That psychic woman's on again, James. I thought you might want to see it.'

Before Paxton could issue an emphatic denial, Tanya was gone again. Knowing her, the decision to change channels was nothing to do with satisfying Paxton's curiosity, and everything to do with keeping the customers drinking. Nothing gave the punters a thirst as much as tales of blood. Paxton tried to ignore it, but Mel waved him over to the TV. Eventually he gave in when people trickled in, watching him expectantly. He could feel the eyes of several tables flicking between him and the screen during the news. If he admitted it to himself, he too wanted to know.

Before *Cross* came on, Paxton caught a preview. The DJ's escape was the number-one item.

Burgess gave the rundown.

'Radio personality Curtis Webb is familiar to all New Zealanders from his days as a music presenter on C4 before he was involved in a bit of a drunken punch-up at Zanzibar. These days Curtis is a morning host at JaFM, the Auckland pop-rock station, along with his late colleague Alicia Schofield, and when the police called round on routine inquiries, he'd disappeared from the studio . . .' Burgess inclined his head noncommittally. 'Where is Curtis Webb? Following those infamous drug-fuelled brawling incidents, Mr Webb has made no secret of his contempt for the police . . . Although police say Mr Webb is not a suspect at this stage, members of the public are invited to call the Auckland Central police if they see any sign of the DJ.'

Paxton found himself wishing he could get hold of the man first, and know for certain. Not to mention *that* bitch.

Cristiana Austin's face was back on the screen, professional and friendly as usual. She'd had a three-page spread in the woman's magazine she was hired by, and seemed to be an almost permanent addition to the Burgess show. She was telling Burgess's fortune. The man was obviously sceptical, but you could tell he was flattered. Of course, anyone who didn't know every detail of Burgess's life story had to be living in another country.

Paxton found himself hating her, filled with an irrational distrust that only increased when they got on to the subject of the murders. To Burgess's obvious disappointment, Cristiana didn't believe either of the two suspects had done it — she stuck by 'George' or 'Jordan' — so Burgess asked her what she thought of Paxton, and why he might have been thrown off the case.

Cristiana sucked in a breath. 'I hate to put someone down just because I don't know them, but the fact is, I *don't* know James Paxton. I've never heard of him, and neither has anyone I've spoken to, either in New Zealand or in the UK, where I've got many friends in the Institute of Spiritualist Mediums. I think that says a lot.'

'All it says is I don't want to be a member of your stuck-up, poncy little club,' Paxton spat at the screen.

'You think he's a fraud.'

'Oh, I wouldn't want to say *that*, Simon. But if someone's not with an established organisation, you have to ask yourself why. Be very, very cautious, that's all I can say.'

'Speaking of someone with important credentials, you're related to the novelist Jane Austen, aren't you?'

Cristiana smiled. 'Distantly, yes. Of course spelling wasn't too standardised back in those days. And I do feel a really close connection with her books. I loved *Pride and Prejudice* when it was on TV.'

Paxton gave an incredulous snort. 'Yeah, okay, then I'm related to the Pastons,' he said to Mel, who was watching beside him. 'They documented half of medieval history, and *I* come from a medieval town. And I did like history at school . . .'

'What a bitch! She was totally slamming you. You should go on the show and get back at her.'

'No thanks.'

Cristiana finished by adding that two more people were going to die before the killer was caught.

'Had enough of the High Priestess of Doom for one evening?' Paxton flipped the channel back to sport.

'Oi! What are you doing?'

Paxton turned to see Tanya in the opening between the bar and the restaurant. 'The programme was finished. I didn't think there was any reason to keep it on this channel.'

'Well just ask me before you do anything like that again, will you? People were still watching.'

Paxton went closer towards her, trying to keep his voice low despite his irritation. 'What's with making me a tourist attraction? I thought you were on my side — you got rid of the reporters.'

'Oh, don't be silly. I am on your side. But the reporters were one thing, and this is another. They were blocking customers and they weren't buying anything. But let's face it, numbers have been up ever since people found out you were involved in all this stuff. And so have the profits, for that matter. Of course I'm on your side. You're one of our biggest assets. What's the harm in trying to cash in, if they're going to be that stupid?'

'How about my feelings? I don't particularly like being stared at and whispered about. Would you?'

'You're a celebrity!'

'I'm reliving my damn adolescence. It's not nice. Please don't do it anymore.'

'I thought you'd be happy to get the publicity,' she said stiffly. 'I even sent a few reporters your way when they called.'

'That was you!'

'What's the big problem? I'm drumming up clients for you.'

'I don't give readings, Tanya. And it's ruining my girlfriend's life.'

'Well, if she can't handle being with you, she should just leave you then,' said Tanya with a shrug.

Paxton turned and walked back to the bar. Her voice followed him.

'Rule number one of hospitality, James. Give 'em what they want and they'll leave you alone.'

FRIDAY ENDED NOT with a bang, but a feeble bubbling sound. It was the sound of a group of detectives standing round the water cooler wondering what the hell else to do. Despite the patchy air-conditioning the temperature fell just below boiling at CIB, and it wasn't doing much for anyone's temper either. Kirkpatrick had requisitioned the one cool spot in the room, which was right under the air-conditioner. No one got too jealous, because they knew the spot would open up in a few minutes, when icicles starting forming in the Senior's cup. The position wasn't so much cool as Siberia.

Stirling was spending his time talking with and second-guessing everyone else, and trying to avoid Rees's eye.

Rees was blithely chatting with Coleman, Paynter and a few of the others, apparently sharing more gossip.

'You all right?' Nielsen asked Stirling, passing by to fill a plastic cup from the cooler.

'Yeah. No. I've put on three kilos since this case started. Interviewing the café owner. I've been trying to put off going back there again.'

Nielsen looked around the crowded space, full of sullen expressions, blank stares and the odd detective rolling their sweating cup against their forehead to soak up the cold. 'Want to go for a coffee? Or an *iced* coffee. Somewhere else?'

Stirling shrugged. 'Sure, why not?'

Never take a secret to someone else's grave. It was drummed into them all from day one. Failure to share your intuitions could mean that another person died. Maybe if he spoke them aloud, his thoughts would show themselves for the fragile little ghosts they were.

The café was less than a two-minute walk away but his shirt was sticking to his back by the time he sat down. His discomfort increased at the astute look in Nielsen's eyes.

'So, are you going to tell me what's on your mind?'

Stirling weighed it up for a while. 'Better out than in, I guess. I'm beginning to have doubts about the café owner. Not *this* café — I mean Arthur Wong, the one whose café all the victims went to.'

Nielsen looked thoughtful. 'It is a bit of a coincidence, isn't it?'

'He knows them all and he's so *interested* in being helpful, so chatty . . .'

'I see where you're going.'

'He sounds like a Kiwi over the phone too. Crazy thing is, I'd never have put him down as a murderer. He definitely ain't the Triad type. He bakes his own shortbread, for Christ's sake.'

'Well, homicidal maniacs don't always froth at the mouth, Andy.'

'You sound like Gardner.'

'Yeah, but in my case I'm not speaking from personal experience.'

Stirling laughed. 'I thought you were telling me to lay off him the other day.'

'Oh, I'm hot and cranky and I've used up all my goodwill for one season. I might not openly argue with the guy, but that doesn't mean I have to like him. What about the DJ? Bit suss, his running like that.'

'Definitely suss. He's hiding *something*. That's what's so wrong with this case. We're beating suspects off with a stick. I'm surprised the cat wasn't in on it.'

'Thanks.'

Nielsen's drink was being set down on the table. It was an iced chocolate in a sundae glass garnished with a chocolate fish and piles of whipped cream. Stirling looked back at his sparkling mineral water. It was already half gone.

'Sorry. Shouldn't be drinking this in front of you, should I?' said Nielsen, pulling off the fish's marshmallow tail with her teeth.

'That's all right. I've got gingerbread men waiting for me at home.'

'Some cops would get an unlisted number.' There was a twinkle in her eye. 'Hard men waiting for you at home . . .'

'Well done, Sarge. Well, it's scary the damage they can do to your body, even if they are only gingerbread.'

'Don't make them then.'

'I don't. It's Nicola — she knows I have a sweet tooth.'

'Your wife is a sweetie. I don't know how she puts up with you. If Brad wants me to do any baking, I give him ten bucks to go to the supermarket and buy a few packets.'

'And here I thought you were Superwoman, juggling the husband, the kids and the career.'

Nielsen burst out laughing.

'Well, just look at your kids! They're not normal.'

They were the most well-behaved children he'd ever met. The eldest was six and the youngest had just started day care, and last time she'd brought them to work every damn crayon had been back in its box within half a minute of her saying 'Time to go'. Stirling had almost fallen off his chair when four-year-old Damian gravely looked up at the cop offering him a biscuit and said, 'Thank you very much. Would you like some?'

Stirling had been quietly shamed into greater politeness until the little freaks went home.

'They're good kids,' said Nielsen with a little smile.

171

Stirling knew damn well that Nielsen's nonchalance was just an act, to fit in. She may not have done the baking, but her kitchen would be as sterile as a forensics lab. Probably more so.

'I'm afraid to have kids,' he blurted out. He instantly wished the words back.

Nielsen was looking at him in surprise. Stirling shrugged awkwardly. 'Nics would be great at it, but . . .'

'You wouldn't need to worry about having any gingerbread men left over.'

Stirling didn't smile. 'I'm a bit — selfish, I guess. I mean, when Hiscocks was talking about his wife . . . How she was out at all hours, he didn't get to see her much ...'

'Have you discussed this with Nicola?'

Stirling met her eyes and guiltily shook his head.

'Do you *want* kids?'

'Well, yeah. Although at times like these I do wonder.'

Nielsen nodded, and was silent for a while. 'The time I saw a boy who fell out of a first-floor window, I wouldn't even let the kids go up the stairs alone. Not for six months. And we have security stays on our windows.' She gave a rueful smile. 'Once you have kids, Andy, you'll find the job doesn't come first anymore.'

The straw made a slurping noise as she reached the bottom of the glass. 'Better go back, I guess.' She stood up, stretched and sighed. 'Well, run it past Graeme, but it couldn't hurt to go and check Arthur out again. As long as you don't eat anything while you're there.'

'Oh hell. He's been so nice to me.'

'How about you get Tony to go with you again? You can't buy him with pastries.'

She noted his unresponsiveness.

'What's up with you and Tony, anyway? You've been a bit funny lately.'

'Oh, just the weather, probably. No, I'll take Tony with me tomorrow. It's a good idea.'

Nielsen gave him a suspicious look, but didn't push it. They walked back to CIB in silence.

That's right, Andy. Nark on a harmless old man, but not on your best mate. And he never would either. He'd be in his own grave first.

They both pricked up their ears at the sound of a siren. Stirling could retire today, and thirty years later his pulse would still rise at the sound of a police car. His anticipation built as he realised it was heading straight towards them. Then he saw it, roaring along Mayoral Drive. Changing left to avoid a slow-moving van, the car abruptly braked and slewed to a halt beside them. Rees was in the driver's seat.

'Quick! Get in!'

Stirling ran for the back door. 'What is it?'

'Curtis Webb. They've found him.'

Chapter NINETEEN

NIELSEN HADN'T EVEN shut the door properly before Rees floored it. Even over the engine, Stirling could hear the radio.

Ten-one, ten-one. Speeder's going east on Leslie Avenue, Balmoral.

They hit Symonds Street, travelling eighty.

In front of him, Stirling heard Coleman groan as comms gave the usual crap about bailing out if it got dangerous, cutting into the commentary.

'Come on . . . Get on with it.'

Stirling was bang on his side. In this city, everyone drove with a permanently raised middle finger and one lead foot. The constable on the radio gave a curt acknowledgement, then got down to it.

Heading south on Sandringham Road in a black Mitsubishi Evo, licence plate Romeo Zero Charlie Kilo Delta Juliet, that's ROCKDJ.

What's the speed?

He's going 115 ks in a fifty zone. Traffic's moderate, but it's a pretty major road.

Unit 258, unit 258, are you able to intercept?

Roger, just on Great South Road now, turning into Greenlane East.

Stirling leaned forward. 'How did they find him, Tony?' Rees answered without turning his head. 'Patrol saw his car at the lights. Believe it or not, he's still driving it.'

Stirling looked at him incredulously. 'You're joking. And then he plays chasey! He's only guaranteeing himself top spot on tonight's news.'

Three cars were in pursuit now, and a fourth was close by, on its way.

He's turned east on to Cambourne Road . . . heading for Balmoral. Almost lost control on that last corner.

This is unit 258. We're on Balmoral — about two minutes away, over.

They heard the Eagle helicopter come in, tracking the pursuit from the air. The constable in the first car wasn't even bothering to narrate the route now, as the streets got even more erratic, winding north again. Curtis wasn't stupid enough to stick to the main road. As the silences drew out, the tension in the car grew. Other traffic went to the kerb as they ploughed a route through. Stirling could feel a pain starting in his back as he bent over his knees. Rees hurtled through a set of lights on Dominion Road just as they turned red, throwing them all against the side of the car as he spun onto Balmoral.

'We're going to land in such shit over this.' Nielsen spoke in a guilty whisper, but Stirling could see she was trying not to smile.

'Not if we catch him,' said Rees.

The next moment he hit the brakes for a queue of cars at the lights.

'Shit!'

Stirling drummed his hands on his lap and Nielsen bit her knuckles. The car seemed too small for them all. After what seemed hours, Reesy pushed a gap in the oncoming traffic. In the same instant, the silence broke.

Got him! He's in a cul-de-sac.

Stirling realised he had the armrest in a death-lock, his knuckles the colour of bone.

A second voice said: *We've blocked off the road, he can't get past us.*

The air in the car was so still that no one was even breathing for fear of breaking the spell. Three . . . two . . . one . . .

Then:

He's crashed, he's rammed into one of ours! Send an ambulance.

Unit sixty-five, please respond. Unit sixty-five, what's your status?

He's out of the car, he's running towards a neighbouring house.

Got the dogs following him, over.

Fragments of different conversations were whirling around like flakes in a snow globe.

Jeff, that's Constable Jeff Mooney, is injured. Cuts and maybe concussion. Or worse. There's blood all over his face. I'm staying with him.

Speeder's over the fence — Eagle, can you see him?

Is he talking?

Go left of the house.

Barely, and I can't repeat any of it. He's in a lot of pain...

Ambulance on its way, over.

Heading south-west.

Need a couple of tow trucks too, we're not driving either of these back . . .

I can hear him!

The sound of barking could be heard in the last message, followed by a lengthy period of white noise. None of the listeners said anything, knowing it would be as much as their lives were worth in this atmosphere. Grimly Rees kept his foot down. Almost there . . .

Got him.

Stirling felt his shoulders unroll in relief. No one killed. It was always a relief.

But there's been a bit of a punch-up. There's a broken nose by the looks of things, and assorted injuries. How far away is that ambulance?

Second that — Jeff's not looking too good.

Grim triumph surged through the quartet of detectives in the car. They had enough to hold him now. Only the news of an officer being wounded held back the cheers.

The whining of the Eagle came in the background. *Can see it from here, mate. Just a few streets away.*

And they were there. Rees brought the car to a halt, and Stirling, Coleman and Nielsen were out before the engine stopped running. It was, predictably, carnage, with the stricken cop and his partner in the middle of the road, the odd neighbour rubbernecking for all they were worth, and now the ambulance wailing onto the scene. Added to that were the profanities coming into earshot from Webb himself as he was dragged back to the waiting cars.

Stirling remained silent, troubled. Rees gave him a quizzical glance, but Stirling — he couldn't help it — looked away. It was ridiculous. Something would have to be done about this. Sooner or later . . .

Stirling was normally immune to abuse, but something about Webb's insults burrowed into his ear.

'I didn't do it! Fuck you, Nazis! I didn't kill her! Let me go! I'll sue all of you fuckers. I am *innocent! I am innocent!*'

THE AIR AT CIB the following morning was as heavy as the smog outside. When Stirling went in search of Kirkpatrick, he found him in Woodward's office, sitting in on the DI's phone conversation. As the office door was open and Kirkpatrick didn't wave him away, Stirling eavesdropped without shame.

'I'm very disappointed about this, Tom. I realise you have a duty to inform the public, but there are some things the public has no right to know at this stage. You're tipping off a murderer about how much we know and removing a very important advantage.'

His expression didn't change as Tom said his piece over the line, his media face still calm and pleasant as ever.

'Tom, do I ever give you advice on how to do your job? Because if we're going to start on that game I might want to ask when you switched the funnies column over to page one . . .' Woodward smiled. 'Oh yeah, we've had a great laugh at some of the stuff you've been printing.'

Stirling wished he could have heard Tom's reply. Woodward's next comment gave him an idea.

'Well, I'd say we have an even greater obligation to the public. You keep your readers informed, we keep them alive. You might want to think about that. I'd hate for you to see any drop in circulation.'

The reply this time was noticeably succinct.

'Look, Tom, we've been friendly for a while, and I don't want to see our good relationship ruined, but if this continues we won't be able to provide you with any more favours. If we can't trust the press, we won't talk to them anymore. And that's the hard truth of it. All you'll have left is that source of yours.'

At those words, Kirkpatrick looked over at Stirling. 'Andy, run and fetch Tony and Vicky, will you?'

Reluctantly Stirling obeyed. There was more to his bad feeling than simply missing out on Woodward's journo-roasting. He knew full well why those two had been chosen — of anyone who wasn't an inspector, they had the best connections in the media. To watch Rees 'help' to track down the mole was going to be tough.

The big man wasn't hard to find; he was standing at the water cooler, chatting to DS Blundell.

'Hey, Tony, Willy wants to see you.'

'What about?'

'The media leak.' Stirling kept his voice casual, but with enough meaning in his eyes to give Rees a scare.

The blond detective didn't show any signs of noticing, only nodding. 'Ah. Well, all the best, John.'

Blundell staggered slightly as Rees slapped him on the shoulder and walked towards Woodward's office. Stirling went and fielded Nielsen from her own office, unable to stop himself tailing her back to the party.

Rather to his disappointment, Woodward's phone call was already over. Rees was in a seat in front of the desk, with Kirkpatrick in his favourite position on the corner of the desk, jiggling his knee.

'Vicky, come in. What have you managed to get from your contacts? Any luck?'

'No, sir. Newshub categorically refused to reveal their source — even when I threatened them with obstruction of justice. They're going to have to find another female face of the force now, or whatever they want to call me, because I'm done with them. She said since nothing was in front of the courts they could run whatever they damn well liked.'

Rees snorted. 'Same at my end. Get bent, copper. If you're not bent already.'

'Bloody journalists and their ethics,' said Kirkpatrick. '*What* ethics?'

'Believe it or not, I'd respect them less if they had told us the source,' said Woodward, sighing. 'It's not like we can do much — we need them, and they know it. But it's bloody annoying. Someone on *our* team is selling us out. And I'm going to find out who.'

Still lingering in the doorway, Stirling glanced at Rees's profile. From this angle it was impossible to see his expression.

Chapter TWENTY

'IT'S JUST NOT the sort of image this school should be projecting.' Veronique shrugged dismissively.

'James isn't some sort of freak — he's not trying to fool anyone. I don't understand how you can say he's tarnishing our reputation.'

Lena kept trying, but she knew it was useless. It was blatantly obvious that whatever she said, she didn't have the slightest chance.

'He is very controversial. Many of our parents don't approve of that sort of thing. They send their children to our school because we are above reproach. How would you feel if all of a sudden our school was seen as a haven for hippies, or communists, or Scientologists? If *Tom Cruise*'s children were coming here, I would want to consult the board and the other parents first.'

Bullshit, Lena thought. *You'd just put his name all through your prospectus and hawk it round Hollywood as fast as you could.*

She kept her voice down for the sake of the people at the other tables in the café. 'Even so, how does what *James* does affect *my* position? I'm not a psychic. Surely it's not fair that I should be punished for something my boyfriend believes? It's like pushing me out of a Catholic school because I'm going out with a Protestant.'

Veronique swallowed a sip of chai latte, her wrinkled, overly made-up face bored. 'But he's not a Protestant, is he?'

181

'Actually he was brought up Church of England,' Lena said coldly.

Veronique shrugged and shook her head. 'This is something very different. You wouldn't have been dragged through the papers if he just went to church. That is the crux of it. It's all the adverse publicity that's got our clients worried. We can't have reporters turning up at our school and disturbing our children, or trying to interview them. Surely you see this.'

'Have reporters actually been doing that?'

Veronique didn't seem to hear her. 'And by aligning yourself with him, you've just made it worse. You've proven to the parents that you think just like him. Do you think they'd want their children to be taught these way-out kind of ideas?'

'I'm *not* teaching them way-out ideas!'

'All that matters is what they *think* you're teaching.' She spread her hands and shrugged again. Lena noticed her long nails, like a cat's. 'I'm sorry, Lena. I'm going to have to be firm — as long as you continue to see this person, we cannot have you teaching at the school this year. I hope you won't take it too badly.'

Lena gazed at her steadily for several seconds. 'Is that what the parents think? Or what *you* think?'

'It is the same thing.'

Lena stood, leaving half of her coffee still in its cup. '*Merci beaucoup, madame*. The French always know what's in or out, don't they?'

As she coldly turned her back, she heard Veronique call gaily after her, 'And you are Swiss, my dear — *you're* not supposed to take sides.'

'BITCH, I HOPE she chokes on a frog.'

Paxton's hands had curled into claws. Lena looked too angry to even be upset. She scooted forward to the front of her seat, unable to sit back.

'How dare she dictate who I go out with? It's none of her damn business. It's not like *you're* the serial killer or anything.'

'So what are you going to do?'

Lena let out a long breath. 'It's the best job I've ever had. I can't very well go teaching at a high school without extra study. I'm not qualified. But I don't want to lose you, and I don't want to work for someone who would treat me like this. Sylvie reckons I should take Veronique to court for discrimination. But it's really not worth it.'

'Some people are so *stupid*. I shouldn't be surprised at it any more. Tell you what, I'll tell Burgess she's next. Bet she'll take it more seriously when people are ringing up asking how she feels about getting an axe through her head shortly.'

'You're a jerk, James,' said Lena. She gave a fleeting smile.

Paxton rested his face in her hair. 'At least Sylvie's on your side now. Is she the one with the long, straight brown hair?'

'Yeah. She's really lovely. I'll invite her to my leaving party.'

183

For almost an hour they sat in total silence, each of them thinking their separate thoughts and getting steadily more depressed until he made the excuse of having the washing to do and left. It fooled neither of them. They both knew he often rinsed his shirts out and whacked them in the dryer half an hour before work.

Paxton might as well have asked himself what he was going to do next. His life seemed stuck on repeat, waking up every day waiting for his guts to be ripped out like Prometheus. It wasn't any better here than back in Telford now; still causing embarrassment to his few friends and loved ones, for nothing but an unfortunate birth defect. Still playing the devil or the Messiah.

Back home, Paxton sat in front of the TV, flipping the top of his beer bottle up and onto the back of his hand, then tossing it up and catching it again. If he'd never gone hunting out the killer, he wouldn't be losing Lena. If he hadn't gone hunting a killer, he'd never have found her in the first place. Heads you lose, tails you lose again. But he couldn't let the crap in his life spill into hers. For the first time in his memory, he was going to do the responsible thing. The difference was this time he'd be walking away, not running away. It didn't make him feel a damn bit better. He felt his eyes burning.

A news bulletin came on, followed by an ad for *Cross*, featuring Simon Burgess's smiling face. In a sudden rage, Paxton grabbed the remote and punched it off. He kept staring at the screen for a long time.

WALKING TOWARDS THE water cooler for his third cup of the day, Stirling caught sight of Rees in front of it, looming over Little John Blundell. Together they looked, as ever, like cops from a skit show. He casually veered off course, aiming for the printer instead. With an empty plastic cup in his hand, it wasn't much of an act.

'Hey, Andy!'

His heart sinking, Stirling looked up. Blundell was waving him over, his face unusually cheery.

'Come here for a minute. We've had some new information from Curtis Webb. I had a hunch, and went with it. Turns out I was right.'

Stirling looked at him sharply. 'Oh yeah?'

'Something just didn't add up. I think it's his usual style — in all his previous escapades, he's got drunk in a bar and lashed out. He hasn't exactly been following women home. Tony agreed with me, so he suggested another stunt. And it worked beautifully.'

Stirling looked at Rees, but the big man didn't say anything.

'I don't know how Tony thought of it, but he suggested I try mentioning that Joel — that other guy from the radio — had told me all about the drugs. And blow me down if he didn't throw one hell of a wobbly!'

Now Rees smiled. 'He's in the music scene, he's always in and out of clubs, he really doesn't like cops.'

'You're due a promotion, Tony, that's all I can say.'

'So he was a dealer. *That's* why he ran.'

'That's exactly why he ran, Andy. Though of course that doesn't exactly rule him out of the equation. For all

185

we know, he could have got himself hopped up on P and done everyone on the list. He swears he was at a nightclub. However, it seems like our friendly nark Joel Moorside isn't so spotless either. God, you should have heard Curtis shouting.' He dipped a hand in his pocket and pulled out a mini tape recorder, then thumbed play. For a few seconds Blundell's own voice could be heard on the tape, mentioning Moorside's name. Then Curtis cut in.

'That little bastard! He bought stuff off me every other week. He and Leash used to do it at home, when her boyfriend was out. He told me all about it, rubbing it in, the smart little prick. If anyone killed her, he did — she had a boyfriend and he didn't like it. He wanted her all to himself, just like everything else. Why don't you go and ask him where he was, the fuckin' arsehole?'

Click.

'Joel didn't mention that one, did he?' Rees's face looked quietly satisfied.

'No, he did not. And afterwards, Curtis made the case that Mr Moorside might have been rather jealous of Alicia's boyfriend. She lived with him.' He waved the tape recorder meaningfully.

'You might not want to play that too often,' said Stirling, trying to make it sound jokey. 'Don't want the leak getting hold of it.'

'No,' said Blundell, with a wry smile. The smile became real. 'But I know I can trust you and Tony.'

Stirling swallowed, hoping neither of them could hear it as loudly as he could. 'Bit worrying when you can't trust

186

your friends, isn't it?' He couldn't help his gaze flicking towards Rees as he said it. He saw the blond detective's eyes widen, then as quickly narrow. Stirling turned away to fill his cup with water.

Paynter's whistle as he came through the door seemed to come from another planet.

'Morning, fellas. Have you heard the news?'

Blundell, Rees and Stirling stared at him.

'We've got some new stuff on Stuart Fletcher.'

'Who's that?' Blundell wanted to know.

'Charlotte Hiscocks's lover boy? I visited your Chinese café owner, Andy. Confirmed what you said, all right — he picked Fletcher out straight away. But not from six months ago.'

Stirling automatically glanced at Rees, startled. He saw Rees was doing the same to him.

'Did you never ask him that?' said Paynter. 'Last time he saw Fletcher, he wasn't with Charlotte — it was just before Helen McCowan was killed.'

Blundell was aghast. 'You're not serious!'

'But wait, there's more. The motel people said he went out the night she was killed. The bloke on the front desk distinctly remembers Fletcher walking down the driveway, because he thought it was strange a man would go for a walk on his own at that time of night. It was just before ten — it was already dark. And he didn't have a rental car.'

As the three of them continued to stare, Nielsen arrived, promptly catching her toe on a curling square of carpet that had come unstuck and spilling her coffee.

'Oh *bugger*. Bugger, bugger, bugger.'

Paynter smiled, calling across the room. 'Why can't you just say fuck like the rest of us?'

Nielsen looked up, sidestepping the puddle. 'I can't. I have kids now. I've trained myself out of it.' She grabbed a handful of paper out of a printer and got on her knees, ineffectually blotting the floor.

'Hey, Vicky, did you hear this about Fletcher being seen in the café? Ciaran was just telling us.'

Nielsen straightened, tiredly hurling her takeaway cup and the soaking paper into the bin beside the cooler. 'That's right, Tony. Course, he could have been simply mourning the death of his girlfriend, in the place they always went to . . . But then again, he could have been looking for his next victim. He never told us he was there, did he?'

Stirling tried to keep his guilt from showing too strongly on his face. *Why* hadn't he asked? But then, Rees hadn't asked either, had he? That bit about staying at the motel and falling into a drunken coma had sounded just a little too pat as well. It stung that Paynter had shown them up. He always seemed a bit too *Starsky and Hutch* to be taken seriously. But what if Arthur was lying, throwing the blame on Fletcher, just to keep himself out of the equation?

'I *hate* cases like this!' cried Blundell, crossing his arms, unknowingly echoing Stirling's earlier thoughts. 'Now *I've* got another chief suspect as well. We're just going round and round in circles. I thought bloomin' forensics was supposed to take the donkey work out of policing. And what have *they* got for us?'

'This time we really can blame television,' said Rees. 'Criminals know more about cover-ups than we do. Forget about a psychic investigator — we should be hiring a scriptwriter to tell us how they bloody did it.'

'I'll say!' Paynter said.

'I don't think we should have got rid of James in the first place,' said Stirling, unable to stay quiet. 'It wasn't my idea to bring him in, but you can't argue, we need him even more now than we did before.'

'I was impressed,' Nielsen said, nodding.

'But he didn't name us either of our suspects, did he?' said Paynter, still smiling. 'Can't say he's been much use. For all we know, *he* did it, just to get involved in another murder case. He was probably getting bored — been too long since the last lot.'

Stirling stared at him in disgust. 'You don't know what you're talking about.'

Rees's voice rumbled behind him. 'I still think it was Ray. He's pissed at Graeme for getting the promotion and wants him to look like an arsehole.'

Nielsen cracked up. 'Now *that* I could believe.'

Even Little John was grinning. 'You've never drunk with him in the Barracks, have you? Ray would never send out those free doughnuts, the tight arse. He always leaves before it's his round.'

Stirling tried to walk as casually as he could towards his desk, but Rees kept pace easily, standing close.

'Have you told anyone your suspicions about me?' he asked quietly.

Stirling stopped and looked him in the eye. 'No.'

'Thanks, mate. I appreciate that.' Rees held his gaze for a moment or two longer, then turned and walked away.

'You bastard, Tony,' Stirling said softly.

Chapter TWENTY-ONE

PAXTON WONDERED OVER and over whether he was making the biggest mistake of his life. First he was ushered into a make-up room to have foundation plastered all over his face, then the man himself was there, shaking his hand as Paxton rose out of his seat.

'Mr Paxton, nice to meet you! We've been trying for ages to get you on the show. Why so shy?'

Although he'd heard how short Simon Burgess was, Paxton was still a bit taken aback. For a man who seemed so much larger than life on the screen, he crammed his energy into a damn small space.

So did Napoleon, he thought. *Don't give the little bastard an inch — looks like he'd take as many as he can get his hands on.*

'I don't much like publicity,' he said bluntly. 'But it seemed like I had little option. If you'll pardon me, there's a hell of a lot of crap flying around these days, thanks to the media. It's about time a few things got sorted out.'

Burgess didn't seem the least bit offended, just nodded, looking pleased. 'Well, that's the idea.'

Someone else was fussing over his sound equipment, with a mike tucked into the collar of his shirt. Conceding that he was out to make a good impression, Paxton had dressed up in a proper shirt and his best trousers. He'd even gone out for a haircut this afternoon, as soon as they'd confirmed his slot on the show.

The floor manager sent him into the studio, directing him to the chair on its plinth opposite Burgess's. This time

191

Burgess didn't even spare him a glance, busy in muttered conversation with one of his studio rats. Paxton's uncertainty peaked. The desire to get up out of this chair and make a run for it was stronger than ever. He recalled the day after he'd channelled a woman who'd been dead for more than 500 years, going into a trance and screaming in her voice in front of his terrified class. The next morning he'd stepped through the school gates knowing, *knowing*, that barely one pupil in the entire place would be ignorant of it. He'd gone inside himself as if back in the trance, knowing his fourteen-year-old life was altered beyond repair, feeling his stomach lurching out of step with his knees at every glance and whisper.

Tomorrow was going to be much, much worse.

When the news ended on the screens behind him and the ads started, Paxton clamped his mouth tighter shut in case his lunch ended up on Burgess's desk. His heart was fighting to get out the same way, and he could almost feel the make-up turning to liquid on his face. The studio lights were like heat lamps.

He was startled to realise his mind had drifted when Burgess's voice cut in.

'Who believes in psychics, ghosties and things that go bump in the night? The police do. Tonight we have an exclusive interview with psychic medium James Paxton, the man who's helping the Auckland police track down a serial killer. Later on we'll be bringing fellow medium Cristiana Austin back to debate with Mr Paxton and share further insights into these dreadful Auckland killings.'

It was as well the cameras were focused on Burgess at that point. The *bastard*. He'd never mentioned having *her* on as well. Paxton knew he'd been ambushed, and he was furious.

'Good evening to you, James.'

'Evening Simon.' It came out more crisply than he'd intended.

'Welcome to the show at last! It's great to have you here. You say you hate publicity.'

'I wouldn't say *hate*. Loathe would be more accurate.'

'And why *is* that?'

'I was just trying to live my own life, and you chose to make it all public without consulting me. Even criminals get name suppression sometimes, but I wasn't even given the chance. And all *I* was trying to do was help the police.'

'Mmm,' said Burgess. 'People have been a bit . . . unflattering lately. I guess you'll have seen the article in Saturday's *Canvas*?'

'Exactly.'

Burgess turned to the camera. 'The article in question was about psychics in criminal investigations, and mentioned Mr Paxton.' He lifted a copy of the magazine section, like a lawyer tabling evidence. 'And I quote: "The reclusive bartender lives in a tiny, shabby ex-state house in a low-income street in Glen Innes. His neighbours say they've never seen clients, and barely any visitors. It's almost as if he doesn't exist."' He carelessly threw the magazine back on his desk with a smile at Paxton. 'Well! What do you have to say to that?'

Paxton gave it a second. 'It's completely prejudiced, and it's probably for the best.'

Burgess bit down hard on whatever he was about to say, trying not to choke on his astonishment.

Paxton didn't even smile. 'I'm finding out who my friends are, and I don't have to pretend about anything anymore, that's for sure.'

'You've come out of the closet, so to speak. Or the coffin . . .'

'It's been good for me, Simon, painful as it's been. I can't say I particularly like people pointing and whispering about me, but maybe it's about time my friends find out who I am. However, what it's doing to my girlfriend is another matter.'

'This would be Lena Bradley, Mark Bradley's daughter?'

'That's right. I came to the studio tonight to break up with her.'

Burgess's eyebrows shot up. 'Is she watching tonight?'

'I didn't tell her about this, but someone's bound to have rung her by now.' Paxton shrugged. 'Either way it doesn't matter, because I've changed my mind. I won't do it. I love her. And I'm here to tell those people who are blackmailing her that they're going to regret it.'

'Blackmailing?' Burgess looked astonished.

'They're saying that if she doesn't dump me, they won't renew her contract at the language academy where she teaches. Basically they're firing her because they don't approve of me.'

'Who don't? The other teachers?'

'Some of them. The head of the academy is called Veronique — she's been pressuring Lena to get rid of me. Don't know her last name, sorry, but the academy is Lingua Europa in Parnell. Apparently it's the parents who've been pressuring the school to drop Lena. And I'm the evil one! I'm not quite sure what I'm supposed to have done, but possibly they're afraid she'll bring my pet demons to work.'

Burgess laughed. 'How many have you got, James? Less than ten?'

'Too many to count.'

'Bet you haven't got as many as I have. But that's blackmail, all right. How do they think they can get away with that?' He was frowning. 'And your girlfriend won't dump you?'

'Not so far.'

Burgess faced the camera. 'Don't dump him, Lena. He's a good man! We'll have to take a look at this.'

Paxton breathed out wearily. 'I hope so, Simon. I've been going through hell these past couple of weeks, wondering if I shouldn't just walk away from her for her own good. But if she's happy with me, as I'm happy with her, why should I have to? It's none of their business who she goes out with — it's not like I'm running a porn ring or something. She's just being punished for something I *haven't* done wrong . . .'

'So what *do* you do?'

'You mean, how does my gift work?'

'Yes. Do you conduct private readings? What's your background? Tell us about *yourself*.'

Paxton sat there silently for a few seconds, trying to distil it all into a few workable sentences. The sweat was forming a moustache under the lights, but he knew it would look foolish or worse, guilty, to wipe it away.

'You're from the UK originally,' Burgess prompted. 'Where?'

'Shropshire — a place called Telford. It's actually made up of some old medieval towns with a big new business park in the middle. It's like a giant conference centre whacked on top of some lovely villages. Strictly speaking, I come from the town of Wellington.'

'Oh really? Have you been to our Wellington?'

'Yes, I was there for a few months. That was long enough.'

Burgess grinned. 'So why come here?'

Paxton nodded. He had to make an effort to look at Burgess when he spoke, and not down at the desk in front of him, especially since he was telling less than half the truth. 'I've always loved travel — I thought it was good motivation to get on with my own life.'

'But why New Zealand? Why *here*?'

Paxton was used to that question from Kiwis; they were perennially kicking themselves in the back of their own heads. 'It reminded me of home, a bit. Without the hassles. And then, of course, there was Lena.'

'Yes.' Burgess smiled. 'Do you love her?'

Paxton blinked. 'Yeah, of course I do.'

'And you won't leave her, even though it looks like she'll lose her job?'

Paxton exhaled slowly, then made himself look up again. 'I'm all she has left,' he said. 'I don't want to sound like she's a pathetic loner or anything — she has some really good friends. More than I do . . . But she's been through so much, and now when she's trying to move on with her life, they throw this at her. It just makes me so *angry*. Her dad's dead, her mother lives on the other side of the world, and so do her brother and sister. Am I supposed to walk away from her too? When you look at it, getting to work with a bunch of snobs doesn't compare with just having someone to come home to. I'm . . .' Paxton shrugged, frustrated. 'I'm not very good with words,' he mumbled.

When he met Burgess's eye, the presenter paused and nodded briskly. 'I think it's time to ask our viewers what they think.'

He turned to the camera. 'James Paxton's partner, Lena Bradley, Lena, whose father was murdered so horribly just six short months ago . . . Lena is about to be let go from her job *if* she doesn't get rid of her boyfriend. What do you think, New Zealand? Is this fair? Is this only to be expected given that Mr Paxton meddles with the other side — bit like Catholic priests, if you want to be frank? Is it right that we should try to separate our impressionable young people from such doings? Or is this a heartless and prejudiced attack on two people who've done nothing to deserve it?'

He rattled off the studio's automated phone number. 'Dial one if you think that psychics are dangerous frauds, or two if they're just misunderstood. I would also like to hear from any parents with children at the Lingua Europa Academy in Parnell to ask them *why* they deemed it necessary to let Lena Bradley go. Message us on Facebook, a text or an email. We'll be back with fellow psychic Cristiana Austin after the break.'

As soon as the cameras were off, Paxton gulped back an entire glass of water and gratefully accepted another. He gave his sweaty lip a swipe and blotted his forehead with his sleeve. 'Here.' The make-up girl suddenly materialised from nowhere, stuck a damp towelette in his direction, then swept more foundation over his face as briskly if she were giving him a spring-clean. As she gave his complexion a critical once-over, Paxton saw Cristiana Austin appear over her shoulder. He had to keep himself from scowling in case he cracked the finish.

Burgess was already shambling over to greet her. 'Good to see you. Have a seat.'

Suddenly Paxton felt a surge of anticipation. He'd be polite, but he wasn't going to nod and smile and agree with the patronising cow. Maybe her abilities were stronger than his, but he doubted it. He saw only a surface — a beautifully dressed woman with a wide smile and an assured air.

Call me a fraud again and you won't be going home smiling . . .

'And Cristiana, this is James Paxton, the guy who was involved with the investigation.'

From the look on her face, Paxton saw she hadn't been expecting him either. She looked positively panicked for a second.

Paxton didn't stand up, but made himself more comfortable. 'Hi.'

'Hello.'

The call went out that the ads were nearly over, and everyone scrambled back to their places. Cristiana perched herself in her seat, quickly smoothing her skirt down over her knees, even though no one could see it. Paxton felt eerily calm as Burgess smiled at the camera.

'Welcome back, and welcome to our next guest, well-known psychic Cristiana Austin. Hello again, Cristiana.'

'It's good to be back, Simon.'

'Now, you've told us you get your messages by seeing images on a sort of screen in your head, just like our viewers at home are watching us on TV . . .'

'Not quite as precise at that, Simon, but yes, that's right. Sometimes I just get a strong feeling about something, or I hear a voice in my head.'

'So how does it work for you, James? Do you see images too?'

'No, actually, I don't. That's what you call clairvoyance, but I've never pretended to be one of those.' Paxton chose his words deliberately. 'I'm clairaudient — that means I hear people. And I do sense things too.'

'Do you have a spirit guide?'

'I think we all do. It's just that most of us aren't listening. I spent years ignoring mine.'

'Cristiana says hers is a Maori chief, a tohunga — was it Tama?'

'Te Mahia. But I have others.'

'Who's yours?' Burgess's hands were crossed expectantly in front of him.

Paxton took a deep, silent breath. What little credibility he had wasn't going to outlive this evening. 'I don't tend to use him, as I said, but from time to time I do communicate with a man named Septus. He was from Roman Britain, way back before the Dark Ages. I used to be able to see him as a kid. He was my not-so-imaginary friend.'

'Really?' Burgess's eyebrows met the wrinkles of disbelief on his forehead. 'And has Septus told you anything about these murders? Did he help you the last time?'

'He did help me last year, yes, but I don't really make a habit of talking to him. Most of the time I get by well enough. I really prefer to just live an ordinary life.'

'But *why*?' Cristiana looked at him like he'd just put his hand up to the murders himself. 'If you have gifts, you can't just turn your back on them — that's like being a fantastic piano player and refusing to play.'

Paxton smiled. 'I've never heard of a fantastic pianist who doesn't play the piano.'

'You know what I'm getting at! Refusing to play in public. People are given gifts for a reason. With something like this, it's almost criminal not to help them.'

'Well, when I *did* try to help the police, oddly enough I got dragged all through the media. And so did my girlfriend. This is exactly why I prefer to stay quiet.'

Burgess cut in. 'But without revealing what you told the police, is there any new light you can throw on the murders? Are you getting other feelings about the case?'

'I can't really tell you that, Simon. I'm sorry. It's not really the right time or place.'

'Does it hurt that the police have just dropped you like this?'

Paxton shrugged. 'I have to say, given public opinion, I can't really blame them. They have a certain image they need to uphold. They've been copping a lot of flak lately.' A split second later he realised. 'No pun intended.'

Burgess snorted with amusement, but Paxton didn't join him. It did sting. *They couldn't run fast enough.*

'Well, what about you, Cristiana? What else can you tell us?'

She looked at her hands, and paused. 'I'm seeing a loner, someone with no friends, and with a previous criminal record.'

'As you've told us before,' said Burgess, unimpressed.

Cristiana didn't miss a beat. 'Yes. What I'm sensing definitely reinforces that. I think he's lying low because of the media interest at the moment, but as soon as the heat dies down, he'll be at it again.' She paused, then nodded. 'Twice. Twice more. Can you give me some more details?' She nodded again. 'In roughly the same area.'

Paxton was hard pressed not to roll his eyes. Burgess turned to him.

'Would you agree, James? Surely you must have some intuition on the matter.'

Paxton opened his mouth to deny any knowledge, when he saw Cristiana's expression out of the corner of his eye. Suddenly he found himself saying, 'No. I don't agree. I think he'll kill once more, but the second time he'll be caught.'

He was as surprised as they were. The tightness of Cristiana's mouth was worth it, though. She sneered.

'No, I'd have to say you're wrong there.'

'My sources are wrong, you mean. As you know, we mediums only channel messages from spirit.'

She had to keep her temper in front of the cameras. 'Has he told you anything about the killer?'

Paxton's mind went blank — then someone else filled it for him. He thought he knew who it was. 'He's almost a charity worker — he thinks he's doing the world a favour, getting rid of the cheating women.'

'He's just fulfilling his own sick fantasies!'

'No. There's a lot more to it. Every time he kills he sees her — he knows it's illegal, but he thinks he's right.'

'And is his name George or Jordan?' Burgess asked.

'No,' said Paxton automatically. He waited for the confirmation in his head, but it didn't come. Cristiana and Burgess were watching him, waiting. 'I can't tell you what it is,' he said lamely.

Cristiana smiled.

'Is Cristiana your real name?' he asked suddenly.

'Of course it is!' *Bullshit*. She looked at him, her mouth smiling, but her eyes like a stalking cat's. 'So how is the next person going to die?'

'Your turn, isn't it?' said Burgess. 'Ladies first.'

Paxton had a momentary flash of fellow feeling for the man, though he quickly suppressed it. He'd always thought the TV host was little different than an undertaker, making money off other people's grief. It was just that he made more and cared less.

Unruffled, Cristiana closed her eyes for a few seconds. 'In her own home, as usual . . . She'll be discovered by another deliveryman.'

'And when will this be?'

'One week. Possibly just over.'

'No. It'll be tonight.'

All three of them looked stunned, Paxton included.

'*Tonight*?' said Burgess.

'I don't know where that came from. Sorry.' Paxton tried to clear his mind, but the feeling wouldn't lift. He looked straight at Burgess, his voice disbelieving.

'Another person is going to die tonight.'

Chapter TWENTY-TWO

IT WASN'T POSSIBLE to bash his head against the steering wheel and drive at the same time, which was the only reason Paxton wasn't doing it. What the hell had he been thinking? He'd have looked less of an idiot if he'd announced that his guide was Elvis Presley. Every time he replayed his last declaration in his head, he wanted to die himself. His conviction that someone was about to become number four had gone now, leaving a cold ball in his gut. It was his own damn stupidity.

What the *hell* was Lena going to say? Far from causing an uprising at her mistreatment, he'd probably just guaranteed her a career waiting tables.

To postpone the inevitable, he took the long way home, past Anubis. He felt guilty, seeing it so crowded after taking the night off, but the contrast between it and the streets hit him hard. The waterfront was strangely empty. Despite the heat, no one was out walking, watching the lights in the fountain or eating ice creams on the beach. Those Paxton did see were heading straight from the restaurants to the carparks, in packs. Had they been watching his announcement in the bar, or had they been like this for a while now? Three women dead, and a fourth on her way. No one needed that said.

Paxton pulled into his driveway and sat for a few moments before going inside. He stuck the key in the lock and snapped on the hall light, shuffling into his bedroom. So engrossed was he in his own thoughts that he didn't even notice someone was there, waiting, invisible in the pitch black. Two hands suddenly went round his neck.

Before Paxton had time to cry out, a mouth pressed hard against his, and the arms tightened their grip, then finally let him go. Paxton's heart was cracking his ribs.

'Holy shit! You scared me!' he told Lena breathlessly, as her face came into focus.

'So did you! Arsehole, I thought you were breaking up with me.'

'You saw me on TV?'

'Bev rang me,' she said.

Bev Davenport was Lena's godmother, married to her father's best friend, Colin. If anyone else would be on his side, they would. He'd become fond of them both, when their cat turd of a son wasn't home.

Paxton flipped on the light switch, blinking for a moment in the sudden brightness. 'But wait a minute — I didn't see you. Where did you park your car?'

She grinned slyly. 'In the side street. I wanted to surprise you.'

He grinned back. 'You wanted to scare me.'

She kissed him again, lightly. 'Thank you. It was really sweet what you did. You idiot. Did you think I was going to break up with you for *that* bitch?'

Paxton didn't respond right away, loosening his grip. 'We got together so fast,' he said slowly. 'I helped resolve your dad's murder. Are you sure this isn't just a case of misplaced hero worship?'

Lena looked back at him for a second, then burst out laughing. '*Hero worship?*'

205

Paxton felt his face flushing. 'Well, I . . . That's not exactly what I meant . . .'

'A martini — shaken, not stirred. That'll be eight dollars, please.' She doubled over, losing it completely.

Paxton looked at the floor, his jaw tightening with embarrassment. 'That's just it.'

She caught the expression on his face, and all the laughter went out of her. Paxton hesitated before he said anything, but just as he started to speak there was a familiar noise — Lena's mobile.

'Here we go . . .' Wearily, Lena went to fetch it from her handbag.

'Hi, Mandy. Yeah, I saw the whole thing.' A few seconds went past, and Paxton saw a frown bloom on Lena's face. She looked over at him and away again. 'He wasn't trying to get me fired, he was trying to help me! He *knew* it wasn't going to work, he's not stupid — he just wanted to make them squirm a bit, and it serves them right.'

She gave it another second, her expression getting positively scary, then glanced at Paxton again and hit the speaker button. Mandy's voice blared out of it, in full spate.

'. . . at him, raking in all the publicity he can get! He's loving this, Lena — all the problems he's causing you are just more chances for him to blow his own trumpet. He doesn't care about your feelings, just about getting his face on TV.'

'All I can say is that you don't know him at all. If you'd bothered to talk to him, you'd know how totally off the mark you are. Don't you remember how quiet he was when I introduced you? He's shy!'

There was a moment of agonised silence. 'Lena, I just don't know how I can get through to you! Does a shy person go on *Cross*? Think about it for a moment, please.'

Now Lena had her back entirely to Paxton, and her shoulders were stiffer than a corpse in ice. Her voice was deadly cold. 'Why would he do it? Try being so loaded with guilt by other people that he thought he'd ruined my life. That's *your* doing, Mandy. You're just as bad as Veronique. You made him feel like he had nothing left to lose. He's been kicked so many times by ignorant people like you he just couldn't take it anymore, even if it meant messing up his own life! Why don't you just fuck off and leave my boyfriend alone.'

She punched the off button with her thumb and flung the phone across the room, where it landed on top of her bag. Paxton sat in silence until she turned around. Then suddenly the biggest grin broke out on his face. He knew it was insensitive, under the circumstances, but it was impossible to hold back. He stood up to grab her in his arms, and she hugged him with surprising force.

'*I love you*.' Eventually she pulled back and stroked his cheek, and gave a small smile. 'Hey, even Dad likes you.'

Paxton's gaze slid sideways. 'Actually, he says he likes me better than you.'

She burst out laughing again, shoving him. 'Bastard!'

Paxton hugged her so tightly she almost stopped breathing. 'So you're not angry with me for completely blowing my credibility, and *your* job?'

'This was never about you in the first place. It's about *them*.' She ruffled his hair, as she always did, with a half-smile.

'You'll give me a bald spot doing that,' Paxton replied, unbelievably happy.

'Too late.'

'Whoooh! It's not too late to change my statement. I'll just call Burgess back, shall I?'

A small frown appeared on her face. 'So, was it true, what you told him? About someone dying tonight?'

The smile disappeared from Paxton's face. He'd actually forgotten. 'I hope not. I just opened my mouth, and — out it came. I'm wondering if it wasn't just sour grapes. And anger. God, that Austin woman pisses me off.'

'I kind of sensed you didn't like her.'

'Her head rotates 360 degrees.'

Lena laughed, but the worry returned. 'So you don't think someone really *is* going to get murdered tonight?'

Paxton planted another kiss on her forehead. 'Don't lose any sleep over it.'

'I don't intend to. I took your phone off the hook.' Paxton laughed. 'Fond of doing that, aren't you? What if there's something important?'

'Do you want me to put it back?'

'No.'

He took her hand, switching off the light.

'Glen's in the lounge,' she whispered into his ear. 'I didn't want him home alone tonight.'

'Awfully sure of yourself, aren't you?' Paxton said, kissing her. 'You just want to sleep with me because I was on TV.'

'Are you going to send me home?' she asked, kissing him back.

Paxton smiled, his voice lowering even further. 'Home is not where I had in mind.'

HE HEARD THE sound of the door opening. The man stepped out first, turning to kiss her goodbye, smiling, as she gently pushed him away. Then she stood, waving, as he got into the car in the driveway and reversed into the road.

Goodbye, sweetie, goodbye! Come back and screw around with me behind my boyfriend's back soon! Tee hee hee . . .

He stopped pretending to look at a road map, and edged the car forward, closer.

He was looking forward to this. He checked the clock on the dashboard. Only about half an hour before the little tart's boyfriend was due home. Any minute now . . .

He got out of the car without haste, as soon as the cheating bastard had disappeared down the road. Briefly he wondered if the poor sod who lived here would be taking the same street home, held up in traffic, crawling past the same man who'd been christening his own sheets with his own girlfriend. Would they recognise each other? Were they best friends? He felt his blood pressure rise, giving a mental nod to the other man. *This one's for you, mate.*

He carefully watched the road, and the windows all around. Darkness was finally encroaching, and all the curtains were shut. It was just a little side street — lucky to see a car every hour. He'd done his homework. It was perfect. He walked up to the door, knocking firmly but politely. Within seconds she answered. He wanted to smack her, right there in the doorway, where anyone could have seen. Her face was still flushed — her expression was positively expectant, but fell when she saw who it was. Or rather, who it wasn't. There was a wary look in her eyes, as if she was afraid she'd been caught.

'Oh. Hello?'

He kept his voice down, considerate of the neighbourhood. 'Hi. Sorry, I'm here a bit early. I was expecting your boyfriend.'

There was just the tiniest flicker of guilt in her eyes. 'Oh, sorry, Luke's not home yet. He usually gets home around nine-thirty.'

Recognition dawned on his face, and he smiled. 'It's Shannon, isn't it? I think we met at someone's party.'

'Yeah, that's right!'

She plainly had no idea who he was, but seemed pleased to be remembered. She couldn't have known that he'd overheard her name while she ate at the café, over the course of a few dirty lunches. Slut slut slut . . .

'Sorry to come round unannounced like this. Luke invited me over for a beer, but I forgot whether it was nine or nine-thirty.'

'Typical of him not to tell me. Come in. He shouldn't be long.' She was fully relaxed now. He smiled suddenly, in very good spirits. She was far too easy in every sense.

She waved him to a seat on the couch. 'Can I get you a drink while you're waiting?'

He wondered if she'd ever done it on this sofa. Probably. It gave his anger an extra edge.

'Oh, yes please,' he said politely. 'Have you got Coke or something?'

'We've got Sprite.'

'That'll do. I'll come and help.'

He followed her into the kitchen. It was a bit eighties, with lino — it actually reminded him of his old flat. It wouldn't look like this after he'd done some redecorating.

'Any idea who else is coming?' she asked him. 'So like him not to give me any warning.' She rolled her eyes, with a silly laugh.

'Just me.'

'Oh really?'

'Yeah. See, it's kind of a surprise.'

Her head was in the fridge; she didn't quite get that. She looked around at him, confused but still smiling pleasantly, clutching the bottle of Sprite.

'Hey?'

She frowned. He was pulling on a pair of gloves.

'It's him I feel sorry for.'

Her eyes went from his hands to his face. His voice was conversational, but his eyes were flat and cold. 'Do you enjoy making a fool out of Luke while you fuck around before he gets home?'

Shannon's jaw dropped. 'You creepy bastard. You were spying on me! That's bloody stalking!'

'That's doing your boyfriend a favour. How would you like me to tell him? Watch his little heart break into pieces? I bet you'd enjoy that.'

Her eyes dropped back to his gloved hands. It was a hot summer's night. She started to back away. 'What were you doing, peeping through the windows?' Now her face was burning red.

'I didn't have to. It was pretty obvious just from watching you on the doorstep — and all the other times you two are together. What's his name? Spike?' He shrugged. 'Dick?'

He'd casually stepped between her and the door. The only place she could retreat to was the corner.

'Get out! Get out *right now*. What the hell are you, some kind of private detective?' She threw the can of Sprite at him, making him duck. She was scared, he could see that. She was making a lot of noise. 'Did Luke hire you? The little prick . . .'

He smiled at that. 'I guess you could call me a private detective.'

She opened her mouth to scream. He kicked her, right in the stomach. She doubled over in pain, groaning and gasping.

'I found out *your* little game, didn't I?' Now his smile was entirely gone, and he was hissing. 'You *slut*.'

He kicked her again, in the head, sending her backwards. There was a crack as her head hit the edge of the bench. She crumpled to the floor as if boneless.

He grabbed her hair, yanking it up to stop her from screaming, clapping a gloved hand over her mouth. 'Tell me why I'm here.' He started dragging her to a set of drawers. 'Tell me . . . what you . . . did to him . . .'

He stood on the backs of her knees to stop her escaping, freeing a hand to pull a drawer open and then another, soon finding what he was looking for. Shannon just barely managed to raise her head as he pulled out a rolling pin, her eyes rolling in terror.

'*Tell me what you did*!'

He took his hand from her mouth. She was sobbing so hard now her words were barely intelligible. She knew it was too late to scream now.

'*I chea . . . I cheated . . . on . . .*'

He brought the rolling pin down. She made a choking sound, which went quiet as he brought it down again. It came down harder and harder.

'*You're just — like — her*!'

When he could see nothing but a mass of red he threw the rolling pin down and gave her another kick, just to make sure. She didn't move.

He checked his watch. Luke should be home any minute.

Poor guy. He'd be horrified at first. But not as much as he would be later on, when the truth came out.

He pulled open a cupboard door and found a blanket, then wrapped her inside it, just in case. Wouldn't do to get sloppy, and get caught. He dragged her into the lounge, an arm around her shoulders. He fetched a tarp from the car, wrapped her carefully and let himself out

213

the front door. The streetlights were spaced far apart, on the other side of the street. He was almost invisible as he walked back to his car. No one was watching, anyway. It was a cul-de-sac, and everybody's blinds were shut.

He laid her carefully in the back seat, and went back for the dented can of Sprite, lying up against the sink. He waited for the foam to stop gushing out, then took a sip. He'd built up quite a thirst. He carefully shut the door behind him as he returned to the car. When they reached their destination he arranged her as he wanted her and stood back to admire his handiwork. As the final bit of garnish, he'd borrowed a knife from the drawer and left it sticking out of her heart. First time he'd done it he almost winced, expecting a rain of blood spraying the walls, but then he realised — it didn't pump if they weren't alive. Cleaner that way, anyway. He washed himself off as best he could, then gave the corpse a last glance.

'You stupid bitch . . .'

Then he went outside to make a phone call.

IT HAD BEEN a quiet night at the Northern Communications Centre. A few drunken hooligans smashing bottles on a beach, a punch-up, a possible drug-related collapse and a loud party that had descended into screaming and curses. Operator Petra Oswald was drumming her fingernails on the desk, trying to stifle a yawn. Opposite her, Chris was on the phone to someone who'd lost their car, by the sound of it. Some nights just weren't worth missing TV.

Another call came through. Petra finished a second yawn before answering.

'Police, what is your location?'

The caller's voice was male, and more wobbly than she'd heard in a while.

'There's . . . There's a dead woman in the Grafton toilets.'

Petra suddenly woke up.

'Are you sure she's dead, sir?'

He started sobbing. 'She's in the toilet. She's face down in the toilet . . .'

Chapter TWENTY-THREE

CONSTABLE REBECCA WILSON turned her face away from Grafton Bridge, where countless desperate souls had leapt to their deaths on the Southern Motorway below. The curved perspex barriers there now only served as an unsightly reminder. She focused on the empty shops across the road instead.

'Hello?' Her partner's call got lost in the dark, between the two halves of the cemetery to the right and left of the road. The soft distant waterfall noise of the traffic under the bridge was the only other sound.

'Can't have been that upset, then. He's gone,' he said.

Rebecca shivered, glancing at the vacant toilet block with the trees of the cemetery looming blackly behind it. 'Can't say I blame him.'

Her partner shrugged. 'Probably a hoax, but we'd better look into it.'

Silently Rebecca gestured for him to go first, into the gents, not unwilling to stay behind. The old brick toilet block was one of the most unique and decorative in Auckland, complete with a mural to brighten up its Gothic glories. In this light, however, the painted tree branches with hunched birds looked positively ghoulish. The place had a reputation as a favourite haunt for the druggies who hung out in the cemetery and in times past had been an infamous cottaging spot. It probably had as many ghosts as its neighbour.

Aside from the empty bus stops and the graveyard behind, there was nothing else on this side of the road for a block. On one of the city's busiest routes, it made its own isolation.

Rebecca's partner was out within seconds. 'Nothing in there,' he said.

Rebecca felt a rush of relief, until he nodded at her. 'Your turn. He could have meant the ladies.'

'What would a man be doing in the ladies?'

He only looked at her, and she felt her stomach shift uncomfortably. 'Unless he was the one who put her there ...'

She glanced at the second doorway. The lock on the women's toilet door was broken and hanging.

'Hello?' Rebecca's turn to call, but more softly. Almost afraid of getting a response. Her partner shone a torch at the outside of the building, pointing high up on the wall.

'Look at that. Someone's smashed the lights as well.'

'Where the hell are crime squad?'

'Don't be stupid. I'm here.' He shone his torch through the doorway, watching as the light glinted off the cold metal walls of the stalls. 'Ladies first.'

Wilson didn't smile. Gritting her teeth, she stepped inside. Was that metallic smell the usual wet-steel odour of sinks and piping, or something else?

It was just a drug thing. Had to be. It'd explain why the bloke had run off, anyway. The creepy feeling tickling the back of her shoulders wasn't so easy to explain. Rebecca took a few steps closer, and saw her, slumped over the toilet as described, her head completely disappearing inside the bowl.

'She's here!'

Instantly Rebecca felt better. This wasn't the work of a serial killer. Just a stupid user who was finding the water in the loo harder to inhale than coke. She took a step closer. But when the torch reached the bowl, and she saw the colour lapping round the girl's head, she knew why her shoulders had tingled. Her partner appeared behind her.

Rebecca pushed past him to the door. When he followed seconds later, shades paler, crime squad was outside.

The car was up on the footpath, two wheels barely touching the road. As DS Gardner stepped out, slamming the door, Stirling saw the look on the uniforms' faces. This wasn't the evening they'd expected.

'What have we got here? Definitely a body?' barked Gardner.

'Yes, Sarge,' said Constable Wilson, whose breathing seemed laboured and deliberate. 'A woman, face down in the toilet.'

'Thank God for small mercies,' Gardner said. 'This'll give the lazy buggers in Drugs something to do for once. Come on, let's get her bagged up.' He jerked his head towards the building, his eyes on his three fellow squaddies.

'Sorry, Sarge?'

'Yeah?' Gardner turned round, looking impatient.

The constable shot a look at her partner, who seemed afraid to open his mouth. He looked pale and clammy in the available light. 'I don't think it's a drug thing. I don't think she did that to herself.'

Without another word, Gardner went into the dark building. The waiting group could see his torchlight moving through the doorway. Within thirty seconds he was back out, his face furious. His easy night had just, almost literally, gone down the shitter.

'Who called this in? Where's the witness?'

Finally the other uniform spoke, his voice quiet. 'He's run off, Sarge.'

It was a curious thing, but Gardner's eyes went straight to Stirling, who was standing a few metres in front of him, just behind the uniforms.

'We thought it was a bit strange that a man found her in the ladies,' the policewoman ventured. 'But then, all sorts happen in these loos.'

'Him, do you think?' Stirling asked, more for form than confirmation.

'There's a knife sticking out of her heart. You be the judge.' Gardner nodded at the other detectives, ringing round them. 'You. Constable. You're OC body.' DC Coleman's face freeze-framed for a second — into a darkened lavatory to hold a dead body's hand . . . 'And Ciaran, you're searching the cemetery. Off you go.'

Ciaran Paynter exchanged looks with Coleman. 'Shouldn't I be OC body? I've had a bit more experience.'

'Time he got some then. Off you go.'

Paynter turned to look at the gravestones. Stirling felt a twinge of pity as he watched him trudge off to the car. If he got a word of sense, or any sign of cooperation at all, from the people who slept in the cemetery, he'd be lucky. On an average night, the place was teeming with people who preferred a grave site to their own homes, but tonight they'd all made themselves scarce. No one wanted to be a scapegoat.

As Paynter fetched the evidence kit, another couple of detectives pulled up, and they too were sent to join him. Stirling felt a strange sense of loss. He'd been praying for something new, almost looking forward to his turn in crime squad, just to take his mind off the psycho running around his everyday life. Heartless as it sounded, a pure and simple OD would have been a breath of fresh air. But the killer had robbed him of that too.

A crowd had gathered round now. In the past fifteen minutes the corner had grown a thousand times in popularity. The uniforms had marked off the police cars with orange cones, separating them from the traffic inching past at rush-hour speed despite the empty roads. Stirling couldn't help looking into each face in the crowd, trying to spot a trace of evil, a trace of something that shouldn't be there. What did a murderer look like? He remembered an early lesson in criminal psychology at training college — *is your next-door neighbour a serial rapist?* Everyone had laughed, until step by step, all the little holes in their knowledge were opened up, and none of them ever looked at anyone the same again, not even the copper next to them. Who was the one poisoned apple who'd called the police, then run away?

The thought almost clanged as it dropped into his skull. It was just like all the others — dial a delivery and then sit and wait. It was just that this time the cops were the ones taking delivery of the corpse. To the killer, they were just as useless as a pizza guy. The arrogant *bastard*. The killer was watching them, enjoying the show, and Stirling knew it.

He stepped down from the kerb and strode across the road, into the other side of the cemetery.

He heard an annoyed yell from Gardner. 'Andy! Where the hell are *you* going?' Trying not to stumble over any headstones, Stirling made random stabs with his torch among the trees. He was probably hiding somewhere, crouched behind a gravestone, a tree, a towering angel. They all looked demonic in the dark.

'Andy!' Gardner's face appeared in the torchlight.

'He's watching us, Sarge. Remember the doughnuts? He's got to be around here somewhere.'

Rather to Stirling's surprise, Gardner nodded, grunting. 'You might be right. As it happens, she didn't die here. Not enough blood — I'd say she got here by car.'

Once again, Stirling realised that for all that he hated the DS, Gardner wasn't a sergeant for nothing.

'Then again, he could be long gone,' said Gardner.

He shouted into the silence, his voice bouncing back off the trees. 'Oi! If you're out there I suggest you turn yourself in. The dogs'll be here any moment.'

A few seconds passed, in dead silence. 'Make sure you keep your eyes out for any evidence as well. No good getting hold of him without any proof to tie him in.'

'Yes, Sarge.'

He waited until Gardner had crossed back over the road before calling softly, 'Time to come out now — I know you're there.'

Stirling didn't expect an answer. He went several paces further along the path, headstones jutting out of the earth on either side. Although it was a warm night, and he was lit with anger, Stirling shivered. He dealt with death on a daily basis, but those bodies were things you could touch, if you so desired, the spent shells of people who lived in this world. The dead who lived in the dark unknown were another matter entirely. He thought suddenly of Paxton. This was the Englishman's area, not his.

Then he stumbled as his foot caught on something. He looked down, and saw something pale and shiny spreading tentacles around his shoe. Bending, he saw a silver vinyl evening bag, its long straps winding round his right foot. Stirling gave a yell.

'Hey!'

He turned and hurried back towards the light, where the other detectives were working, scouring for evidence. The SOCOs had arrived, just taking their orders from Gardner.

Stirling waved at them over the road, beckoning hastily. 'Hey! Check out this side of the cemetery. I've just found a bag.'

A couple of SOCOs made a beeline for him, already suited up for the Apocalypse. Stirling, shining his torch on the bag, noticed something white sticking out of its gaping main compartment. A photographer almost elbowed him out of the way. Then Gardner bent down over the bag, peering at the white object.

'It's a letter . . .' He bent even closer, his expression changing. 'What the fuck?' Using the hem of his shirt to protect it from fingerprints, he quickly pulled out the folded piece of paper, reading the outside. He looked up at Stirling. 'It's addressed to you!'

Stirling stared at him. 'You're not serious.'

He gazed at the piece of paper as if it was a letter bomb, but there was no seal, and therefore no trigger. Gardner held it out to him. Equally carefully, Stirling clutched it in his own hem, nudging open the folds. Gardner shone his torch onto the paper. Then Stirling saw it wasn't a letter. It was a menu. To be precise, the menu from Parsifale. Below Fettuccine Carbonara $19 and Open Steak Sandwich $21, someone had typed in:

POLICEMAN'S SPECIAL:
DOUGHNUTS
WITH A WIDE SELECTION OF TARTS.

Stirling almost screwed it up, before remembering himself. The fucker knew how to get under his skin.

'*Him* again?' asked a SOCO, reading it over his shoulder.

Gardner's face was back to its usual scowl setting. '*Wanker*. Why the hell did he send this to *you*?'

'It's from Parsifale. Who else? I'm the face they always see.' He thrust the menu into the SOCO's gloved hand.

'Here. Get this checked for prints.' He added to himself, 'And I think I know whose prints to look for.'

223

'Whose?' asked Gardner.

'Arthur Wong's.'

Chapter TWENTY-FOUR

AS HE STOOD beneath the shower Paxton heard distant music start up in the lounge, and smiled. He felt the best he had in months. The music skipped, then became voices, then became different voices. Then Paxton realised — Lena was listening to the fallout from *Cross*. At first he pricked up his ears, but it was impossible to hear, so instead he listened to the rhythm of the voices, mingling with the spray, enjoying the lulling peace of it all while it lasted. He'd find out soon enough. No avoiding that.

Rubbing the bulk of the moisture out of his hair, he wrapped a towel around his waist and headed for the lounge. He didn't hurry about it. Fuck them all, so long as Lena was happy.

Her head came up as he walked in. She was perched on the edge of the sofa, arms on her knees, listening. She almost bounced out of her seat when she saw him, her eyes round and incredulous.

'Hey, sit down — listen to this!'

Paxton sat. After a moment his mouth fell open. 'Holy shit, is he talking about Veronique?'

'Yes!'

A strange Mancunian hybrid accent was in full flow: '. . . worked with a more arrogant bitch. She thinks she has God on her speed dial. I swear she thinks she's Joan of Arc reincarnated.'

'That's Bruno,' said Lena. 'He's the Italian tutor.'

'She never consulted any of us about this. And we haven't told Lena, but three of us were going to resign if she lost her job. Sylvie, Thomas and I, we're all sick of her. You know, all four of us have, or are studying for, our university degrees, and she treats us worse than the cleaners.'

When Paxton looked at Lena, there were tears in her eyes. For the first time in days she wasn't just smiling; she was happy. With a wide grin, he grabbed her hand and squeezed it.

'Well, that's certainly damning testimony, isn't it?'

Paxton recognised the voice — yet again — of Simon Burgess, in his early morning radio slot.

'Thank you, Bruno! And now we have Paula Fischer on the line. Paula, your daughter goes to the academy?'

'Can I just say, it is Pow-la — and yes she does. And I think it is terrible the way that poor girl has been treated. I have met her many times and she is always very nice, and a very good teacher. My daughter loves her and says she will not go to the school if Frau Bradley is thrown out. And I agree. Who cares what her partner does; he is not selling drugs to the children. It is all about our children's education, and I think the only person who should go is the woman in charge.'

Paxton whooped. 'Good call!'

'You think Veronique should be fired?'

'Yes I do. She is not Joan of Arc, she is Napoleon.'

Burgess cackled. 'Can I ask you, Frau Fischer, do you believe in psychics?'

'I am willing to be convinced.'

'And you don't think it's colouring your views?'

'Of course it is. But I'm not firing someone because of them. Everyone has a right to their views, and that is something Veronique Rideau needs to learn.'

Paxton sat with his hand still in Lena's, basking in the newness of it all. Never in his life had he experienced anything like it. He could have listened all day.

There was a slight pause before Burgess spoke again. When he did, his voice was changed, brusquer.

'We've just got some news off the wire that should ring a bell with Mr Paxton. The body of a woman has been found on Symonds Street in central Auckland. Cause of death is as yet unknown, but the level of police interest at the scene suggests it may be the work of the serial killer already responsible for the deaths of three other women.'

Paxton and Lena looked at each other, but neither of them said a word. They were both speechless.

'The victim is a woman from Ponsonby. According to our independent source, police are investigating a link with the Parsifale café in Ponsonby, where several of the women apparently had lunch not long before they were killed. Viewers of last night's Cross *programme will recall psychic medium James Paxton making just this prediction. Someone else is going to die tonight, he said. Someone is going to die . . .'*

Paxton leaned forward and seized the stereo remote. The voice cut out instantly.

'This is not funny.' His wet shoulders felt cold.

He sat up, then propelled himself to his feet. 'I'm calling Andy.'

'What? For Christ's sake, haven't you learnt your lesson yet? *Don't get involved*.'

Paxton looked back at her, pausing, and frowned, his frustration showing through. 'I know. It's just that I want to make sure I've done everything I can. It's like I can't rest — this whole thing is hanging over me. It's like doing a crossword and not knowing the one missing word because I'm not allowed to use the bloody dictionary.' He spread his palms out wide, trying to convey something he couldn't quite grasp. 'Haven't you ever — ?' The sentence rolled to a stop, and his eyes widened. 'Hey. Wait a minute . . . Look who put me up to this whole detective business in the first place.'

It was Lena's turn to look guilty.

'You *hypocrite*. You seduced me into finding your father's killer!'

'Well — you didn't *have* to go al—'

'You wouldn't let me rest until I found him, but you'd let a mad axe murderer chop up as many strange women as he liked. It's just because they're cheaters, isn't it? If they weren't all sleazy little tarts, you wouldn't have a problem with me going after the killer.'

'Well, I don't like cheats, but that's not it. No one deserves to be murdered.' Lena let out a long sigh, then gave a rueful smile. 'I have only myself to blame, don't I?'

'It's just a *phone call* . . .'

But as he readjusted his towel and wandered towards the kitchen, he knew this was a lie, and so did she. Whether the cops liked it or not, Paxton was a part of this investigation and had been ever since Stirling had first called. The humidity in here was almost as bad as the shower, making movement and concentration equally difficult. He felt beads of sweat mingling with the cold drops from his hair trickling down his forehead.

Stirling answered without any preamble, clearly reading his caller ID. 'Hello, didn't expect you to be ringing me. I hope you're having a better morning than I am.'

'I heard about the murder.'

'That's not the half of it . . . Hang on. Let me call you back, save you paying for the call.'

Paxton had barely hung up when the phone rang again.

Stirling's voice was rushed and miserable. 'Hi. Sorry, I can't talk for long — I'm at the murder scene. Don't know if you've heard, somehow the name of the café's got out to the media. The shit's really hit the fan this time. And guess who they're blaming for it?'

For a fleeting moment Paxton forgot his own troubles. 'Oh Christ. Why?'

'Well, guess who stumbled across this café in the first place? I've been to every single interview on the premises. I'm the logical scapegoat, really.' There was an underlying anger to his tone that Paxton didn't miss.

'And because of me, they think you might have bleated to the radio.'

'I've already had one going-over by the Senior this morning, no doubt because Woodward got onto him, and his boss was sitting on him . . .' Stirling sounded as lively as a flat can of lager. 'And to top it all off, I got an irate

229

phone call from the café owner. My bloody number-one chief suspect rang up to give me a bollocking for ruining his business! Can you believe it?'

'The café owner's your chief suspect?'

Paxton heard a breath exhaled through the receiver.

'I really can't keep my mouth shut, can I? Shit. I haven't been home this morning.' To emphasise his point, Stirling yawned.

'I've got some news that might wake you up. Dunno if you'll want to hear it though.' He saw Lena standing in the doorway, listening.

Stirling gave a tired laugh. 'Oh come on, tell me. If it's more bad news, just shovel it on me — I'm well buried anyway.'

'I predicted this woman's death.'

'*What?*'

Paxton shifted towards the fridge, reaching for the orange juice with the phone still to his ear. Lena poured them both a glass while he talked. 'I was on *Cross* last night, and I predicted that someone else would get murdered last night.'

Paxton managed to down half a glass before Stirling spoke. '*You* went on *Cross*?'

'It's a long story.'

'And you *predicted* this?'

'Don't ask me how I did it. It just — came out. I'm as freaked about it as you are. And someone round CIB is bound to know about it. It was live on TV.'

Paxton heard a long groan.

'This is just the tip of the iceberg, isn't it? They'll crucify us. We let you go, and now look — someone dies.'

'It's not your fault, Andy. It's no one's fault. Well, except the sicko who's doing this.'

'Fuck fuck *fuck* . . . I've got to go, James. Thanks for ringing. At least now I know what I'm dealing with. See you.'

Paxton put the phone down and looked at Lena, who gazed blankly back.

'Never a damn dull moment.' Paxton shook his head, running a hand through his hair. He wiped it dry on his towel. 'I'm getting dressed.'

STIRLING WATCHED LUKE Thompson plucking blades of grass, one by one, underneath the tree where he sat. In his exhausted state, he found it mesmerising. Thompson shredded each blade methodically as he watched the SOCO technicians march in and out of the house, like a line of ants in paper shoes. He'd been sitting there for two hours, since he'd returned from identifying Shannon's body. Where he sat, behind the fence, he was shielded from the eyes of people passing on the street, looking curiously at the crime tape strung across the yard. Luke wasn't allowed in the house, nor did he want to be, but he couldn't bear to leave the place either. His phone call had come through at a quarter to ten last night — he'd found blood all through the kitchen, and no sign of his missing girlfriend. The splash of vomit in the hallway hadn't been cleaned up yet.

Stirling was about to take his leave, as politely as he could, when he heard another car draw up. Turning, he saw a younger brown-haired man in a T-shirt, his good-looking face scared and bewildered.

'What's going on? What's happened?'

'Do you know the people at this address?' Stirling asked.

'Yeah. I just had a text message to come round!' He reached into his pocket and held out his phone.

Stirling took it, and blinked. The message was from Shannon. It was timed just twenty minutes ago.

'Sarge!' Stirling yelled.

He looked up to see the man staring at his expression. Stirling tried to keep his voice level, his veins rushing with anger. 'I'm afraid I have some bad news. Shannon was killed last night. This message can't be from her.'

Gardner stepped out of the house. Stirling held up the phone. 'Look at this. It was sent less than half an hour ago.'

Gardner focused on the screen, and his face flushed dark red. 'The little *shit*.'

'He's using her phone.'

The young man's face was white. 'Shannon's dead? What happened to her? Was she — ?'

'Are you a friend of hers? Sorry, I didn't get your name.'

'Mike. I'm her boyfriend.'

Gardner and Stirling both stopped. 'Well, it's complicated, but — '

'What the *fuck*?'

232

Luke Thompson had come up behind them, the veins in his neck standing out like ropes. Stirling hadn't appreciated before how well built he was, as if he played rugby. Opposite him, Mike looked slight and frail.

'What do you mean, you're her boyfriend? *I'm* her boyfriend.'

Mike was stammering, backing away. 'Sorry, Luke. Let's just drop it.'

'Are you saying you were sleeping with her?' Luke's face looked ghastly — mostly white, with spots of colour. 'She wouldn't sleep with *you*.'

'Hey, let's discuss this later, okay? This isn't the place ...'

'Give me that phone,' Luke said quietly to Gardner.

'I don't think it's such a good idea right now,' Stirling replied, equally quietly. 'Leave it for the moment.'

'*Give me that phone.*'

'It's my phone,' said Mike, grabbing it from Gardner and trying to hold it behind his back. With a lunge, Luke snatched it from him. Mike took two tiny steps behind Gardner. Silently, just as he'd stripped the blades of grass, Luke scrolled through the message inbox. He stopped to read one message, his expression giving nothing away. Then he looked up, thrusting the phone back into Gardner's hand.

'Thank you.'

Stirling was already starting to move, but Luke got to Mike first. In a split second, Mike was on the ground, Luke's fists hitting his face with repeated sickening smacks, like hands slapping a side of meat. The first blow burst his nose, sending blood pouring down his front.

Stirling dived to pull Luke off, but the man was as single-minded as a pit bull. The speed of his attack was astonishing. Gardner screamed out for help as he joined in, and suddenly a passer-by was jumping the crime tape on the drive, joining in the struggle as one of the SOCOs pelted over from the house. Finally Luke was pulled free, breathing like a horse after a race, Mike's blood all over his front. The other man lay sobbing on the ground, hands over his shattered face.

Stirling felt sick. He knew who'd set this up. He found himself looking round at all the worried faces, into every corner and window. How did he know? Where was he? *Where was he?*

Chapter TWENTY-FIVE

SHE STEPPED OUT of his line of sight for a second; looked like she was going to her chest of drawers. He changed his position on the shed roof, to get a better view. Stupid bitch, didn't she realise net curtains hid nothing if you had the lights on? This wasn't exactly a private backyard. Especially not since he'd arrived. She was asking for it, all right. They all were.

Many's the time he'd sat here when she had one of her boyfriends over, and he joined in all by himself. He already had a hard-on.

It was going to be riskier this time — there were four other people in the house.

Then again, he knew how to keep them quiet. By the time he'd finished, she'd be begging for it.

STIRLING LOOKED AT the room through bleary eyes. Twenty-four hours since the last victim was found, and the atmosphere at CIB seemed even more bunker-like than usual. Stirling's colleagues were like an army under siege, with morale at an all-time low. Standing in the computer room shared by all the underlings without their own office, he could see people making phone calls, looking at screens, tapping pens against piles of notes, all trying to look busy. He knew it was all show. They were a bunch of detectives without a single clue between them. Except him.

Stirling shook his head, his mind full of an all-purpose, unfocused anger, the way it got when you were too tired

235

to nail down any one thought. He remembered what the pathologist had said about Shannon's body. It had been as badly disfigured as Charlotte Hiscocks', the first victim. He'd gone for her face. There was an indentation on her finger too, from a ring that had been removed. The fact that the mark was still there showed the ring had been taken post-mortem. He was collecting tokens — the phone was another.

That bloody Arthur. *Wong*. Who the hell did he think he was? He remembered the Malaysian's voice when he'd rung to complain. As if he were the one hard done by, as if he were totally innocent.

You've ruined my business! I thought you were one of the good guys. Why did you do this to me?

It had been all Stirling could do not to shout back at him. *Why did you kill all those women? You're just trying to throw us off the scent, aren't you, matey?*

Despite that, he'd felt a familiar flash of guilt. What if Arthur wasn't the one? He was becoming like Gardner, trying to wrap up the case with a too-small ribbon, squeezing the evidence out of shape just to get it tied up.

In that case, whoever it was — the bastard who kept running to the press, arrogant sod — had just ruined a harmless baker. One of his own colleagues had a mouth he couldn't keep shut. And it was probably his own best friend, Tony Rees.

The sudden buzz and shrill of his phone in his pocket produced a shot of adrenaline that actually burned in his chest.

236

Wincing and rubbing his breastbone, Stirling pulled the phone out. Unknown number.

'Hello, Andy Stirling.'

'Hello, this is Warren Lucas. Helen McCowan's friend.'

He was the last person on Stirling's mind at the moment. 'Hello, Warren, what can I do for you?'

There was a moment of dead air. 'I was watching TV the other night, *Cross*, and they said something about the murdered women all being cheaters. Well, that psychic did.'

He stopped, seeming to be waiting for a response. Stirling closed his eyes. Oh hell.

'That's right, Warren.'

'I've been thinking about it. Is that why Helen was killed? Did she have — a boyfriend?'

'I'm afraid she did. I'm sorry.' Stirling was seeing the punch-up on the lawn again, all the blood and tears.

'I see.' Warren's voice was steady, but quiet. 'I suppose it's not really all that surprising.'

'It's an awful way to find out.'

'Looks like there's two of us waiting for justice, then.'

'Sorry?'

'Me and the other man. We're both hurt by her death, aren't we?'

Stirling tried to keep the surprise out of his voice. 'So you're not angry with her then?'

'How can I be? She's dead now.' Warren sounded deeply sad, but there was a braveness in his tone that touched Stirling's heart. 'She never meant to hurt me. How are you getting on with the search?'

'I think we're getting closer. Got it narrowed down to a few.' Stirling desperately hoped he wasn't lying. It would have been cruel, somehow.

'That psychic seems a clever fellow. He was dead right about what happened, wasn't he? I hope you listen to him.'

Warren seemed full of surprises.

'Yes, he's a very clever man.'

Warren finally hung up after thanking him profusely for helping to find Helen's killer. Stirling slid the phone back into his pocket, feeling worse than he could remember in a long time. He blinked, scrunching his eyes tight shut, and opened them again. He was still seeing a fog in front of everything, with a few floating spots for good measure. Shit, he wanted to go home. He leaned his head back against the wall, letting his eyelids fall shut.

'Wakey wakey, Sleeping Beauty.'

When Stirling opened his eyes, he saw the unwelcome features of Ray Gardner smirking at him. An insult about nightmares was on the tip of his tongue, but the cave-ins under Gardner's eyes were truly the stuff of bad dreams. Like Stirling, he could only have had two hours' sleep at the most. His voice sounded almost as deep as Rees's.

'Time for the briefing now. In Graeme's office.'

Stirling pushed himself off the wall and followed, breathing in deeply in an attempt to wake himself up. It only made him yawn. Hearing him, it set Gardner off too. They ran into Nielsen in the corridor, talking to her husband, Brad, well dressed as usual.

'What on earth are you two doing here? They haven't called you back, surely?'

'Good help is hard to find these days,' said Gardner. Stirling nodded at Brad. 'How are you, boss?'

DC Brad Nielsen had once been a sergeant above Stirling, on general duties. He'd only taken his detective's course a couple of years ago, when his eldest son Cameron was about to turn five and he realised his wife's bedtime stories were going to sound better than his.

'Christ, you guys look terrible.' Brad was looking from Stirling to Gardner.

'Yesterday we had a murder and an attempted murder,' said Stirling. 'And the guy responsible for both is laughing at us. If I look like shit, it's a damn sight better than I feel.'

Brad stopped smiling. 'Leaves my Thai meth importers for dead, doesn't it? Good luck, fellas.'

'Cheers, Brad.'

He nodded and bent to give Nielsen a kiss. 'Take care. See you, sweetheart.'

'Maybe.' Nielsen sighed, then turned and walked towards Kirkpatrick's office with the others. 'Any idea what this is all about? I've been holed up watching security tapes all morning.'

'From the car park on Symonds Street?' Stirling asked, his heart skipping a beat. The dogs had tracked a scent from the toilets across the road to the parking building. 'What did you find?'

'Nothing.' Nielsen shrugged glumly. 'The footage was so grainy, and the lights didn't show faces very well.

Besides which, a number of people were wearing caps or looking in the wrong direction. I slow-moed it so many times, and I couldn't even tell if it was one of *you*.' She shook her head. 'I'll get the experts to do what they can with it.'

'I thought there was supposed to be a security guard training college in that bloody building!' said Gardner. 'That's typical. The only reason you go into security is because you're too damn stupid to make the police. I might as well not have even bothered with the dogs.' He shot Stirling a sardonic look. 'Mind you, Andy reckons he's got it sussed.'

'Well, we've already got him on the defensive, haven't we?' said Stirling. 'Arthur Wong's threatening to go to the Police Conduct Authority. Somehow it's all my fault — like *I* leaked the name of his café.'

'Well, it is if you've been talking to that psychic friend of yours. New Zealand's latest Z-list celebrity.' Gardner smiled sourly.

'He didn't even know, Ray. I never told him.'

'According to him, he'd be able to find out anyway. I heard about that prediction of his the other night. I'm surprised they didn't offer him a slot as a weather presenter.' Gardner grinned, adopting a cod English accent. 'My spirit guide says there'll be rain on the West Coast and sunny spells in Nelson. And when I say spells, I mean it literally!'

Stirling looked away in disgust, but caught the eye of Vicky Nielsen. She looked spooked.

'James Paxton predicted this?'

The door to Kirkpatrick's office opened. 'Come in.'

Rees was already in there. Surprised to see him, Stirling stood closest to the door, automatically maintaining his distance. Whatever was coming, he preferred being next to the exit.

'Take a seat.'

Crammed into the tiny space were three chairs. Rees was squeezed beside Kirkpatrick at his desk and, to Stirling's surprise, Woodward sat in the corner on the Senior's other side. Stirling, Nielsen and Gardner each had a chair facing them. It felt like a game show. Or a scrum. Stirling tried hard not to shift in his seat. Kirkpatrick gave a quick drumroll on the desk with his hands.

'I've called you back here, Andy, to say that I'll be sending you back to Parsifale café to interview Mr Wong,' Kirkpatrick said.

After this morning's embarrassment, it was the last thing Stirling had expected.

'With Ciaran Paynter, just to keep all our bases covered, and so he's got one more person to worry about. The inspector and I both agree — you've drawn it to my attention that you believe he's a suspect, and it's only fair that you should have the chance to speak to him again. In the meantime, please assure him in person that it wasn't our intention — or your fault — that the name of his café was given to the media. I'll be following that up with a letter. And who knows, either his anger or his fear that we're onto him might get him to drop something he shouldn't.'

'Yes, sir.'

Kirkpatrick nodded. 'Tony, I want you to check out the boyfriends. It's a long shot, but it's got to be done. Take young Coleman with you if you want. You okay with that?'

'Sure, Senior.'

'You don't believe our friend Mr Paxton was behind the leaks?' asked Gardner, reverting to their previous topic.

'It had to be looked at,' said Kirkpatrick. 'But DC Stirling has assured me he never told Mr Paxton a thing, and I have no reason to doubt his word, do you? Or Mr Paxton's. I found him very honest.'

Gardner didn't say anything. Stirling felt a flood of warmth towards the Senior.

'And while you're here, Ray, I have a proposition for you and Vicky. A special mission, should you choose to accept it.' Kirkpatrick was smiling now, rhythmically clicking his pen. 'While Andy's interviewing Mr Wong the usual way, which may or may not come to anything, I want to throw something more interesting into the mix. A sting, in fact.'

'You mean like a drug bust?' Gardner looked at Nielsen, who looked just as bewildered as he did.

'Almost,' said Woodward, breaking his silence. 'Sorry, Graeme, I want to have some of the fun, for a change. This is one of mine.'

'All yours, sir.' Kirkpatrick's smile grew even wider, as they all stared at him.

Woodward laced his hands on the desk. 'I suggested this to Graeme after it became obvious our killer hunts in one spot. Now it's become public knowledge, that might stuff it all up — but I hope not. I thought, the man has a thing for two-timing women, and he seems to find his victims in the same café while they're on their little assignations, so why not play along?'

Out of months of habit, Stirling's eyes went to Rees's, and saw the same look on his face. This time when Stirling looked away, it wasn't out of embarrassment but self-preservation. He'd wet himself if he laughed now.

Nielsen's laugh sounded tinny, more like a cough. 'You're not serious, sir.'

The look of disbelief and sheer horror on Gardner's face was a pleasure to watch. 'You want me to play boyfriend with her? Why the hell didn't you pick someone like *him*?' Gardner pointed to Stirling. 'Or another toyboy like Coleman? Middle-aged women are more into that sort of thing — it's more believable.'

'I'm not middle-aged. I'm only thirty-six.'

'You can't think anyone would take us seriously!'

'Well, that's precisely what you're going to have to work on, Ray. Because that's the plan. We didn't want to hand this to someone as young as Sean — he tends to clown around a bit anyway, from what I've seen. I think you more fit the type of older businessman going for a younger woman at the office, and you have a bit more experience.'

Rees was smiling. 'But has Ray had the sort of experience you're after?'

'Shut up, Tony. Aren't you finished here?'

'What about my own husband?' Nielsen was clearly desperate. 'He's a detective — he's used to playing a role. And it would definitely look more realistic.'

'It can't be Brad — if he's following you home, he'll see straight away that he's your husband. You're both adults, I'm sure you can handle it. We're not asking you to spend the night together, just put on a bit of a show.'

Kirkpatrick looked uncomfortable. 'But we will have to ask you to spend a few evenings together at Ray's. Just in case he's following you. We'll have people close by watching.'

Gardner shook his head in disgust, huffing out a breath. 'Jesus.'

Stirling looked steadily at the floor; Rees was doing the same.

Woodward looked at Gardner. 'You've been divorced for years now, what are you worried about? You're not going to upset anyone, and you get to spend time with a lovely young woman.'

'That's what's upsetting *me*,' Nielsen muttered.

Kirkpatrick frowned. 'Well, if you really want, I could get someone else to do it. Stephanie Harris, maybe . . .'

'God no,' said Gardner fervently. 'She's like a walking armpit.'

'If you can't handle crap flung at you, Ray, stop handing out shit pies.' Woodward crossed his arms and sat back. 'Are you in or do we have to find someone who can handle it?'

'I'll do it,' said Nielsen. 'When I'm not working I usually spend my evenings reading anyway, between sorting out the kids. This way I'll just be combining all three.'

'What's *that* supposed to mean?'

'Are you up to it, Ray?' Nielsen gave him a challenging look.

'It's not a case of not being up to it,' Gardner flung back.

'Right, then. You'd better start acting like a team.'

'I was trying to think which actor you remind me of, Ray – and unfortunately, it was Kevin Spacey...' Gardner glared. 'Might be the hairstyle. You're quite a bit like him, actually.'

Stirling pressed his lips together and focused on a corner of the desk, desperately trying to force his mind to go blank.

Rees nodded. 'Was that as the hitman, the serial killer or the guy who wanked in the shower?'

This time Stirling lost it. Nielsen couldn't help giggling too, and once she started she couldn't stop, until she was hunched over and gasping for air. The others were almost as bad.

'Get the fuck out of here, Tony.' Gardner's scowl was dangerous.

'Hey, Spacey played a detective sergeant in *LA Confidential*,' said Kirkpatrick. 'That's what I was thinking of.'

'Speaking of which, if you want to do any detecting, you'd better get yourselves over to the café,' said Woodward. He turned a critical eye on Nielsen. 'Vicky, go get a bit of lipstick on, get yourself a bit tarted up. Not over the top — use your discretion. If you want to buy some new clothes, charge it back to us later. Can you be back here in' — he looked at his watch — 'half an hour? I want you in place when Ciaran and Andy arrive.'

'Best be off then.' Nielsen scraped back her chair and promptly left.

If Nielsen pulled this off, Stirling thought, she'd deserve a medal. Romancing Gardner was well above and beyond the call of duty. If she had to actually kiss the man she deserved hazard pay.

Chapter TWENTY-SIX

DESPITE A SNEAKING desire to see his superior dressed up like a hooker, Stirling knew he was bound to be disappointed. As usual, Nielsen had taken the sensible middle ground, keeping the white blouse she'd had on, and her hair was its usual shoulder-length dark blonde. Her sole purchases were a designer skirt that came down to the knee and a cheap pair of very low heels. A necklace she'd borrowed and a dash of lipstick, and that was as sexy as it got. Stirling suspected she wasn't quite as prudish as it looked. If he were a female working opposite Gardner, there was no way he'd be wearing a miniskirt and a low-cut top either. Nor if he were trying to attract the attention of a killer who hadn't slipped up yet.

When Stirling walked into the café, followed by Paynter, he couldn't help vaguely scanning the interior as if pretending to look for Wong. There weren't many full tables, he noticed. The novelty value of dining in Death's café had worn off. Many a woman who'd done nothing more than eye up a picture of Johnny Depp would be keeping away until this was over.

A burst of laughter drew his attention to one corner, and he saw them. Nielsen looked greatly amused by something Gardner was saying; only those who knew her would realise that the bubbliness was overdone. For his part, he actually seemed to be enjoying it. *Loves the sound of his own voice so much he thinks its bloody Christmas,* thought Stirling.

'Well I never,' Paynter murmured, his eyes flitting to another table.

'Mr Stirling.' Arthur Wong stood in between the food cabinets and the cash register. He nodded sideways, towards the back room. 'Shall we talk in here?'

The office was a mere cubicle, with a set of plywood shelves, a stack of flour sacks piled up in a corner and two scruffy chairs, one of which Wong pulled out from behind the small desk. As soon as he shut the door behind them Wong gestured them to seats and fixed his eyes on Stirling, crossing his arms. The genial little man from the other day was entirely gone.

'As I said to you on the phone this morning, I'm very disappointed. I understood your investigations were being conducted in the strictest confidence.'

'Have you noticed a drop in customers today, Mr Wong?' asked Paynter.

'As a matter of fact I have. I thought you had more integrity.'

'I apologise for that, Mr Wong, but I believe DC Stirling's already told you it's not intentional. Whoever leaked this information is being hunted out and will be dealt with, I assure you.

'By the way . . .' Paynter rested his elbows on the table, leaning forward. 'Doesn't this whole thing disturb you? Apparently you have a killer stalking your café. At least this way people are being warned.'

'Of course it disturbs me! I even thought about shutting down. But that's not the point. The point is that I trusted Mr Stirling not to reveal the name of my café to the public, and he, or someone else, has. That makes it very hard for me to trust you.'

Stirling had to grit his teeth at that point. The hypocrisy in the room was choking.

'And what about you, Mr Wong?' said Paynter. 'How do we know we can take you at face value? Can I ask why you didn't shut down?'

'What are you suggesting?'

Paynter let his silence speak for itself. Wong darted a glance at Stirling, who still hadn't said a word. After a moment he gave a sigh that filled the room.

'You think I could be the killer? Because it's my café? Why the hell would I do something like that? Just because I have a yellow face doesn't mean I'm a Triad, you know.'

'It'll be easy enough to rule you out, Mr Wong. Undoubtedly your wife could tell us where you were when these killings happened.'

Wong gave an impatient shake of his head. 'I don't have a wife. Not anymore. She's back in Malaysia.'

'You're divorced?'

Now Wong paused. 'Not exactly.' He realised what he'd been led into saying.

Whoops. There it is . . .

'Have any of these women been in to the café?'

Paynter pulled another deck of photos from a brown envelope, fanning them out on the table. Stirling barely recognised a mugshot of Shannon Lawrence. With a face.

Wong's eyes shifted again to Stirling, who was watching him intently. Wong's own expression was unreadable. 'I don't think I'd better say anything without a lawyer. I'm entitled to have one present.'

'That's your call, Mr Wong. That'll be all for now anyway. We'd best be going, I think.'

Paynter started to rise from his chair, with an audible creak.

Wong looked at Stirling, who was doing the same. 'At least you know where to look, don't you?' he said suddenly, his voice cold. 'You're blaming *me* for not closing down, when you don't want it either. It's making your job easy, isn't it? All you need to do is watch whoever's in the café. The more people who die the better, because it gives you more clues.'

'I wouldn't call collecting dead bodies easy,' said Paynter.

Arthur ignored him, still looking at Stirling. '*You* haven't said anything. Why did you even bother coming? Hoping I'd give you more cake?'

'I'm watching my weight, Arthur.' Stirling turned his back.

As he began to walk from the café, he noticed the young woman, Lauren, beckoning to him frantically from a corner. Intrigued, Stirling headed towards her, with a glance at Paynter to follow.

'Hey!' She murmured at them, trying not to make it too obvious. 'That's the guy I was telling you about. The creepy one.'

Stirling and Paynter twisted their heads to look. Sitting alone at a table was a pale, stocky man in a T-shirt. He was engrossed in a ratty women's gossip mag that looked like it came from the café.

'He's always in here,' Lauren said. 'It's like he doesn't have a life.'

'What kind of things does he do?' Paynter asked.

'Well, he does look at people. I think he probably eavesdrops on them. I've seen him crack up laughing at the same time as other people, so it's pretty obvious. Sometimes he doesn't even have a magazine — he just sits there.'

'You haven't seen him follow people out of the café, anything like that?'

'No,' she admitted, with clear reluctance. 'But he's always talking to *me*. He just drones on and on — I have to pretend to be interested, because he's a customer, but he's just *dodgy*.'

'Being lonely isn't a crime, unfortunately,' Paynter said. 'But I'll have a chat with him. You never know. We'll have to talk to everyone in here.'

Stirling watched as Paynter went over to the man's table, pulling out his exercise book. The man seemed surprised, but on the whole delighted to be distracted from his magazine. Judging from his manner, he couldn't have been more eager to please. It was probably pointless, but Stirling noticed Arthur watching the interview closely from behind the counter. If it put the wind up him, then well and good.

'How about your boss?' he asked Lauren casually. 'How's he been taking all of this?'

'It's really stressing him out. He's not been himself, lately, eh? Usually he's always smiley and joking a lot, but I think this has him spooked. Can't say I blame him. I mean, there's a murderer coming to this café.' Lauren didn't look so perky now. 'I don't want to work here anymore, but it's been the ideal job.'

'Have you noticed Arthur talking to the customers — including the people who died?'

No matter how he phrased that, it was always going to sound suspicious. Lauren frowned harder. Then Nathan passed with his hands full of coffee cups. 'Hi, Mr Stirling! We've got orange and almond cake today. Want some?'

Stirling met Arthur's eye. 'Better not today, thanks, Nathan.'

Nathan's smile vanished as he saw the look on Stirling's and Lauren's faces. 'Hey, what's wrong?'

'He thinks Arthur might be the killer!' said Lauren incredulously. 'There's just no way; he's friendly to *everyone*!'

Nathan looked at Stirling, astonished. '*Arthur?* You might as well pick me, or Lauren, or Morgan. We're in the café almost as often.'

'Exactly!' Lauren said. 'Except Nathan's been with his girlfriend for the past four years, and I faint at the sight of blood, and Morgan is, like, this really staunch Christian.'

Stirling fought the urge to roll his eyes.

'But whoever it *is*, I hope you find them soon,' Nathan said helplessly. 'I'm getting really paranoid — I'm always positive he's in here. I'm so glad Tessa's in London.' He glanced at Lauren. 'I've just bought my plane ticket,' he admitted.

'My parents keep telling me to quit,' said Lauren unhappily.

When they'd both cleared off, Stirling noticed Paynter had finished with the dodgy man, and was chatting to a couple of women who looked like colleagues on their coffee break, jotting down names and numbers and whether the customers had seen anyone or anything suspicious. The usual donkey work — as Paynter said, sometimes you got lucky. On Stirling's side, there were only Nielsen and Gardner. Gardner was still talking. Nielsen's eyes were slightly glazed, but at least it could have passed for something else.

'Excuse me,' he said politely, showing his badge. 'My name is Detective Constable Andy Stirling. I'm investigating the murders of several women who were patrons of this café. I don't know if you've been following the news?'

Gardner frowned up at him, with the same fuck-off expression Stirling had seen on so many teenagers. 'Yeah, I've seen it.'

'Was it *this* café, then?' Nielsen interjected, realising it was all part of the show. Stirling also thought she looked a little relieved.

'Have you been here before?'

'No. But if this is the murder café, we'll have to come back. I'd love to catch the killer.' Nielsen flashed Stirling a dazzling smile. 'Eh, Ray?'

Stirling tried not to laugh. 'Here's my card. Let me know if you see anything.'

A text message came through on Nielsen's phone, startling them.

'I'll let you know when I've solved the murder for you,' Gardner said, sticking the card under his saucer.

Stirling kept the smile on his face. 'Just leave all the dangerous stuff to those who can handle it — won't you, sir? Don't do anything stupid.'

Nielsen deleted her message. 'It's my husband,' she announced, with a disparaging smirk. She pressed the call button. 'Hi honey, how are you? I'm just having lunch with Jenny.' She met Gardner's eye and gave him a flirtatious grin. Stirling smothered another laugh. Unless that was Woodward or Kirkpatrick on the other line, someone was going to be extremely confused.

Paynter was waiting by the car.

'How did it go with that guy?' Stirling asked him.

'Believe it or not, he said he was home with his wife for all the murders.'

'He's *married?*'

'Yep. According to him, they run a business from home. He sells computer parts, she sells New Age stuff over the internet. On the nights in question, he and his wife were home watching DVDs. Apparently he's writing a fantasy novel as well — the café is where he goes to study dialogue.'

Stirling snorted with laughter. 'Well, that explains a lot, anyway.' He got into the passenger's seat.

A text message sounded from Paynter's pocket as he got in beside Stirling. He checked his phone, and smiled. 'Did you notice Vicky got a message when you were in there?'

'That was *you*?'

'Thought I'd help them out a little . . . The husband had to come into it somehow. I suggested Vicky give him a call.' Paynter looked down at his phone again. 'I asked her how she's enjoying her one-on-one time with Ray.'

He held out his phone, with Nielsen's text message still lit on the screen.

IF THE KILLER DOESN'T SHOW UP, I'M KILLING MYSELF.

Chapter TWENTY-SEVEN

COLEMAN WASN'T HAVING the best morning. Like Gardner and Stirling, he'd been hauled out of bed for the morning shift after the horror of last night. After his first ever taste of being in charge of the body, he was itching to pour mouthwash through his ears. Or at least sleep. He'd come straight from the morgue to CIB, which struck him as eerily similar. Most people seemed to be on the road, leaving their desks quiet and empty. It was almost a relief when Rees corralled him. Left to his own devices, with no one to talk to, he'd have gone straight to sleep.

They had a shopping list of suspects to tick off on their rounds.

'The banker, the baker, the record-rotator . . .' Rees mused as he waited for the roller doors to let them out. 'Like a bad joke.'

'It's all digital now, Tony,' said Coleman, his eyes shut.

'Who cares? What I want to know is, how come we have to go to people's offices and they get a cushy café? What did I do?'

Coleman grunted sleepily. 'I spent last night in a public toilet and at the morgue.'

'Was that on or off duty?'

'Up yours, sir.'

CHARLOTTE'S EX-LOVER WAS first. He'd got himself another job now, but it was a bit of a comedown for a one-time corporate banker. When Coleman and Rees walked in to the combined post office and Kiwibank, he was standing behind the counter, selling a young couple stamps for a postcard to Britain. As soon as he laid eyes on the policemen, Stuart Fletcher's face went blank for a second. He waited until the couple were well away before speaking.

'It's not really the best time right now . . .'

'Sorry, Mr Fletcher — won't take a minute. Could we go into your office?'

Fletcher gave a suffering glance towards his two colleagues, who were both busy serving. 'It really can't be any more than a few minutes.'

He came around the counter and opened the door to a tiny glass office, with blinds all down the side. Looking like he was tempted not to, he left them open. He spread his hands wide on the desk as Rees and Coleman sat wearily in the customers' chairs.

'Now, what else can I possibly tell you?'

Coleman ostentatiously flipped open an exercise book on his lap, clicking his pen down. In the five-second pause, Rees examined the man's face, especially the reddened skin on his nose and around his eyes. His shirt was crisp, his hair tidy, but he needed a drink.

'Tell us again about Charlotte. You loved her?'

'At one time I think I did. Now, of course, I know what she was like.'

'What was she like, Mr Fletcher?'

'I don't think you need me to tell you. I wasn't the only man in her life, was I? Not even the only *other* man.'

'So you don't miss her?'

'No. She was out of my life long before she died.'

'You didn't miss her even then?'

'I got over it.'

'About two days after she was murdered, was it?'

'Eh?'

'You went to the café. You were seen. The same day Helen McCowan was killed.'

Fletcher looked trapped.

'You knew Helen, I hear,' added Coleman. 'Like to tell us where you were the night she was killed?'

'I don't remember! I was drunk. But I woke up in my motel room, and there's no way I was in a fit state to do anything to anybody. How could I? Helen McCowan was killed in her home — I don't even know where that is.'

'That's what you told the last pair of detectives. Except you told them you were drunk and incapacitated for *three days* after Charlotte was killed. Never went anywhere, you said. You didn't tell them about your trip to the café.'

Fletcher steepled his hands together on the desk, then touched them to his nose. 'I thought it would sound . . .'

'Incriminating?'

Fletcher breathed out through his nose. 'I wanted to say goodbye. It doesn't really make sense when you say it out loud. I kind of thought — go to this place, see that it's not magical, it doesn't mean anything to you anymore. Just let it go, leave all of the bad stuff behind.' He bowed his head. 'I was drunk. Even at that time of day.'

Rees nodded. 'What about the following night, then? When you left the motel?'

The look Fletcher gave them was wary, and just a little frightened. 'What are you talking about?'

'Because witnesses say you did.'

The banker's complexion went grey, tinged kiwifruit green by the decor. He looked back and forth between both of them, surprised and really unsettled now. 'I don't remember.'

'Are you sure about that?'

Fletcher shut his eyes tightly. He did the same gesture with his hands: it almost looked like he was praying, or diving. 'I have blackouts,' he said at last. 'I can't remember where I was or what I did. All I remember is that I woke up back at the motel. But that doesn't make me a murderer!'

'Did you take your own car?' asked Rees.

Fletcher silently shook his head. 'Must have got on the bus. Didn't have a car then.'

'That's good to hear.' Rees paused. Fletcher seemed to be telling the truth so far. 'Can you say for sure you didn't murder Helen McCowan, as well as Charlotte? What if you were too drunk to remember? You might have caught the bus, or a taxi.'

Fletcher looked up at them, his brow furrowed. He'd finally lost his temper. 'Does that sound likely to you? If I was so dead drunk I couldn't remember, I somehow flagged down not one but two buses to the correct addresses — one of which I didn't even know — *plus* I got home again, and managed to conceal any bloody weapons or clothing I had on me?'

'You could have thrown the weapons away, taken a change of clothes. You could have followed Helen home previously or obtained her address some other way.'

Fletcher closed his eyes again, then looked at the desktop. 'Maybe I was in a drunken rage against Charlotte, or that poor English lady. Maybe I had a secret grudge against both of them for screwing more than one man. But I was cheating too! How on earth does that make sense? If I had something against evil homewreckers, why the hell didn't I turn a gun on myself?'

Coleman and Rees exchanged glances. Someone rapped on the glass partition, making them all jump. The door opened, and an Indian woman peered round.

'Stuart? There's another customer to see you when you're finished. Sorry to interrupt.' She gave them all a brisk smile, then closed the door softly.

Rees's mind went back to what Fletcher had just said. He had a point — there didn't seem much sense in attacking someone else for behaving the same way you did.

'And as for Alicia Schofield, I don't even know what she looks like.'

'You might have seen her when you were there last,' said Coleman, but there was no force behind the punch.

'Possibly I did, but I wouldn't remember.' Fletcher's voice sounded smooth, but self-loathing seeped through the cracks.

***

'IT'S ALL THE effing around that started this mess. And now we're still doing it,' said Rees.

Coleman grunted. He waited until the shopfronts were sliding past the car window before he said, 'I'll admit, he doesn't seem like the killer. But how do you know?'

Rees sighed. 'True story, Sean,' he said. 'It was about my third or fourth year on the job, and we were down at the local Farmers, in Papakura, seeing to some fourteen-year-old who'd been shoplifting. My sergeant and I were walking back through the store with this kid, looking at the displays a bit — it was Christmas — and we went past the Christmas shop.' Rees wore a slight smile. 'There was a guy in a Santa suit, little kids on his knee, and I was just wondering what it'd be like to have his job, when he looked up and spotted us. Our eyes made contact — the whole eyes-meeting-across-a-crowded-room scenario — and I recognised him. Beard and all. We had a warrant on him for armed robbery.'

'Oh no, Tony. I'm not believing this one.'

Rees just gave a dry chuckle. 'He knew I knew who he was, and the two of us froze. I didn't know what the hell to do. I wasn't going to arrest Santa! My sergeant hadn't even noticed. I've just turned my head towards him, started to say something, then our guy panics. *Throws* this little boy off his lap and makes a run for it. Only problem is, he's in this grotto thing. It's an enclosed area, and the only way out's through the front. Without even thinking I block him off and do a rugby tackle — guy must have been about half my size without the pillow down his front

261

— and bring him down, and then because he's struggling, my sergeant comes running over and he's just yelling and whaling away at him, really giving it to him, and all these little kids are screaming and crying.' Rees shook his head. 'We get the cuffs on him and start dragging him away, and all these parents are giving us the evils and the kids are screaming at us to leave Santa alone, and the shoplifter's legged it while we were busy . . . I tell you, my face must have been about as red as that Santa suit.'

Coleman was half laughing, trying to spot the tell. 'You saw that on TV!'

Rees gave another grim laugh. 'I wish I had, Sean. It was the most embarrassing day of my life.'

Coleman burst out laughing. 'You arrested *Santa*?'

'Hey, I heard of one bloke in Manukau who brought in Ronald McDonald.'

Coleman laughed harder.

Rees stopped at the lights. 'But the point I'm making is you can't always tell what a person's like from the outside. You ask me, they're all bloomin' murderers.'

Chapter TWENTY-EIGHT

THE PUB WAS pretty crowded by the time Stirling sleepwalked in, but there was room at the table for him. Coleman waved him over.

'Hey, Andy. Looks like you've had the same kind of day I have.'

Stirling sank into his seat. 'Do me a favour and don't tell me about it.'

'What'll you have?' asked Kirkpatrick. 'I'll get it.'

'Just a Heineken. Cheers, Graeme.'

They'd all been a bit wary about letting their senior officer into their unofficial club, but the fact was, Kirkpatrick had been sitting at this table longer than Stirling had been with the police. The fact that he'd been promoted didn't ban him from having a drink.

'Shame Vicky and Ray couldn't join us. I've been dying for a rundown,' said Paynter from his end.

'How long do they have to spend together?' asked Coleman.

'Two weeks. Some evenings as well — back at Ray's.' There were guffaws from all round the table, but they didn't last long. No one seemed in the mood.

'Vicky's sister's helping Brad with the kids.' Kirkpatrick took a good long swig of his pint. 'But how did *you* go today? Anyone say anything useful?'

'Count the beer glasses, Graeme.' Paynter indicated a line-up of two empty glasses and a half-full one in front of him. 'What do you think?'

'Looks like you're pacing yourself today, Ciaran,' said Rees.

Paynter boomed with laughter. 'Damn right — I was just being polite, waiting for Andy. Drink up, mate, you've got a bit of catching up to do.'

'Just the one for me today, I think,' said Stirling. 'Any more than that and I'll fall asleep at the table.'

'Oh good, someone can grab his wallet,' said Paynter, and laughed at his own joke. Despite the solid buzz of conversation around them, the laughter seemed too loud.

'I can't figure it out,' said Coleman, frowning down at the table. 'There are too many damn suspects, and no witnesses! I didn't feel good about anyone today.'

Rees swallowed his beer. 'The way things are going, I'm going to lock everyone up just to make sure.'

'Still think it was the café owner?' asked Kirkpatrick, watching Stirling.

'You bet.'

'I've put in a request to Interpol. Could take a while, though.'

Stirling nodded, but he was finding it hard to get enthusiastic, even about this. He was absolutely shattered. He finished up his beer as quickly as he could and left. It must have been late — dark didn't come on till nine these days, but he had to turn his lights on. It was a relief not to get pulled over by Traffic on the way home; he was more than half asleep at the wheel. By the time he reached the driveway, he could already feel the cool pillow against his face.

Before he even had a chance to turn off the ignition, his mobile rang. Mumbling a curse, Stirling groped in his pocket and finally located it on the final ring.

'What's up, Tony?'

At the answer he blinked, suddenly wide awake. Moments later he reversed straight back out of the driveway.

'TELL YOU WHAT. He says he'll meet you at the cemetery, round midnight. Oh — and bring a spade.' Adam started giggling, and had to slam down the receiver.

'You're such a git.' Paxton turned to face the drinks on the wall.

'Hey. Mr Psychic. *Without looking around*, how many fingers am I holding up?'

Paxton laughed, then it turned into a sigh. 'I can't handle this. Every damn phone call, it's another person wanting me to solve their problems.'

But when he turned round, Adam's attention was on a woman with greying hair, one of the millions out there who all looked alike unless they were your mum. 'Can I help you?' Adam asked.

Paxton wasn't entirely surprised to see her eyes flick from Adam to him. 'I was wondering whether I could talk to Mr Paxton. Sorry, I realise you're working,' she said politely.

'What did you want to talk about?' asked Paxton.

The woman's eyes lit up, and she dropped the formality. 'I've been coming here for a while, actually, and I've always thought you seemed like a nice young man. I had no idea! I was watching *Cross* and there you were!' she said. 'That was incredibly brave of you. What did your girlfriend say?'

'She said the same thing,' Paxton replied, hoping his face wasn't red.

'I should think so. And of course the poll results were marvellous, weren't they? How does it feel to have the whole country behind you?'

'Pardon?'

'The poll results. From the show. About two-thirds of the viewers said your girlfriend's boss should be fired. And just over fifty per cent said they believed in psychics. Didn't you see that?'

'No.' Paxton almost missed her next sentence, trying to process it.

'Yes, I thought it was great. And you seem much more reliable than that Cristiana woman. She's far too smooth. What do you charge for a reading?'

'I don't do readings. Sorry. It's just not something I'm comfortable with.'

She looked taken aback. 'But why on earth not? You don't mean to tell me this is your only job?'

Off to his left, Adam stared gormlessly into space and pretended to scratch his bottom.

'Yep.'

'Maybe you should tell Tanya to give you some time off, then. Cut back your hours — I'm sure she'd be really understanding. Then you could concentrate on your other abilities.'

'You know Tanya?'

'Yeah, she's a friend of mine. She told me to come and see you — she thought you might cut me a deal on a session. I'd be interested to hear what you had to say.'

Paxton tried to remain polite, but he was boiling. 'Sorry. I'll have to tell Tanya not to do that.'

'Oh, that's such a waste! I have to agree with Cristiana — you should be using your powers! What are you doing in a place like this?'

'I have no idea. Excuse me.' Politely but deliberately, Paxton went on to the customer waiting behind her. After a few moments the woman left. Two minutes later, however, Tanya appeared in front of him as he cleared the tables.

'What's this about telling Trish you weren't going to help her?'

'I don't give readings to *anyone*, Tanya. I told you, I'm not after publicity. I'm just trying to do my job: why won't you let me?'

'So you'll help the police, but you won't help a friend of mine who lost her son three years ago? What good is that?'

Paxton gritted his teeth. 'The thing is, where does it end? If I let you refer *one* woman to me, I've got to let everyone else. Haven't I? And if I don't tell them what they want to hear, then it offends a good friend of yours and therefore you, because they won't come back here, and we're worse off than when we started.'

'Then don't tell them the bad news! I thought all psychics were supposed to only say the good stuff — like if someone's going to die, you just tell them to go on a world trip so they get to live a little. Just make something up.'

Paxton stared at her in disbelief. 'Why don't *you* give the readings then, Tanya? You seem to know exactly what you're doing. Just rig up a curtain in a corner of the bar — it'd be better than a slot machine!'

Tanya's face was mean. 'Don't talk to me like that.'

'Well, how about this then? I wish to tender my resignation, effective immediately.'

Tanya scowled.

'Thank you for employing me, have a nice life. Polite enough for you?' Paxton turned and walked directly to the bar, setting down his handful of glasses.

He clapped Adam gently on the shoulder. 'See you, mate.'

'Eh? Where are you off to?' Adam looked round from the till.

'I quit.'

'*Eh?* Why? What happened?' Adam shot Tanya a look of dismay, but she flapped her arms contemptuously, then crossed them.

'I'm tired of being a sideshow. Keep in touch, eh?' He looked at Brent, who had just walked up to the till.

'I'll see you later.'

Brent looked surprised. 'Where are you going?'

'Sorry, Brent. Ask Tanya.'

Without waiting for a goodbye, Paxton walked away, leaving both men staring.

***

HE HAD TO keep his breathing quiet as he watched her, but it was difficult. Once he thought he saw her glance towards the spot where he squatted, under her window, but she kept moving around as if she hadn't seen. Whore. She had guys looking at her all the time, and she knew it. Well, he'd had enough of waiting. Tonight was the night, fuck the flatmates. The bitch's time had come.

'I LIKE A bit of irony, but this is just cruel,' said Lena, playing with her glass of wine. 'You leave your job because of your boss, just as I get my job back.' She shrugged sadly.

'Well, I didn't *have* to resign,' Paxton muttered. He wasn't much in the mood for talking. Lena had offered to let him stay, and it made him guilty. He couldn't help thinking of Mandy.

'No, but . . .'

'I promise I'll be paying my way until I find another job. Then you can turf me out again if you want.'

'Look, don't worry about it. You spend almost all your time here anyway.'

'Honestly, I've got a bit saved up. I'm not a freeloader.'

'What were you saving for anyway?' asked Lena suddenly.

She looked at Paxton's startled face. 'You were saving to go away again, weren't you?'

Paxton realised it was true. 'I've — always saved my money.' He frowned at his glass. 'Just a habit, I guess.'

Lena didn't say anything for a moment.

'Are you against being a medium because of what happened with that woman back home? The whole being run-out-of-town thing?'

Maybe.' Paxton looked into his barely touched wine again. 'I guess . . . I just don't feel qualified to work as a counsellor. 'Cause that's basically what you are. You pass on the messages, and then you've got to deal with all the emotions. It's . . . tough. So many times I went to my gran's, and she had someone sobbing in her lounge. I'm really not up to that.'

'But you handled it fine with me.'

'Well, yeah.' Paxton grinned. 'But a sexy brunette crying on my shoulder's a bit easier to cope with.'

'You're always selling yourself short, that's your problem.' She shook him gently, smiling in exasperation. 'You never believe you're capable of anything, and then you do it! You know what? I think you should go and prove this Cristiana Austin wrong.'

'How do you mean?'

'I've always been against you putting yourself in danger, but enough is enough. This case has caused you so much trouble, I think the least you can do is get it over with.'

'Yeah, but I can't go nosing around anymore, remember?'

'But couldn't you get Andy to bring you a piece of evidence? You know, a handkerchief that belonged to one of the dead women or something. You're good at that, I've seen you.'

Paxton stared at her. 'Psychometry, you mean?'

'Yeah! Hang on.' Seeming more animated than he'd seen her in weeks, Lena pushed herself off the sofa and went into the next room, coming back with a solid-looking paperweight. She held it out. 'Here, have a go with this.'

Reluctantly, Paxton took it. 'This doesn't hold all the answers, Lena. It's usually really vague . . .'

'Stop whingeing and just try it.'

Letting out a long breath, Paxton held the paperweight, and looked into it. It was a rich, dark green, with different shades and lights in it, unexpected sparkles like sand and, somewhere in the middle, a drop of bronze. It felt cool, as if it had been out of the sun. He let his eyes go out of focus as he gazed into it.

'I'm getting . . . glass,' he said. 'Sort of rounded. It could be a Christmas tree ornament of some sort, but it feels heavier . . .'

'James.'

Paxton closed his eyes. He let his back relax until he could no longer feel the sofa, and hear only the sound of his own breathing. Gradually his awareness of the surroundings faded until he might have been floating in space, or asleep. He smelled salt, the salt of the sea, and words dropped into his consciousness, foreign, like music . . . Then, like a curtain dropping, it cut to black, and an all too familiar sound that made his heart leap.

The sudden blast of the phone snapped his eyes open. Lena went to take it as Paxton waited for his heart to start beating again.

'Yeah, he's here.' Lena was looking at him, her face concerned. 'Are you all right?' She was speaking not to him, but to the person on the phone.

Paxton couldn't hear the reply.

'I'll hand you over.' She brought the phone over to him. 'Andy.'

'Hello?'

'We've found someone, James.' Stirling's voice managed to be tired and energised at the same time. 'He was caught sneaking round a property in Grey Lynn. Turns out he's not new to this. We've had him in on a whole bunch of stuff. Including male assault on a female, and there's a previous acquittal for rape.'

Paxton sat up straighter. 'You sure it's him?'

'God, I hope so. I don't know what to think right now, to be honest. I just thought you should know.'

'Shit, I hope he's the one.'

'Unbelievable how just one chance call-out can lead to an arrest. Thank Christ the woman had her wits about her. She thought she was being watched a couple of times.'

Paxton nodded, suddenly feeling let down. 'Sorry I wasn't more help.'

'Hey, we can't always be right. I didn't see this coming either — he's not the sort of guy you could see hanging out with any of these women. Sort of rough and dodgy-looking.'

That snagged a memory in Paxton's brain. 'Funny, that. The other psychic reckoned he'd be Maori.'

'Gee, that's insightful. Given, statistically speaking, more than half the prison population is Maori.'

'I know. She also said he lived near water, and had a wooden house.'

Stirling snorted. 'I heard about that.'

'His name's not Jordan, is it?'

'No, it's George. George Huia.'

Paxton stopped smiling. 'Sorry?'

'George Gordon Huia. Gordon *does* sound a bit like Jordan, though. Maybe you're on to something.'

Paxton took a moment to find his voice, his pulse rising in his neck. 'I don't believe it.'

'What?'

'She was right. She was bloody right.'

Chapter TWENTY-NINE

'JUST THERE TO do her a favour, were you? Like you did a favour to Belinda Jansen? And Michelle Crossan? Gagging for it, weren't they?'

'Oh, man, that Shelley . . . Fuck, she was a whore. She was screaming my name, man. I had to give it to her twice, just to shut her up. Get the file if you want the details. Something to get your nuts off on.' Huia looked past Gardner at Stirling, giving him a slow, satisfied smile over the table. 'You get off on it, eh? You're just jealous I get the girls and you don't.'

Stirling looked back at him from the corner, trying to be objective. The man was a turd in the gene pool, who bobbed up all too often. Had up for assault, both physical and sexual. Nine months for removing half the teeth in another man's mouth, acquitted on a technicality for rape, let off on diversion for his first foray into amateur porn eight years ago. Pervert. Basher. Psychopath. A narrow face with prominent cheekbones, greasy hair and a leer that was never long absent. And a psychic had dobbed him in days ago . . .

Gardner had, with unprecedented generosity, let Stirling in to watch the face-off. Stirling's explanation was that he wanted to learn interrogation from a master. Gardner probably wouldn't have been fooled, except for his relief at having escaped the café. If he could prove this was their man, he'd never have to play the lunchtime lover again. If he failed, he was facing another two weeks of it. Huia wasn't going to find this easy. However, they'd been sitting here for the past two hours, and Huia hadn't given a millimetre. Gardner's canines were beginning to show. He leaned forward, sneering.

'They like it so much you have to kill them now? "I'm so happy being dicked by a sad ugly Maori bastard I could just die?"'

Huia didn't bat an eyelid. 'You're a racist, bro. I should report you to the Police Conduct Authority. That lady officer who brought me in, she wouldn't mind a bit of Maori in her, I tell you that.' He giggled. 'Asked me for my phone number and my address. Nice tits. I might go round sometime. Give her a turn in the handcuffs.' He giggled again. The sound of it grated on Stirling's nerves.

Gardner smiled nastily. 'I know your mother fucked around, George. She's the biggest slut there is.'

Huia leaned back lazily. 'Not arguing there, bro.'

'Is that why you killed those women? Eh? What kind of guys did she bring home for you to play with? Bet they were fun, eh, George?'

'Did you like the doughnuts, bro?'

The skin tightened over Gardner's cheeks. 'You think that was fucking funny? We got your DNA on those doughnuts, boy. We can get you for that.'

Huia wiped his nose on his arm and smiled. He'd know that if they had his DNA, they'd have pulled him in long before now, seeing as he was on file. He stared dreamily at the watermark near Stirling's head while Gardner kept at him, looking like it was a day at the movies. He'd walk away from this too, and he knew it. As the sergeant's voice rose, Stirling stood. Both men ignored him as he left.

Kirkpatrick was outside the door, looking anxious. He kept his voice low, just in case a sound got back to Huia. 'I've been watching from the other end. We don't have enough to keep him yet. Not for murder, anyway. And his parole's already expired so we can't even hold him on that.'

'He's not stupid, sir. He's all "man" and "bro", but that's just front.'

Kirkpatrick jammed his hands in his pockets to keep them still. 'We can get him on trespass, at least. Having that psychic woman get so close, it's got my attention.'

Stirling nodded, saying nothing, and turned to go. Kirkpatrick stopped him after two steps. 'Oh, by the way. How's your friend? Mr Paxton?'

Stirling turned back, uncomfortable. After a moment he realised he was an exact mirror of the Senior, with his hands in his pockets. 'I had to let him know. In case the media got on to it somehow. He was a bit embarrassed. This has really shown him up, hasn't it?'

'Show me one of us who's a hundred per cent accurate. There'd be a lot more people alive today if that happened. Tell him not to feel bad.'

Stirling thanked him, but oddly, he felt worse.

PAXTON SAT WITH his head bent and eyes closed, as if that would somehow bring him closer to Shannon Lawrence. He had his hands pressed to the dead girl's face, willing her to respond. It was a grainy photo, cut out of the newspaper, but it would prove if he was good enough. He'd half expected the phones to ring as the media got news of the arrest, but all was silent. They had nothing more to say to him. It was Cristiana they'd be calling now. He shut his eyes more tightly, trying to focus, and at the same time let himself go.

'You don't have to do this, James. You've got nothing to prove.'

Paxton opened his eyes and looked at Lena, who was standing in the doorway to the lounge.

'That paperweight was your dad's. I felt it. I felt his last moments, for God's sake, I felt him hit me on the head. I felt him die! I should be able to do *something*.' He looked down at the paper girl, breathing through his nose.

Lena looked shaken, but said nothing.

'How come that *bitch* was able to predict this and I wasn't? How come I'm so fucking useless?'

'Hey, you're not useless,' Lena said firmly. 'And you know it.' She came to sit beside him on the sofa, laying her head on his shoulder.

Paxton closed his eyes again. 'When I try to ask Shannon what happened, all I get is a crushing headache. No proof George did it, no proof it wasn't him either. All I have is this horrible feeling that everything's wrong.'

There was a knock at the door, then Paxton heard Stirling's familiar tones. Seconds later he was in the lounge, carrying a black briefcase.

'I need your help,' he said, without any preamble.

'Captain Helpful, that's me,' said Paxton sourly.

Stirling didn't answer. Instead he sat on the chair opposite, putting his briefcase on the coffee table and flicking the clasps open. From it he pulled a photo and a sheet of paper, and placed them in front of Paxton. The photo was a black-and-white of a man with a narrow, expressionless face and dark complexion. The other was a list. Looking at it, Paxton saw it was a menu. More precisely, the menu from the café all the dead women had been to. Stirling was watching him.

'You think this guy might be him?' He looked at the man in the picture, who could only be Cristiana's killer. George Gordon Huia. It might have been a passport photo, but it was undoubtedly a mug shot. He had a stubbly excuse for a moustache and eyes like holes in the paper. There was so little to read in his face that he looked capable of anything.

'He might well be.'

Paxton looked again at the face, with its flat, dark eyes. 'All right. Let's give it a go.'

He picked up the photo, feeling ridiculous with Stirling watching. He tried to clear his mind, and, to his surprise, an impression came to him almost at once. He wanted to let go of the paper, which felt like it was soiling his fingers.

'Shit, this guy is twisted. I feel really dirty. Scared. He wants me to be scared; he likes it.'

Stirling listened patiently, and Lena was so still she might not have been breathing.

'Are you getting the murders?'

Paxton waited, so long it seemed like he'd fallen asleep. 'No,' he said at last, disappointed and frustrated. He dropped the photo back on the table. 'Only that this guy is not what you'd call normal. There's violence in his whole being — past, present and future. It's warped him. He hates women too. I feel that. If he's never raped or killed something before, I'd be very surprised. He's definitely capable.'

Paxton could see Stirling trying hard not to question him further. 'All right. What about the menu?'

Paxton sighed, frowning dubiously at it. 'I don't know. I mean, this doesn't have a special connection to anybody. I might as well try analysing a train timetable.'

'This isn't just any menu. Take a closer look.'

Paxton peered at it, wondering what Stirling was getting at. Then he saw it: POLICEMAN'S SPECIAL.

His head shot up. Beside him, he saw Lena's do the same thing. 'The *killer* did this?' she said.

'Holds us in great esteem, doesn't he?'

'You've got to admire a man who thinks killing people is normal, and the height of comic genius is a pizza with a funny name.' Paxton shook his head. 'I thought *I* was fucked up.'

'This guy makes Ray Gardner look like Eddie Murphy.'

Paxton looked at the typed message again and picked it up. He almost let go. The warnings came as soon as his fingers touched the paper, battering his brain and howling in his ears, voices jangling and overlapping as they tried to be heard. He blinked, trying to block off his mind. The pain in his head was so intense he almost blacked out.

After two seconds he couldn't hold it any longer. He dropped the paper back on the table, unconsciously wiping his fingers on his trousers. He felt beads of sweat standing on his lip.

'Are you all right, James?' Lena looked pale, rubbing his shoulder.

'This is your killer, all right.' Paxton exhaled, giving his head a small shake. 'That wasn't pleasant. I heard them. All the women's voices. I felt him too. The guy's so far gone he doesn't realise he's evil. He doesn't see anything wrong with what he's doing. He's like a Masked Avenger type — somewhere, somehow, a woman did him wrong, and now women like her are evil. He's *angry*.'

'Anything specific? His car?'

'Nothing like that. I don't get pictures, remember.'

'What about his name?'

Paxton looked up at him. 'You're positive Cristiana's right about this, aren't you?'

'Two days ago — no. But now . . .'

'You don't think she could be wrong?'

'Where are you getting this information from, James?' Stirling's frustration had finally come to the surface.

'It's just — *there*. I just know.'

'Just like you knew that bloke you beat up was a killer last time?'

'Hey, *I* did that, not James. And that prick deserved it.' Lena had her arms folded, glaring at Stirling. 'I thought you were grateful! You wouldn't have found the killer if it wasn't for James.' She raised her eyebrows coldly. 'And I'd be dead.'

Stirling winced. Still he ploughed on. 'But it shows he's not always right, doesn't it? I know I'm not. I've been really impressed with some of the stuff you've told me, James. But can you tell me you're *one hundred per cent* certain that your own feelings aren't prejudicing you on this?'

'Well, no, you can never be one hundred per cent of anything.'

'And I was right about *you*. Despite Ray Gardner.'

'Yeees.'

'In fact, I'm willing to bet I'm right this time. Fifty bucks, James. This guy's our killer.'

Paxton raised his eyebrows. 'You take it personally, don't you?'

Everyone takes it personally. Anyone who says the latest dead body's just another file has got to be joking. Even Ray takes it personally. If he can't solve a case it's like . . . Well, you know what he's like.'

Paxton looked out the window.

'So what about Arthur? I thought you were after him.'

'I was.' Stirling's temporary buoyancy faded. 'But he's not a serial rapist.'

'You sure?'

Stirling looked at him, startled.

With perfect timing, the phone rang. Paxton groaned with frustration.

'I'm going to pull that damn thing out of the wall and smash it to death with a hammer . . .'

'Is that you, Brent? Sure, just a moment.'

Lena held it out to him. Paxton took it, immediately regretting his departure without a proper goodbye. He'd been meaning to call tonight.

'Hi, Brent.'

'Hi, James. How are you, all right?' Brent sounded cagey about something.

'I'm okay. Thanks. Sorry to walk out on you like that last night. It's not your fault, it's Tanya.'

'About that . . . I've been to Regan, and he's decided to swap restaurants. From next week he'll come over to Anubis, and Tanya'll handle The Chandlery. He said you're welcome back anytime — of all people, he knows she can be tough to deal with. And he'll handle all the unwanted visitors, he said.'

Paxton was struck dumb with surprise. 'Thanks. I thought you'd be glad to get rid of me after all that.'

'Nah. You're a good guy. We protect our own . . .' Brent cleared his throat. He seemed to be psyching himself up for something. 'Speaking of which. Don't suppose you're still friendly with the police?'

Paxton's eyes jumped to Stirling. 'Why? Has stuff been going missing?'

'No, no, nothing like that. But if you could bring one down here with you, I think it'd be a good idea. They might want to take a look at it.'

'Look at what? Are you at work already?'

'They called me in. Mel couldn't help taking a quick look.'

Paxton could feel his heart beating. 'What is it?'

'I think you'd better see for yourself.'

Chapter THIRTY

BRENT LOOKED STRANGE wearing colours. Paxton was used to seeing him in his uniform black. Today he wore a red polo shirt and faded blue shorts. Even stranger was the tight look to his features. If it wasn't on a sports field or in a bottle, Brent Palmer didn't give a damn. That wasn't true today.

'Brent, what's with all this secrecy? Just tell me what it is.'

'Come out the back.'

He was already leading the way without waiting for a response.

'Hey, this is my friend Andy Stirling,' said Paxton as they went. 'He's a detective. He was there when you rang, luckily.'

Brent turned to look at Stirling, and paused long enough to shake his hand. 'Hi. I've already touched it, sorry. Just as long as you don't think it was me who sent it.'

At the word '*sent*', Paxton saw Stirling's brow crease. Now, as well as alert, he looked positively grim. 'None of the staff have disappeared, have they?' he asked quickly.

'No, thank God.'

Paxton saw Brent send him a doubtful look. They reached the office door, and came across Mel standing guard, with her arms folded. Her hair had changed since Paxton last saw her, just two days before. It was now dark brown layered with crimson; the colours changed as often as Adam's girlfriends. Paxton expected her to let loose with a flood of description, but at one glance from Brent she said nothing, merely stepped aside to let them through, with a worried look at Paxton.

Then the door opened. All Paxton saw on the desk was a piece of paper, trying to fold itself back up. It looked like a letter.

'Is this it?'

'Yep,' said Brent.

Paxton realised he'd been holding his breath, and let it out. The dull cream of the office walls was almost shocking to the eye, his mind having prepared him for an overload of red. He went to take the letter, but Stirling held out an arm to prevent him.

'Uh, better not contaminate it any more. Just in case there's prints.' He took a pair of gloves out of a small kit he'd brought with him and put them on. Very, very gently he pressed the edges of the letter flat on the desk. Paxton read it over his shoulder.

It was laser-printed neatly on a sheet of plain white paper, in large bold letters that looked very familiar.

DEAR MR PAXTON,
HOW MUCH DO YOU REALLY LOVE YOUR
GIRLFRIEND? TO DEATH? BECAUSE HERE'S MY
PREDICTION: IF YOU DON'T STOP LOOKING FOR
ME, LENA BRADLEY WILL BE THE NEXT TO DIE.
BACK OFF, FREAK. I KNOW WHERE YOU WORK, I
KNOW WHERE YOU LIVE, AND I WILL GET HER IF
YOU DON'T STOP NOW.

I WILL DO WHAT I KNOW IS RIGHT — NOW YOU
DO WHAT YOU KNOW IS RIGHT.
???
P.S. HI, DETECTIVE STIRLING.

'I'll get him. I will so *get him*.' Shaking with anger, Paxton snatched the letter from Stirling's resisting hand.

'Careful, that's evidence!'

'The — ' Paxton couldn't speak, crushing the letter where his hand held it, pacing back and forth.

'We will get him, James. I promise you, we're close! But we're not going to convict if we don't have evidence. Give me the letter.' Stirling held out his hand. There was almost no colour in his cheeks. 'It probably doesn't have any prints on it, but we need to check.'

'What's going on? What's he doing back already? He's not due till next week.' Tanya was in the doorway of the office, giving Paxton a dirty look.

Paxton rounded on her with a speed that made her take a step back.

'Do you see?' He waved the letter in her startled face. 'Now the killer knows about me, and he's after Lena, all because of this fucking publicity! Do you see why I just wanted to be *left alone*?'

Brent broke the long silence, putting a hand on Paxton's shoulder. 'You don't know this is the killer, mate. This is probably some freak of nature who thinks he's funny. I'm sure it happens a lot, eh, um . . . ?' He looked at Stirling for back-up.

Stirling slowly shook his head, scowling. 'It might happen sometimes, but this is him. How else could he have known to put my name at the bottom? The DI's the one who's been on TV. And he's sent me these little notes before.' He looked at Paxton. 'Don't worry. Just sit tight. We'll catch him. All you need to do is keep yourself and Lena out of harm's way. All right?'

Paxton was quiet for a second. 'No. *I'm* gonna find this bastard.' He gave a small smile. 'What kind of dickhead killer sends something personal to a psychic? I can feel the desperation through the paper.' He tossed it back on the desk. 'He's pissing himself — and he should be.'

To himself, however, Paxton admitted the truth. He was even more terrified. It made it worse when Stirling got on the phone to CIB.

'Our killer posted a letter last night,' he said to whoever picked up. 'I want a warrant on Huia's house. If we can find the printer that did it . . . *What?* How?' He listened in appalled silence for a few moments, then shook his head angrily. 'Bloody bleeding-heart judges. Why do we even bother to do this job, Senior?'

He pressed the hang-up button with more force than was necessary. When he looked at Paxton, his mouth was a thin line. 'They let Huia go on bail. He managed to get a hot-shot lawyer who pointed out he's committed no crime but *trespass*.' He spat the word.

'So both men you think could be the murderer are roaming free.' Paxton said it as a statement. His skin felt cold.

'Don't worry, James. We'll get him.' Stirling sounded as if he was convincing himself.

PAXTON SAT LENA down and told her about the letter, which Stirling had carted off for testing.

She went very still, and her eyes looked large in her face. 'Do you believe him?'

Paxton knew she was remembering several horrible minutes alone with a serial killer, hearing him tell her all the things he was about to do to her as she sat there, helpless, and all the things he would do to her boyfriend — if her boyfriend ever came.

He held her face between his hands, trapping her eyes on his. 'I want you to go and stay with someone. Just to be safe. Who's got a spare room?'

She hesitated a split second. 'Mandy does.'

'Then ring her. Ask her. I'll stay here in case he comes.'

Lena took a long breath to compose herself before Mandy answered the phone. The conversation was brief and emotional, and full of apologies. Mandy promised to come round straight away.

Lena came to wrap her arms round Paxton's neck, and kissed him long and hard. 'I'm going to miss you.'

Paxton smelled the apple shampoo in her hair, and finally let her go. 'You'd better go and pack.'

When Mandy arrived, she didn't say a word. Paxton walked past her to her car with Lena's suitcase, taking a good look round at the street, peering into every property his eye could reach. He couldn't see anyone, but there was still that crawling feeling of being watched. Something was close. He could feel it.

'I'll see you soon. As soon as we catch him.' He gave Lena a parting kiss. 'Take care, all right?'

She squeezed his hand, looking scared. 'It's you he's got a grudge against. Be *careful*, won't you?'

'If he comes here, I'm calling the police.'

With a glance over her shoulder, Lena got into the passenger's seat.

'Thanks for taking her, Mandy. I appreciate it,' said Paxton seriously.

'Why don't you show your appreciation by pissing off back where you came from?' she said softly. She lowered her voice even further so Lena couldn't hear her. 'Why is she in danger, James?' Her tone was pure malice. 'If she gets killed, it's your fault.'

Paxton blinked, then leaned in closer, making eye contact. '*Go. Fuck. Yourself.*' He turned back to the house. 'No one else will.'

Lena was looking between them, wary and anxious. Mandy shot Paxton a look of hate and slammed her door. Paxton watched Lena's face in the window until it disappeared into the distance, then walked inside, feeling childish and angry. He went straight to the table, where the picture of Shannon Lawrence stared up at him. He took it to the sofa and sat, shutting his eyes tight.

THE FEELING OF being one step behind the tiger haunted Stirling as he drove to Parsifale. He was on its tail, but it could turn at any time, without warning. And a word from the staff could send them back to square one quicker than another dead body. Huia's name was too big a coincidence to pass up — even Paxton acknowledged that. But Paxton was right. He couldn't forget Arthur Wong just yet.

The Malaysian was nowhere to be seen — probably out the back, baking. Stirling felt a huge sense of relief. The freckled girl, Morgan, was helping today. She reached him first, her face solemn.

'Hello. Have you got any leads?'

'Maybe. Are you able to take a look at these pictures? Tell me if any of them comes into the shop?'

He spread out eight photos on an empty table, moving the sugar out of the way. He tried hard not to look too intense, so as not to scare her. Morgan frowned down at them, her face a picture of concentration. 'They all look so alike.'

'I know. We want to be absolutely sure we get the right person.'

She looked up at that, her eyes widening. 'You've got someone?'

Stirling held up a hand. 'Metaphorically speaking.'

She bent her head again, studying the faces even more closely, her nose almost touching the photos. At last she gave a rueful twist of her mouth. 'I'm really sorry, I don't recognise any of these people. But I only work Tuesdays, Fridays and Saturdays. I'm a student. You'd have to ask the others.'

Not letting his frustration show, Stirling glanced over at Nathan, who was making coffees. 'Are you able to swap with Nathan for a moment?'

Morgan looked relieved. 'Sure.'

The young man was just as eager to please. 'You must be getting close if you're showing us these. Good job. I'm just real pleased you don't think it was Arthur any more — honestly, if you really knew him, you'd know it couldn't have been him.'

'The question is, was it any of *these* men?'

Nathan looked down at them. He took a long time over it, silently comparing the differences between each one. Finally he straightened. 'I've definitely seen one of these guys in here a bit,' he said.

Stirling couldn't help his eyebrow twitching.

Nathan returned his gaze to the photos, frowning. 'I've been trying to work out which one. It could just be he hasn't shaved or something . . .' He pointed his finger at one of the eight. 'But I'd swear it was either this guy . . .' He looked up at Stirling again, nodding thoughtfully, then pointed to another. 'Either him or that one. It's a close call, but I've definitely seen him or someone very like him before, and recently too.'

'Thanks, Nathan. You've been a huge help.'

'Was I right? Is one of them the guy you're looking at?' Nathan's face was hopeful under its emo haircut.

'Can't tell you that, I'm afraid.' But Stirling couldn't help smiling at him. 'Arthur in?'

Nathan followed his glance to the back of the store. 'Sorry, he's out for a few minutes. I could get him to call you?'

'That's all right. Thanks again.'

Stirling gathered the photos into a neat pile and walked back towards his car, his heart sinking. The first photo could have been Huia's brother. The second was Huia himself. And everyone knew that rape was petty murder — they were both about power, both about something other than simple bloodlust. The knives stabbed through the women's hearts . . . any fifty-dollar shrink would draw parallels with the act of rape. And everyone knew rapists often graduated to the next level. Could he have been so wrong about the clues that screamed it was Arthur? Deep in thought, Stirling almost crashed into a couple on their way into the café. He apologised automatically, before he realised that it was Nielsen and Gardner, back for another cosy lunch. For someone supposed to be enjoying a bit on the side, Gardner didn't look happy. Stirling didn't let the recognition show, but as he passed them he felt something else drop in his stomach. Sheer hard determination. Whoever the killer was, he'd find out. Even if he had to call up the dead to do it.

Chapter THIRTY-ONE

'*MONTHS?* HALF THE women in the city will be dead by then!'

'Sorry, Andy,' said Kirkpatrick. 'That's bureaucracy for you. At least it's Malaysia and not China or Russia or something. Trying to get anything out of them is like bashing your head against a brick wall.'

Stirling kicked his toe rhythmically against the corner of Kirkpatrick's desk, full of pent-up frustration.

'So Interpol's basically a no-go then. I hope we'll have caught him by the time *they* come through.'

'That's the way to look at it. Whichever one it is. I'll see if we can't assign someone to look out for Lena, okay?' His expression cheered slightly, and he sat up straighter. 'But we have got one bit of good news. It's definitely not Stuart Fletcher. Believe it or not, his ex provided an alibi.'

'You're kidding.' In all the latest mess, Stirling had forgotten the banker.

'She came in to tell Willy. On the night Charlotte Hiscocks was killed, Fletcher was out of his mind drunk, trying to get his wife to take him back. That's the irony — she was actually on the point of calling us. Poor sod doesn't even remember.'

'And she's telling us *now*?'

'She knew he was a suspect, but she never thought it was serious. As soon as she found out, she rang to let him off the hook. She's still here, actually, giving John a statement.'

Stirling looked thoughtful. 'Guess she didn't hate him as much as she thought she did.'

As he was walking back down the corridor, he bumped into Rees.

'What are you doing at work so early? I thought you were supposed to be off till one.' Rees checked his watch.

'I got a letter.'

'Dobbing someone in?' Rees's eyebrows shot up.

'Not quite. It was from the killer.'

'What?'

'It was sent to James Paxton.' Stirling took a chair in front of one of the computers, swivelling it to face Rees. Despite all he suspected about Rees, he couldn't help hoping the big man would make him feel better, as he used to. 'He threatened James's girlfriend if he didn't stop helping us. Looks like he heard about *Cross* and got a bit spooked.'

Rees frowned at the carpet and folded his arms. 'He could always have been *watching*, and got inspired. It was right after that that Shannon was killed.' He looked up and saw Stirling's expression. 'Sorry to offend you — I'm just throwing ideas out there.'

'You don't think James predicted anything, do you?'

Rees smiled. 'I'm a typical detective, I guess. I need evidence.'

Stirling didn't smile back. 'I used to think the same way you did. But if you'd seen what I've seen, you'd believe him too. Whoever leaked his name to the press should know that it isn't a joke. It could get him or his girlfriend killed.'

Rees nodded, his smile gone.

'This guy isn't scared of us, or anyone. He's killing women right under our noses, with all this public scrutiny. For God's sake, he's still taking them out of the same café! And people keep *going* there . . .' Stirling realised his hands were clenched. He shook his head.

'Look on the bright side — they get killed off, future generations get smarter. Survival of the fittest.' Rees looked at him more closely. 'So has Paxton told you the name of the killer?'

Stirling hesitated.

'Hello, Andy. Don't you ever go home?'

Stirling had never been more pleased to see Ciaran Paynter. 'Morning, Ciaran,' he said, forcing himself to look easy. 'Yeah, I'm putting in overtime. I'm owed a holiday and I need to make up with my wife.'

'Shame,' said Paynter. 'Women just can't understand playing second string to a dead person.' He turned a chair backwards and sat on it, facing them. 'So who do *you* think the guy is, Andy? I'm thinking of starting a bet.'

'I'm starting to believe more in our mate Huia,' said Kirkpatrick, appearing behind them. 'Believe it or not, I just got a phone call. There's a woman in an interview room. Says she was raped and beaten by Huia — left for dead. A report was filed a few years back, but she never gave us his name.'

Stirling stopped slouching. 'So why'd she change her mind now?'

'The media.' Kirkpatrick gave a wry smile. 'It wasn't the TV networks or the papers this time. Someone who doesn't give a shit about suppression orders was at the courthouse when Huia was up for bail, and it ended up on a blog. And guess who decided to screw us over a bit more and blurt it all out on the radio?'

'That *arsehole* Webb,' said Rees.

Kirkpatrick nodded. 'His suspension lasted a long time, didn't it?'

'So you think it really is Huia?' Stirling asked.

'He's cocky enough. He won't even give us an alibi for any of the murders . . . This woman certainly thinks he's it. She's damn scared.'

'I can't believe they let the little shit go,' said Rees. 'Some people just never get what they deserve.' His tone was slightly off.

'What if it wasn't any of them?' asked Paynter suddenly. 'What if it wasn't even a man? Have you considered a lesbian who *identifies* herself as a man?'

Everyone looked startled.

'You're a worry, boy,' said Kirkpatrick.

'No, no, think about it. It makes sense. She's killing cheating women because another *woman* stole her partner. This is all about jealousy, right? A man would kill the guy who stole his girlfriend. But who else but a woman would go round blaming the *other woman*? I'm telling you.'

Rees smiled. 'It's a nice idea.'

'And a woman would be more likely to let another woman into the house,' said Kirkpatrick. 'It's plausible. They've all been afraid of a *man*.'

'*And* if she had kind of a gruff voice, she could easily be mistaken for a man on the phone . . .'

'For God's sake, Ciaran, stop fantasising about lesbians. You couldn't get a straight woman to sleep with you, let alone one who hates men.'

Gardner stood by the doorway, scowling. He looked in an even sourer mood than usual. 'Have you listened to the 111 call he gave us? If that's a woman, then I'm Claudia Schiffer.'

It had to be a first — Gardner had actually made Stirling feel better.

'What are *you* doing back here?' Rees asked. 'I thought you were supposed to steer clear of the place for a while.'

Gardner pulled over a wheely chair and sat down as if he were trying to hurt it. 'No point now. He potted us.'

'*What?* The killer?'

'Did you call her Sergeant in bed or something?' asked Paynter.

'Oh, very funny, Ciaran. As a matter of fact, he recognised me straight away. Bloody *waste* of time. I knew it.' He crossed his arms.

'Hi everyone.' Nielsen came in, dressed to the nines in a skirt and heels, her face defeated. 'Anyone want a bunch of roses?'

Stirling stared at her. 'Oh, tell me he didn't.' Nielsen nodded.

'There a note with them?'

'Sure was. How did it go, Ray? "Dear detectives, thanks for the laugh. Like the ring tone."'

Stirling remembered — 'The Pink Panther'.

Gardner smacked a desk with the flat of his hand, making them all jump. '*Bastard*. It had to be Huia. Who else would have recognised me?'

'Are you sure you didn't give it away somehow, Ray?' Paynter asked. 'I mean, no offence, but you're not exactly what I'd call the affectionate type.'

'Hey, don't blame *me*. Vicky was the one who was hamming it up. I felt like telling you sometimes, Vicky, but I couldn't exactly say anything in there, could I?'

Nielsen looked at him in disbelief. 'Maybe you just don't know what a woman in love looks like because you've never actually *seen* one.'

'I've pressed *your* button, haven't I?'

Stirling had never seen Nielsen lose her temper before. Her face flushed, and she slapped her palm down on the neighbouring desk. 'You could have leant over the table and told me whatever you liked, and it would have looked perfectly appropriate, but no, you just kept yabbering away with your opinions on everything else. No wonder the killer wasn't fooled — anyone would have thought you were in love with yourself!'

Gardner bared his teeth. 'Maybe I had to keep talking because you never said anything worth listening to the entire time! No wonder your husband works late.'

'Steady on, Ray,' said Kirkpatrick, with an anxious look at Nielsen.

She was pale now with rage. 'You're just a selfish, evil —'

'Here, here, what's all this about?' Woodward was standing in the doorway, his brow furrowed. 'I can hear you from my office.'

There was a moment's silence.

'Sorry, boss,' said Nielsen in a low voice, then hurried past him out the door.

Gardner looked a little ashamed.

Kirkpatrick sighed. 'I'll go see how she is.'

'It's all right, I'll go,' said Stirling. 'I want to talk to her.'

'What's happened?' asked Woodward, looking at the door.

'Graeme?'

Stirling saw the door to Interview Room Two swing shut. He gave two quick knocks to warn her, then, without waiting for an invitation, he pushed his way in. Nielsen was sitting in front of the blank screen, struggling to stop the tears rolling down. Stirling shut the door quietly behind him.

'He gets to everybody,' he said. 'You're just lucky you didn't punch him like I did.'

Nielsen wiped her eyes. 'I don't know why I'm letting it bother me. My kids are used to me working funny hours. But it was Damian's birthday yesterday and I couldn't even be hhh-ome . . .'

Stirling waited until the sobs quietened down. 'You're a great cop, Vicky. You've got so much more patience than I have.'

'It was all for *nothing*. That's what gets me.' She raised her red face from the desk. 'Usually I can handle Ray — we get on all right. I think he's a bit of a joke. But he wouldn't even let me read at his place, he just kept talking about the case. And then the flowers . . .' She shook her head.

'Sad when the only time we get flowers in our job, they're from a serial murderer.'

Nielsen actually smiled at that. Stirling was relieved.

'What did Brad say about you spending your evenings alone in an apartment with Ray?'

Nielsen rolled her eyes. 'He just laughed and kept texting me dirty suggestions.' She smiled, more easily, wiping her face. 'He's just busted a massive drug ring from Thailand, so he's in a great mood lately.'

Stirling felt a firework explode in his head. 'Hang on!' It was all he could do not to jump up and down. 'I'll bet Brad has a lot of contacts in Asia,' he said.

Nielsen gave him a quizzical look.

'Could he use his contacts in Malaysia to find out information on Arthur Wong?'

She narrowed her eyes, sitting up. 'I bet he could . . .' She looked at him sharply, now fully on the alert. 'You think he sent the flowers?'

'Let's find out, shall we?'

Chapter THIRTY-TWO

FOUR HOURS LATER, Stirling was in the Drugs corner of the floor, actually feeling sick with anticipation. Brad was standing next to his chair, with an expression that said he hadn't come up empty, and the desk in front of him was full of paper. He was reading a printout still warm from the machine.

'There was a complaint filed against Arthur by his wife. She says he killed her dog.'

Stirling's heart stopped. 'Did they say why?'

'There was a nasty separation, apparently. He caught her screwing around with the chef in their restaurant. It's all in the report.'

Stirling exchanged looks with Nielsen, who was on the other side of her desk. 'And there's our motive . . .' His insides were filling with champagne.

'*Did* he kill the dog?' asked Nielsen.

Brad shrugged, shaking his head. 'They never found it. I had them double check. But I *did* find out what happened to his wife — she's still alive.'

'Did they talk to her?' asked Stirling.

'Yep. She says he killed her dog because it loved her more than it loved him. Oh, and get this. She says when Arthur came across her and the chef, he got into a screaming match and threatened them both with a cleaver. She would have taken out a restraining order, but as the guilty party, and the wife, she wouldn't have had much luck.'

'Bloomin' heck,' said Nielsen. She shook her head. 'Polite little Arthur. He was so lovely to us at the café.'

'Ha. Wait till you listen to what his wife had to say: "The only reason I got away from him was because I hid. We didn't tell him where we were going. We went to Brunei for six months." The "we" is her and the chef — they're still together.' Brad read the next line, and smiled. 'And you're gonna owe me big for this, Vicky.'

'What?'

'Guess when they were married? Just under two weeks before Charlotte was killed.'

HOW COULD SOME people be so evil and look so normal? It never failed to give Nielsen the creeps. Her eyes fell on the photo on her desk, taken just this Christmas — the kids and Brad on a day at the beach. Parents knew nowadays, didn't they? The friendly youth group leader who took the kids out for ice cream, the old man who liked to feed the birds in the park, right by the swings. It could be anyone. Anyone.

Her mobile rang suddenly. Breathing deeply to clear her head, she reached for the phone in her bag.

'Hello, Vicky Nielsen.'

The voice was quiet, as if afraid of being overheard. 'Hello, is this the detective who was in Parsifale this morning?'

Nielsen's pulse took off. 'Yes.'

'Hey look, I don't want to scare you, but do you have children?'

Nielsen's eyes went back to the photo. He was reading her mind. 'Who is this, please?'

'Oh sorry, it's Nathan. I work at the café.'

'Oh, right. How did you know I was a detective?'

Nathan sounded surprised. 'My boss told me. Weren't we supposed to know? We get detectives through all the time.'

Wong told him. 'What's this about my kids?' Nielsen asked sharply.

Nathan's voice was nervous now. 'Well, I'm just here closing up. Arthur's gone down to the bank to make a deposit. I was looking for some more rubber bands in his office, and I saw these photos . . . I can't believe this . . .' She heard him breathe into the receiver. 'You're in them. You and that other detective you were with. I recognise both of you together. And there's some other pictures of kids clipped to them. Really little kids. Didn't you say once you had kids? I remember you buying some extra . . .'

Nielsen's chest was hurting. 'How many?'

'Kids? At least two.' He sounded scared by her tone. 'I can't tell if one of them is the same as the other one. They've both got blond hair, but they could be the same kid. Sorry.'

Nielsen could hear her own breaths through the phone now. 'When do you expect Arthur back?'

'He can't be more than five minutes away. I'd better get out of the office.' His panic was coming through. 'Shit. I can't believe this . . . Um, do you want to meet me somewhere? I can bring the photos.'

'If you can get them out safely, I'll meet you in ten minutes.'

'Okay. I mean, maybe they're nothing. I mean — *Arthur*. There's no way. This is stupid!'

'There's a school just by you, isn't there? How about I meet you there? Ten minutes.'

'All right.'

Nielsen thumbed the off button and almost ran to the door. As she strode through CIB, she kept an eye out for Stirling. This was his catch too. She sped up, jogging to the door of his office, but when she stuck her head round, he wasn't there. He'd be angry to miss this.

Nielsen made sure to get an unmarked from the garage, and tried not to speed too much as she drove. Between the heat and the nerves, her hands were sweating badly on the steering wheel. She switched on the air-con, directing it towards her face. Even the bottleneck felt twice as bad this afternoon. It seemed to take an hour just to get down Ponsonby Road. Nielsen heard herself humming, wired tighter than a mesh fence. At last the school crawled into view. She drove to the back, towards the reception area, and parked. The only people in sight were a couple of older kids bouncing a basketball.

She saw the movement just a split second before Nathan opened her door. She sucked in a startled breath.

'Hi,' he said, clambering in with a nervous smile. 'Sorry to scare you like that.'

'It's okay — we're both a bit keyed up at the moment.'

'Tell me about it.' He breathed out. 'Have you got back-up?'

'Not at this stage. I'm not making an arrest just yet. Why?'

'I just found some extra stuff in the safe I think you might want to take a look at. Necklaces and things. It's really starting to give me the creeps.'

Nielsen, trying not to show her excitement, spoke calmly. 'You did the right thing calling me, Nathan. You have nothing to be afraid of. Did you bring the photos?'

'I was just grabbing a bag to put them in when he came back. Sorry.' He looked a bit less frightened now. 'But luckily he's gone home. I was there when he locked up. I can let you back in with my key, and we can both take a look.'

'All right.'

He took a look out the window at the road. 'Might as well leave your car here. Walking'll be quicker.'

Nielsen set the pace, walking briskly on her short legs. Nathan had to trot to keep up.

'This feels so unreal,' he confessed.

She smiled at him vaguely. 'Wait until you're a cop. After you've been to a few drug labs and gang houses, normal life seems completely unreal.'

Parsifale was in sight now, locked up and dark, but in the still bright sunshine it didn't look like the headquarters for evil. Nathan took a set of keys out of his pocket. After motioning Nielsen inside, he looked around carefully, then shut the door behind them.

'Cloak and dagger stuff.' He gave her a sudden fleeting smile, clearly trying to brighten the mood. There was something vaguely creepy about a café after hours, its chair legs pointing to the ceiling on top of the tables, cases empty, the clink of cups and noise of chatter missing.

Nathan led the way into the office, snapping on the light. It was small and windowless, with the usual in and out trays, and invoices clipped together and pinned to a cork board on the wall. Much the same as Nielsen's own desk.

'The stuff's in the safe,' said Nathan.

Nielsen realised she was holding her breath as he wound the dial. The safe opened with a clank, and Nathan pushed open the thick metal door, crouching to take out an ordinary-looking cash box. He turned round and set it on the desk, then looked up at Nielsen.

'I wondered why he'd got another cash box lately. I thought it might have been a spare or something, and there wasn't any key. But then when I was looking through the drawer after finding those photos, I found one and tried it out.' He held up a little square silver key, and stuck it into the lock. 'Tell me if these look familiar.'

As he lifted the lid, Nielsen saw a necklace, just a plain curl of silver on a chain. Lying on top of it was a ring, set with a bright green stone that looked like peridot. A chunky pendant made of shell lay in one corner, with another, plainer ring beside it. Nathan stretched out a hand to take a closer look, but Nielsen quickly took hold of his arm.

'No, you don't want fingerprints on them. You might get rid of any other prints.'

Nathan quickly dropped his hand.

'There's no chance these could just be valuables that have been left behind?' But Nielsen knew how ridiculous that sounded. What was the likelihood of two people leaving rings behind, let alone two necklaces as well? She wasn't surprised when Nathan shook his head.

'No, the lost and found's all on that shelf.' He pointed and behind her Nielsen saw a sad collection of baby toys, a neatly folded cardigan and a couple of single earrings, next to a pair of designer sunglasses. No other jewellery.

'Now show me those photos.'

Nathan nodded. 'Wait here. I hid them in a paper bag behind the till.'

Nielsen looked at the jewellery again, especially the rings, remembering the indentation on Shannon Lawrence's finger. She slowly strolled around the open safe door, peering inside, trying to spot God knew what among the bags of change. The rings would be enough for a search warrant, and for a case to be brought, but she wanted more, especially because of the photos. The photos of her own damn kids. Damian had just turned three . . . Nielsen's fingers flexed. She wanted his cell locked so tightly the door rusted shut.

A soft footstep announced Nathan's return.

The safe door slammed shut on Nielsen's head just as she started to turn. Woozily, she registered the blinding pain at the same time as a hand cupped the back of her head and rammed it back into the door.

THE SOUND OF his mobile going off was a welcome respite from the acres of case notes and sod all. Gardner massaged his sore neck as he picked up.

'Sergeant Gardner . . .'

PAXTON WAS FLOATING in the darkness. Voices came from all around him, through his ear and straight into his mind.

I thought he was good . . . I knew his face.

It's okay, Alicia. It's okay. Just tell me what happened.

She didn't respond.

Alicia, I need you to help me. If you —

The sudden ringing made Paxton's head jerk up, so fast that he cricked his neck.

'Ooh! *Christ!*'

He sat for a few seconds, wincing, until the pain receded. He'd been sitting so long in the same position that his whole body hurt when he unfolded it. Alicia and the others were gone now.

It was Stirling. 'Hi James, how are you?'

'Exhausted. I haven't stopped to eat anything since breakfast.'

'Been trying to get hold of Shannon again?'

'Yeah. Not much luck with her, but I've kind of got bits of the others, through her. They're all linked now, you see. All tied to the same killer . . .' He rubbed the left side of his face.

'Did the name Arthur come up?'

'Pardon?'

'I just rang to tell you. He caught his ex-wife cheating with one of his staff. That's why he came here. It was getting too hot for him back home.'

'It all comes back to the café. That much I know. He's like an evil spirit over the place. But I can't tune him in.'

Stirling seemed to be thinking. 'He thinks he's doing some good, right? He thinks he's saving other men from being hurt by these cheating women. In his own mind, he's doing something truly . . . I don't know. Charitable. Does that make sense?'

'Yeah. I guess you could be right.'

'And someone saw a man take Arthur's ex's dog just a week or so after she moved in with her lover. It's never been seen since. But God it's annoying — we still don't have enough for a warrant.' Stirling sounded like he was speaking through gritted teeth. 'All we can do is keep an eye on him, and wait. By the way, I've spoken to my boss about the letter you got, and he's getting an officer to look after Lena, all right? I've given him her number.'

'Thanks, Andy.'

'Arthur or George, the guy's bloody dangerous, James. Just because he's mad doesn't mean he can't be clever. Keep your eyes open. If anything happens, give me a call.'

'I just wish there was something I could *do*!'

Stirling sounded tired. 'Yeah, I know.'

PAXTON DRIFTED AIMLESSLY over to the sink, washing the black ink off his hands, then opened the fridge. There was last night's leftover Chinese, which he put in the microwave. He sat at the table while it was heating,

308

aware of the absolute emptiness and stillness of the place. Now he knew how Lena felt, all by herself in the house. He felt a low-grade nausea. Just worry, or his growing awareness of the killer? Whatever the man did was poisoning his bloodstream. He was so close he was getting beneath Paxton's skin.

Paxton wondered how Lena was, but with Mandy there, he didn't dare to call. He hadn't realised how accustomed he'd become to having someone to talk to. He tried to watch TV, but it only half held his interest. He should have been working tonight. Without that, without Lena, and with this horrible feeling trying to get his attention, he didn't know what to do with himself. At midnight he still wasn't tired. The ringing of the phone wasn't a relief but a shock, sending Paxton jumping out of his skin. He looked at the clock on the stove as he picked up. 12:36.

'James! Thank God. Are you okay? Have you seen anything?' Lena's voice sounded breathless and frightened.

'No, why?'

'Please come over here, now. As soon as you can.'

'What's wrong?'

'He found me! He knows I'm here!'

'*What?*'

'He left me something. Please, just come.'

'Hang on.' Paxton was running out the front door like a shot when Glen, thinking it was a race, barrelled after him, barking.

'No! *Inside*, you stupid dog.'

309

He made a few sweeping movements to shoo the dog inside, but then reason took hold. He had no idea when he'd be back. Best to take Glen with him. He let the dog in the back seat, then reversed out of the drive with his foot almost flat to the floor.

All the lights were on when he got to Mandy's. A blue-shirted policeman was pacing near his patrol car at the foot of the driveway. Paxton could see the man's hackles rise as soon as he pulled up.

'What's going on?' Paxton called out. 'I just got a call from my girlfriend.'

The cop looked at him more closely than he should have. 'You're James Paxton, aren't you? I remember your voice. I saw you on TV.'

Paxton nodded. 'Yeah.'

'I'll still need some ID.'

Fighting back a sharp comment, Paxton quickly dug his wallet from his pocket, and showed him his New Zealand licence. 'Can you tell me what happened? Lena sounded —'

At that moment the door flew open, and she came down the drive to meet him. 'James!'

Before he could speak, she grabbed him by the hand and dragged him towards the house. 'Come and see this.'

When they reached the door, instead of taking him inside, she closed it. Immediately Paxton saw why. Nailed to the outside was a card, attached to a note. At first Paxton thought it was a playing card, then he saw the familiar figure. Death, on his pale horse.

'Oh for God's sake. How naff can you get?'

But his insides were iced with fear and rage. He read the note underneath it.

I SAW THE DETECTIVE AT YOUR HOUSE. CLIP CLOP, CLIP CLOP.

'He thinks he's so bloody clever!' Paxton sneered at the beckoning skeleton. 'And I'm not afraid of *him*.'

But it was a lie. Funny, he was used to the idea that the dead were watching, all the time. The thought that a living person was following them, wishing them ill, was far more frightening. The dead were just shadows; it was the living who held the guns and the knives.

He turned and frowned at the policeman, still at the end of the drive. 'What I don't understand is how he managed to get this here right under the cop's nose.'

'That's because he wasn't here when the killer showed up. He only came afterwards, and I had to yell out the window.'

'You're serious?'

Lena nodded. 'Apparently he was only told to drive past every half hour or so. Doing double duty.'

Paxton snorted in disgust. 'Fuck. If you were dead you'd get at least five, plus a photographer. Come on, I'd better get you out of here.'

Lena looked profoundly relieved. 'I thought you were going to say I should stay here.'

'Hell no.' Paxton thought quickly. 'What about Colin and Bev? And I'll get you some decent protection. Bring me your mobile.'

Fresh hope surfaced in Lena's eyes. 'I'll go and call Bev.' Somewhere in Paxton's wallet was the business card

Kirkpatrick had given him. Rather to his surprise, the mobile was answered after only two rings. The detective sounded tired but alert.

'Hello, Graeme. It's James Paxton here.'

Kirkpatrick seemed to throw off his tiredness at once. 'Hello. What can I do for you, James?'

'I don't know if you're aware of this, but my girlfriend received a death threat from your killer today.'

Kirkpatrick sounded oddly disappointed. 'Yes, I was aware of that. I sent a patrol car to check on the house.'

'I know, the man's here now. But unfortunately the killer beat him to it.'

The pleasantness entirely vanished from Kirkpatrick's voice, which was sharp as acid. 'What? Is she all right?'

'Yes. Luckily. He nailed a tarot card to the door. I'll let you guess which one. He also sent us a note saying he'd seen Andy Stirling round at Lena's house earlier.'

There was no reply for a few seconds, then Kirkpatrick spoke briskly. 'Right, James, I'll be sending round some more cars. I'll get someone to investigate where you are right now, but I also want to make sure you're safe. Do you want to stay where you are, or would you rather move? I'm quite happy to sort out a motel.'

'No, that's all right. We've got another place.' He gave Colin and Bev's address to Kirkpatrick.

'We'll be round there in fifteen minutes. Thanks for ringing.' There was an uncertain pause. 'Listen, there's something I think I should tell you. Two of our detectives haven't been seen since this afternoon. Not answering their phones, can't reach them on the radio. We're getting pretty worried.'

'Who?' asked Paxton, feeling sicker than ever.

'Ray Gardner and Vicky Nielsen. You've met them both, haven't you?'

'Yes,' said Paxton. He couldn't say anything more than that. His mind was spinning.

'If you have any ideas at all, we'd be very grateful,' said Kirkpatrick frankly. 'We haven't even had one of his usual tricks. No deliveries, nothing. I don't think anyone's gone home in the last twelve hours.'

'I'll do anything I can to help.'

'Just stay safe, for God's sake. Don't go anywhere, and make sure you've got people with you.'

Lena came out of the house with her bags and made for the car. Glen was sniffing at the few centimetres of air coming in through a rear window.

'What if he's still watching us now?' Lena asked, staring out at the darkness.

Paxton followed her gaze. 'Don't even think about it.' He didn't tell her the news.

Colin and Bev were waiting for them when they arrived and, to Paxton's relief, they didn't fuss. Seeing Lena was worn out, they put her straight to bed, and Paxton went with her after answering a few more of their questions. Colin insisted on sleeping on the sofa in the lounge downstairs, as an extra precaution. Lying in bed, Paxton could hear the knock on the door as the police arrived, and the murmur of several voices.

Anger, confusion and frustration all took their turn at keeping sleep away, and after at least half an hour of sweaty tossing and turning the bed was roasting. He knew what he would have to do in the morning. When sleep finally came, Paxton dreamed of fire.

Chapter THIRTY-THREE

COLIN DIDN'T WAKE from his guard post by the door when Paxton slipped past at six-thirty. Months ago he'd nicknamed Lena's godfather Cuddly Colin, and asleep the man really did look like an overgrown teddy bear. Glen opened an eye from his spot on the floor, but stayed where he was.

He swung by Lena's house, where he had a quick shower and changed into a clean shirt. Then he flicked through the phone book until he found what he wanted: Parsifale.

It was a good twenty-minute drive before he reached Ponsonby, and Paxton felt his blood pumping faster through his body as he turned onto Richmond Road. He kept his eyes on the shopfronts as he went past, then, between a tiny boutique and a Chinese restaurant, he saw it, with a painted wooden sign hanging underneath the awning. At this time of the morning, the tables were empty, and there was a space right outside. If Stirling was right, he was walking straight towards a psychopathic killer. Despite less than five hours' sleep, Paxton hadn't felt so awake in days. All the rubbish floating through his head would finally make sense – it had to.

The tension as he got out of the car was nightmarish. He was sweating almost as much as he had last night. He paused as he saw the door was ajar. Heart thumping harder than ever, he stepped inside, then stopped short, his eyes widening in shock.

'What are *you* doing here?' Stirling had just appeared from the back, looking as surprised, and exhausted, as he was.

The place was otherwise deserted. Paxton walked towards him, keeping his voice down. 'I was going to ask you the same thing. I thought you were looking for your friends.'

'He was. He thinks I have an underground cell or something.' A little Asian man stood stiffly behind Stirling's shoulder, his arms crossed, watching a young curly-headed detective sift through the drawers of the small office.

'A car last issued to Detective Sergeant Nielsen was found just over the road, sir. Care to explain that away?' Stirling's eyes bored hotly into the man's head.

Paxton stared. So this was Arthur Wong, Stirling's killer.

The other detective gave a sudden exclamation. 'Come and have a look at this, mate.'

Stirling turned quickly to the drawer his colleague held open, and Paxton followed. He could feel the waves coming off it before he even looked in. Sudden, violent death and sick anger poured from the box, though all it contained was a few small pieces of jewellery, and three mobiles.

'They're from the victims,' he whispered. He felt nothing but shock.

Coleman was peering harder at the mobiles, his brow creasing in a frown. 'Those are the same model we get.'

Stirling darted a glance at Arthur, and brought his own phone out of his pocket. A scared look suddenly came over Arthur's face, as he looked between Stirling and Coleman and the drawer. Stirling's thumb hit a button, and seconds later, the first few electronic bars of 'The Pink Panther' started up. Coleman almost dropped it.

Stirling abruptly flung his phone on the desk, with a look on his face that frightened Paxton. He wasn't sure how far the DC could go.

'You'll have to come with us,' he said to Arthur. 'You have the choice of locking up, or letting your staff mind the shop.'

Arthur stared at the box Coleman was holding, his face pale. '*What?* Where did those come from?'

Stirling put his face in Arthur's, shutting him up. He cut off each word with his teeth. 'My colleague's mobile is in that box. Where is she?'

Arthur stared back into his eyes, swallowing, but didn't say a word.

'*Where are they?*' Stirling screamed.

'Stop it!'

The three of them turned to look at Paxton, whose anger had suddenly returned tenfold.

'He's not your killer.'

'What?' Stirling looked at him like he was speaking in tongues. 'But you just said — '

'I know what I said. He's still not your killer.'

'For God's sake, James!'

'There's someone else.'

317

'He's got the motive, he's got the damn murder victims' items — you just said so!' Stirling was shouting again. '*I am not leaving here without arresting this man!*'

Paxton, so angry with Stirling he could have hit him, tried to hold back his frustration. 'Then you're letting the killer go free, and your colleagues are going to die.'

Behind Stirling, he saw Coleman looking at them both in surprise. Then Paxton saw him nod at someone behind him. Paxton turned, and saw the door to the kitchen was open. A young man with dark hair was peering round it, looking concerned by the noise. Their eyes met for a split second, and Paxton felt like he'd been doused in ice, and then in fire. For that one second, he felt dizzy, weak, nauseous. His own feet didn't even seem connected to the floor. Before he was able to speak, the young man had quietly disappeared again. Paxton turned slowly to Arthur.

'*Who was that?*'

The little man was watching him in shock. 'That was Nathan Carter. My employee.'

All three were once more giving him identical stares. Paxton tried to speak calmly, forcing himself not to run after him as fast as he could.

'That's him.'

'Who, *him*?' said Coleman.

Arthur was frowning at Paxton in astonishment. 'Who *are* you?'

'James Paxton. I'm a psychic.' Wasting no more words, he walked quickly towards the kitchen.

318

Arthur stared after him. 'Why would Nathan kill these women? He has no reason. He has a girlfriend.'

Paxton pushed open the door to the kitchen.

'Then where is he?'

In two steps Stirling was beside him, staring into the empty room. The rear fire escape hung open. The back lot beyond was empty, home only to two miniskips and not much else. Stirling was speechless. Paxton strode back inside to Arthur.

'When was the last time you saw his girlfriend?'

Arthur tried to think. 'It must have been several months ago. She's in London.' He looked horrified. 'He had a plane ticket.'

'He served all the dead women, didn't he?' Stirling demanded sharply.

Arthur nodded dumbly.

'We need his address.'

Arthur gave him a quick, scared look, then ran into the office, bringing out a printed list. Nathan's previous address was crossed out in pen, replaced by a new one.

Taking the list, Stirling ran out of the café, closely followed by Paxton and Coleman. Neither of the detectives complained when Paxton jumped in the back of the car. Coleman floored it, lights flashing, radioing a description of Nathan to Comms.

'*Fuck!*' said Stirling. 'How could I have missed him? I thought I had good instincts.'

'You can't see what doesn't want to be seen,' said Paxton. 'He kept that well hidden.'

'He never mentioned his girlfriend by name. I didn't even notice. He was so friendly. *Please, officers, how can I help you?*'

Stirling looked white. 'It's exactly why I went after Arthur,' he muttered.

Coleman's eyes were looking at Paxton's in the rear-view mirror. 'Do you think Vicky and Ray are still alive?' he asked softly.

Paxton's gaze met Stirling's as he craned his neck. Paxton didn't dare speak. He couldn't help thinking of the pale rider on his pale horse. *Clip clop* . . . Tick tock. The sick knowledge that Nathan had fled because he'd recognised Paxton was uppermost in his mind.

Stirling turned round again, staring out the windscreen. 'Don't even think it.'

Nathan was clever, and he was angry. And he was mad. Nothing could stop a man from killing, who wasn't afraid to die. *Dear God, let Lena be all right.*

The five-minute drive seemed to take half an hour. Nathan's house was a tiny, decrepit villa on a long driveway. It was a paint job in waiting, surrounded by rented clones. Stirling jumped out and took a look around, but the door was locked and there was no sign of anyone.

'What happens now?' asked Paxton. 'Do we wait?'

'No,' said Stirling after a moment.

'He knows we're onto him,' said Coleman. 'Where would he go?'

Paxton's stomach lurched.

'I'm going in there,' said Stirling suddenly. He twisted round to face Paxton. 'Hand me that torch, will you?'

Paxton dived to retrieve it from the floor, and got out, determined not to be left behind. He passed the torch to Stirling, who strode towards the house. Coleman jogged to catch up. Stirling jiggled the doorknob for half a second to make sure it was locked, then shrugged and paced right to the window. Grimacing, he lifted the torch and shattered the glass, smashing out all the shards until they could climb through.

Coleman was in like a flash. Paxton glanced at Stirling. 'After you.'

But when Paxton stepped inside, it felt empty. Coleman's yell, 'Anyone here?' made a sort of dull echo, flattened by curtains and carpet. Stirling was already going through the rooms, one by one, opening doors. He shook his head tersely as Paxton came up behind him. 'Can't see any sign of another person. It's like he lives here alone.'

'Makes you wonder what's happened to the girlfriend,' said Coleman.

Something was furiously shaking Paxton's brain, trying to get his attention. He wandered in circles, half seeing. He stared at the walls, the bare walls, which were no help. The bare walls . . .

'A studio,' he said.

Stirling and Coleman stared. Paxton looked back at them sharply.

'He's an artist. There's a studio somewhere.'

He didn't wait to ask himself how he knew, he just ran. As he got to the front step, he ran left, towards a bald square of concrete for an extra car, and a daisy-covered lawn. There was no sign of an outbuilding. Stirling stopped short behind him.

'Damn, nothing!'

'*Shit!*' said Coleman, his eyes widening. 'The other address!'

Stirling was already starting to run, Paxton and Coleman behind him. Paxton's nausea had returned full force. He closed his eyes and willed himself to breathe as Coleman violently flung the car round the corners. All at once Coleman swung into a driveway, his left hand jerking up the handbrake as his right fumbled at his seatbelt. It was an old weatherboard, white with a green trim, like so many others.

A car sat in the drive. Stirling felt the bonnet.

'Warm,' he said shortly.

Paxton beat him around the corner of the house, willing himself to see what he knew had to be there. And across the lawn, half grown over by trees against the back fence, there it sat. It was a large cottage, an old sleep-out really, its windows intact, sheets hung over the glass. All Paxton's nerves were standing on end.

'Nathan!' he called. 'Come out!'

At his back now, Stirling and Coleman stood in silence. A few seconds of absolute quiet passed, then suddenly there was a yell, then a scream, higher — a woman's. It too was cut off abruptly. The detectives didn't waste a glance, sprinting for the door at the side of the little

322

house. Stirling tried the knob, but it was locked. He looked at Coleman. 'Ready?'

Coleman was already taking two paces back. 'One, two, *three* . . .'

Under their combined weight the door imploded, and the detectives stumbled to regain their balance, almost tripping as they went bursting through. Paxton brought up the rear, half afraid of something he couldn't put into words. What he saw when he came through the door was bad enough. Empty frames leaned against one wall. An easel lay on its side near the window, at angles to a half-finished oil painting of a boat, a jagged hole smashed through its centre. A watercolour study was in tatters on the worktable beneath the window, tubes of paint and bottles of water scattered all over the surface.

Painted footprints, the tread of boots, led across the room to where Nathan stood beside Nielsen. She lay slowly curling up on the wooden floor, her mouth open in almost inaudible sobs, her blonde hair soaked by a pool of her own tears. She was bound hand and foot with thin, strong cord, the sort used for hanging mirrors and paintings. Gardner was beside her, blood all over his face, streaming from his nose. Nielsen had a purple bruise, almost black, down one cheek, and fresh paint marks down the sides of her loose old shirt, the same hazy blue as the paint on the floor, and on Nathan's boots.

Nathan's eyes, an intense blue, were fixed on the three other men. An open bottle of turpentine was squeezed in his bloodless knuckles, the fumes adding to Paxton's light headedness.

Coleman lurched forward. Nathan flung his arm out wide, dousing the front of Coleman's shirt and everything within a two-metre radius. Paxton instinctively ducked further out of range, but Stirling was closer. Splashes of solvent soaked through his pants and the hem of his shirt. Nathan's hand went into his pocket and brought out his lighter. He flicked it on.

All of them stood there as if painted into place. A living tableau, just. Nathan's gaze focused on Paxton.

'You saw it in me, didn't you? You looked straight through me and saw the truth. Man, I wish I was you.'

Stirling's eyes were on the lighter, which flickered off again. 'Put the lighter down, Nathan. Let's talk about this somewhere else, okay?'

The flame reappeared in Nathan's hand.

'No.'

'Nathan, just let them go. They're not the ones who hurt you.' Nielsen's raw red and purple face was turned up towards him, her voice clear.

Gardner too looked up, his mouth dripping blood. 'What happened to her, mate?'

'*Stop pretending you care!*' Nathan's boot struck the side of his ribs with a force that had all three onlookers starting out of their places. He whirled round ready to face them, the flame arcing in the air. His cheeks were glistening wet.

'She doesn't deserve your pity, the heartless fucking whore! She doesn't give a shit about anyone but herself!' Breathing hard, he looked back at Paxton. 'So unless you can control fire with your mind, I suggest you don't . . . fucking . . . move . . . again.'

Paxton didn't twitch a muscle, making the world just him and Nathan. 'Stephen King is meant to be a genius, my friend. This is just stupid. Are you going to let what one chick did mess up the rest of your life?'

He saw instantly he'd made a fatal error.

'What if that one chick damn well was your life?' Nathan wiped his eyes with the back of his left wrist, which was trembling. 'What if she took your life, and your house where you lived—' he waved at the room around them — 'and everything that made you happy, and just smashed it all to bits?' His chest was heaving. 'I saw her with him! She'd been doing him for months, laughing at me behind my back. The bitch! She told me she was scared of me, that she'd never loved me. Like I was *nothing. She smashed me into pieces with her own bare hands and walked away without a scar.'*

He kicked at Nielsen, roaring over her scream.

'Tell them what you did! Tell them what you did to me, you lying two-faced *bitch*!'

Tears ran freely down Nielsen's face. Her shoulders jerked as she tried to gulp down enough breath to speak between sobs.

'I . . . I . . . haven't done *anything* to you . . . I'm not her. Nathan, I'm not her.'

Paxton looked on, sickened.

'You're all the same!'

Paxton knew it was all over for Nathan Carter. And for anyone else he could take down with him.

Slowly Nathan bent over Nielsen's body, his gaze all the time fixed on the three men standing in front of him. Nielsen wriggled desperately back and forth, trying to roll out of the reach of the flame.

'*Nathan.*' Stirling tried to halt his progress with his eyes, but Nathan kept moving. Stirling whipped out his phone, dialling 111. Nathan made no move to stop him. Coleman shifted nervously on his feet, his voice stretched tight.

'Don't do this, mate. It's not worth it. You've been through enough.'

I saw that on a trailer for *The Bill*, Paxton thought, his mind beginning to separate itself from what it saw. This is all just a horrible cliché.

Nathan wasn't listening. Paxton wondered that the vapours hadn't caught already in the enclosed space. The flame was waving closer to Nielsen's turps-soaked shirt. Coleman was dancing on the balls of his feet. Stirling was clenching his fists as he shoved away his phone, then pulling at his hem, tempted . . . The flame was inches away. Riveting them all. Slowly descending . . .

Paxton flew forward. Startled, Nathan jerked away from Nielsen, towards him, his thumb still pressed on the striker. Paxton's T-shirt smouldered, then was smothered as his body met Nathan's. Paxton cried out at the searing pain in his abdomen as they went down. Beneath him Nathan tried to re-ignite the flame, to torch him off, reckless of the fire against his own skin. Paxton grabbed his wrist and beat it against the floor, trying to make him let go of the lighter. At the same time he noticed that the lighter rested right by Gardner's head. One small spark and he would blaze up like a Guy on the top of a bonfire. And they were rolling in the turps.

Stirling appeared in the corner of his eye, dragging Gardner and Nielsen to safety. Just as Paxton registered this, Nathan's thumb reconnected with the button. In the same instant, Coleman grabbed the lighter in his hand.

Flick.

And the world turned to flame.

Fire whooshed across the floor, following the path of the turpentine. Nathan was screaming beneath Paxton, as the shoulder lying in the turps went up. Flames shot from his thrashing head, brushing Coleman's trousers and eating up his body with terrifying speed. Coleman's voice mingled with Nathan's in an unholy discordant howling. The smell of burning flesh rose to Paxton's nostrils as he scrambled to his feet.

Released from his weight, Nathan leapt up and jumped onto the worktable, shattering the glass through the sheet as he dived through the window, his body still blazing.

Stirling seized Coleman's shoulders and threw him to the floor, forcibly rolling him over and over as Paxton grabbed for a bottle of mineral water from the table and twisted off the cap, pouring it all over his flaming clothes until it was empty. There was a sizzle as the water met the burning floorboards. The fire continued to throw smoke, strong with solvent and worse, into the air. Retching, Paxton glanced towards Nielsen and Gardner, near the doorway. He picked Nielsen up and carried her to the safety of the verge at the foot of the drive. Given the kicking Nathan had inflicted on her, it must have hurt, but she didn't make a sound. Still struggling to clear his lungs, gulping in breaths of untainted air, Paxton saw Stirling set Coleman on the soft grass beside her. Coleman's breathing was rapid and shallow, and his eyes were shut. It was almost a relief to turn his back on the sight and return to the house. Smoke was already issuing from the open door, and breathing it in had the same effect as a hand around Paxton's throat. The heat promptly turned his skin pink as he bent to get clear of the smoke and find Gardner.

'Here!'

Gardner's cry was followed by a series of coughs, and Paxton scuttled forward, almost tripping over the sergeant on the floor. He hoisted Gardner over his shoulder with a grunt, nearly fell over with the weight, but managed to keep his feet. As quickly as his legs would carry him, he made it outside, into the cooler air. He had to put Gardner down on the drive before he reached the others, fighting for breath.

He heard Stirling speaking softly to Coleman.

'You'll be all right, mate.'

Paxton took a few steps closer. 'Shit . . .'

Stirling had ripped Coleman's flaming shirt off, exposing a singed chest. To Paxton's unpractised eye the burns looked fairly minor, the brunt of the fire having been borne by the cotton fibres, but they were nevertheless bound to be painful. The worst would be Coleman's legs. Stirling hadn't dared remove the blackened fabric around them, for fear of what else he might strip away.

Stirling coughed, breathing as hard as Paxton, and turned his hands over slowly to gaze at them. The skin was scorched and blistered.

'Are *you* all right?' Paxton asked him quietly.

'I'll live.'

Stirling's eyes went back to Coleman, lying still on the grass. Nielsen too had rolled over to look, the tears drying on her face. The smell of roasted flesh reminded Paxton horribly of a Christmas ham. He closed his eyes, bending to suck in more air.

A metallic sound recaptured his attention, along with a grunt of pain. With excruciating delicacy, Stirling was extracting his keys from his pocket, teeth clenched in agony as he used his hands. Silently Paxton took over, opening the pocketknife attached to the keys. He knelt down in the grass beside Nielsen, holding the cords away from her skin as he sawed her free, then went to do the same for Gardner.

'Thanks,' Gardner muttered, very quiet.

He got slowly to his feet, his face furrowing in pain, and walked carefully over to Coleman. 'Bastard,' Paxton heard him say. *'Bastard.'*

The first fire engine arrived a minute later. Stirling went to brief them.

Paxton wasn't there to hear him, already round the side of the main house, in front of the burning studio. The leaves on the trees overhanging the roof had gone up in

329

flame, dry and crackling. But Paxton stood staring at only an empty lawn hazed over with smoke. Nathan was gone.

Chapter THIRTY-FOUR

AN EDDY OF warm air and citrus fragrance blew in the entrance of the burns unit at Middlemore. Lena let the door swing shut behind her, lost. She gazed uncertainly at the institutional stretch of lino and walls with many doors. Down the hall, Paxton stood to let her see him, and she came forward almost at a trot, wrapping her arms around him and pressing her face tightly into his chest. Paxton closed his eyes. Her voice was muffled and breathless.

'God, you smell of smoke! Are you really okay?'

Paxton ran curled fingers along her cheek. 'I'm fine.' He drew back a little and raised his shirt, exposing the small red burn on his stomach, glistening with salve. 'Won't even leave a scar.'

Lena pulled him closer again, kissing his cheek and resting her face against it for a long moment. Then she turned her head, seeing Stirling inside the room, legs dangling over the edge of his bed. She took in the bandaged hands resting in his lap and took a breath to speak, but Stirling forestalled her.

'Not bad going. Second holiday in six months.'

Lena exhaled slowly. 'You're in the wrong ward, Andy. Psychiatric's somewhere else.'

Paxton rubbed her shoulder, just as heels tapped hastily on the lino behind him. 'James, thank you so much for calling me. Where is he?'

Paxton barely had time to turn round before Nicola had swept past him, enveloping her husband in a hug.

'Hey, sweetheart.'

With his bandaged hands Stirling was unable to hug her properly back, but Paxton saw his eyes close tightly as she held him. Nicola eased back, gingerly touching his hands.

'How bad is it? Are you all right?'

Stirling gave a defeated laugh. 'Well, I'm a bit dopey at the moment — they've given me morphine.'

'He says he wants to go mountain climbing these holidays,' said Lena.

They all watched as he raised a swaddled hand and realised he couldn't separate the fingers. Stirling's face took on a pained expression. 'They say it's not too serious. I shouldn't even need grafts. It was all over pretty quickly. I'm not nearly as bad as Sean.'

They'd rushed Coleman straight into theatre. He was going to be there for a good six hours. Not only had he sustained burns to a large part of his body, but there was inhalation damage to his nasal passages from the heat. The team at the emergency department had told them he was lucky to be alive. Paxton found himself wondering.

THEY BROUGHT NATHAN Carter into the emergency department half an hour later, already hooked up to an IV, a pair of uniformed constables trailing behind. Stirling wasn't supposed to be down there, but that hadn't stopped him jumping in the lift as soon as he heard.

'Hey!' He called over one of the constables, careful to keep his hands hidden. 'Pete, what happened? We've just come from that fire.'

'Hello, Andy. Was that *you*? Christ, you were lucky to get out of there. Looked like the centre of hell.'

'I got out fast. Not as fast as him, though.' His eyes returned to Nathan, just at the moment the young man looked in their direction. He jerked a bit, forgetting himself, as he caught sight of Paxton waiting beside Stirling. Nathan gazed at him unfathomably for several seconds before turning his head away, his face twisting as if at a sudden chop of pain.

'How did you get him?' asked Stirling.

'Dogs. Found him in someone's yard, trying to cool his shoulder under a tap. It looked pretty bad. He was crying.' His partner waved at him, and he nodded back. 'Better go. But well done for finding him, Andy. Another big feather in your cap.' Smiling, the constable clapped Stirling on the shoulder and strode back to Nathan.

'Not *my* cap,' said Stirling.

Paxton looked grim. 'Don't be jealous of what I've got. You can shove that frigging feather any damn place you like.'

As Nathan was wheeled away, his eyes were drawn back to Paxton. Only the door shutting behind him broke the connection.

'My gran had an expression.' Paxton was still staring at the closed door. 'She called it the darkness looking back. You look into the eyes of an outwardly harmless, unremarkable human being and, suddenly, there's a monster at the controls.'

'You felt sorry for him too, didn't you?'

Paxton met Stirling's glance.

'Funny, isn't it?' he said quietly.

THE SMALL BARE room to which Paxton had been summoned was empty of patients, but full of visitors. Those who were sitting all stood as Paxton entered with Lena. All five faces were sombre.

Paxton nodded warily to the tallest of them, a face he'd seen once before. 'Hello.'

'Afternoon, Mr Paxton,' said Rees. 'Another lucky escape, I'm told. Must have a guardian angel. Or whatever.'

Paxton gave a weary smile. 'Something like that.'

Rees turned his head towards the silent man in the centre, dressed in blue, and as Paxton looked at him, he suddenly recognised the man from the TV. 'I might as well introduce you. This is Detective Inspector Woodward. The Senior you know . . .' Kirkpatrick nodded to him. 'And Vicky.'

Nielsen had found new clothes somewhere, and her wet hair smelled of shampoo. The bruise was still startling on her face, and she moved gingerly, but she shook Paxton's hand with a bright smile.

'And this is Detective Sergeant Paynter.'

'Hello.' Paxton glanced at Lena. She looked as puzzled as he felt by all the attention.

'Do you mind if my girlfriend stays?' he asked, unsure to whom to address his question.

Woodward answered him. 'Not at all. She's welcome to stay.' He gazed down at Lena, solemnly assessing. 'Miss Bradley, isn't it?'

'Lena.'

Woodward nodded. 'Nice to meet you.' He shook her hand and didn't automatically look back at Paxton, as others often did. 'How are you doing?'

'I won't say things are back to normal — they can't be. But I'm fine anyway. Thank you.'

'Fine is all you can ask for, most days. And there's nothing wrong with that.' The inspector returned her smile, showing all the lines on his tanned brown face. Then he did look at Paxton.

'We all wanted to come and thank you personally for what you did this afternoon. There's hardly a detective left in the office. Andy's told us all about it.' He extended his hand again, and the others followed suit.

Paxton hesitated a moment. 'Thank you.'

'And don't you *dare* feel guilty for anything that happened, all right? It would have been a lot worse if it weren't for you. We still wouldn't have caught him.'

The acuity of Woodward's gaze rattled him. Again Paxton was reminded, bizarrely, of his gran.

'We have a proposition for you,' said Kirkpatrick. 'How would you like to be a permanent on-call — *paid* — consultant for the police?'

Paxton blew out a breath as he tried to regain his composure. 'Well, I'll have to think about it . . .'

'Not for too long. We need you,' said Nielsen.

'That's a great idea,' Paynter said. 'Make a good reference for your CV. You could start your own TV show.'

'Would he be forced into any more situations like this one?'

335

They all turned to look. Lena's arms were folded. She focused on Woodward. 'This is the second time he's been to hospital in six months. Both times he's been bloody lucky. I don't want any strike three.'

Kirkpatrick smiled gently. 'Believe me, Lena, being a detective isn't — *usually* — a high-risk job. All the dangerous part is over: the crime's already happened and all you've got is a body. You've just got to do all the spadework.'

"Allo, 'allo, 'allo, what's all this then?' Heads turned as Stirling walked into the room. 'There's bloody cops in the hospital! I thought there were hygiene standards.'

'Is Sean out of theatre then?' Nielsen asked as Kirkpatrick rose to let Stirling have his seat.

'Cheers, Graeme.' Stirling sank into the chair, his false levity disappearing. 'Yeah, his family's in with him now. He's still doped up, though. Apparently it all went well, but they don't want him awake just yet. He's in for a nasty time.'

Woodward broke the silence.

'We've just been thanking Mr Paxton here for everything he did today. Whatever reservations anyone might have had in the past, I think we've all got to accept he did something pretty incredible.'

'So where's Ray Gardner?' Stirling asked, scowling. 'I don't see *him* lining up to shake James's hand. The man saved his life.'

'Ray's overseeing Carter's arrest,' said Kirkpatrick. 'I told him he should be resting. He's had two ribs broken and he's badly dehydrated.'

'Well, that's a few more inches for the *Herald*,' said Nielsen. 'Whoever's selling our stories.' She looked embarrassed. 'I thought it might have been Ray, actually.'

Kirkpatrick looked thoughtful. 'You know, that's what I don't get. How on earth did the *Herald* get hold of the idea that there was some homicidal lesbian on the loose? I mean, most of it was spot on, but that . . . Good grief! I'm wondering if it was that ghastly Austin woman. There's no *way* anyone attached to the inquiry would have said something like that.'

Stirling gave a sardonic grin, looking anywhere but at Rees. 'Come on, Senior. They're reporters. They made it up. Sales must have been flagging that week.'

'No, it's true!' Paynter's eyes were alight with amusement. '*I* should be so lucky in my retirement. Apart from her love triangle with the two old guys, Helen McCowan actually had a lesbian thing going on with some other woman. Ask Tony, that's exactly what happened!'

'No, Ciaran, that's just what I told you happened.'

Total silence fell. All eyes went from Rees to Ciaran Paynter. He was gazing at the big man, locked in a long, horrible stare. Stirling felt rocks begin to slide loose in his brain.

'I wasn't sure it was you,' said Rees. 'I just heard you asking a few questions, and I got curious. So I played my usual trick with suss reporters — feed 'em something dodgy, swear them to secrecy, and see if they can be trusted.'

Paynter was examining the wheelchair in one corner, meeting no one's eyes. He gave a dry-mouthed swallow.

Maybe it was just the pain relief, but Stirling's head seemed light.

Rees's face was, as ever, unreadable. 'I'm sorry, all of you . . . I should have said.'

His gaze met Stirling's. And suddenly Stirling understood. Rees wasn't a nark either.

Woodward came up quietly at Paynter's side. 'I think we should talk later.'

Chapter THIRTY-FIVE

PAXTON WAS VISITING Stirling when the tall figure of Rees came through the door, immediately taking up half the tiny room. He said hello to Paxton, and pulled another chair over to the bed.

'How are you, Andy?' he asked. 'I've got some more news. We found out how Nathan got their addresses. They ran a business card competition — put your card in the box and you could win a free coffee. All he had to do was match her surname with her after-hours number in the phone book.'

'It was that bloody easy?' cried Stirling incredulously.

'Believe it or not, we actually found the name Nathan in Charlotte's diary — for two days *after* she was killed. Nathan admitted he actually booked in a meeting with her, pretending to be buying a house, and found out her husband was away till Wednesday, and bang. Helen he just had to follow, of course, because she walked. Ooh, have you got chocolates?'

'Seeing as you lot bought them, you can have one I suppose. Greedy sod.'

'You'll get fat in that bed, eating chocolates all day,' said Paxton, his own cheek distended. He held out the box to Rees.

Rees took a chocolate, then nodded at Paxton. 'Still don't know how you did that.'

Paxton felt himself being scrutinised by someone who wouldn't be happy until he had the answer, but would let it slide anyway.

'Can you tell me what happened to the girlfriend?'

'I don't think she's dead,' said Paxton.

'She's not. She really is in London. And Nathan really did have tickets.'

No one said anything to that.

'She's still living with the guy she left him for. A fellow jobbing artist. He used to deliver for Hell Pizza.'

'But why did he kidnap Vicky and Ray?' Stirling asked. He frowned down at his sheets. 'He must have known it was a huge risk.'

'I've thought about that,' said Paxton. 'He liked the attention, didn't he? All those letters. He liked being smarter. When Huia showed up, it took the limelight off the café. He'd already set Arthur up for the fall. He had to do something desperate. Isn't that what they say? There's not much fun in being a serial-killing genius if no one knows who to admire.'

'Not to mention,' said Rees, 'that he'd run out of victims. Only a finite number of cheating women in any café. But by then he was so damn crazy he just couldn't stop.'

The next visit was from Arthur Wong. Stirling couldn't have been more surprised to see the little man there, hesitating outside the door to the ward, as if wishing to find him asleep. He looked ten years older and, above all, Stirling thought, as if he were grieving. He felt the guilt well up at the sight of him.

'I rang your mobile number, and your wife said you were here,' he said, standing awkwardly by Stirling's bed. 'When do you leave?'

'Tomorrow,' Stirling said. 'They were trying to save me a skin graft. We'll just have to see.' There was a long, awkward pause. 'I'm so sorry for treating you the way I did. I was so sure . . .'

'I don't blame you,' said Arthur. 'It must have seemed like it was me, even though what my wife said about me was lies. She was Muslim — she was afraid of her *own* family after her behaviour. Not me. I loved that dog.' His face was tired. He studied the white sheets in front of him, and shook his head. 'I still can't believe it. He was such a lovely boy. Like a son.'

Stirling couldn't get rid of his pressing sense of shame.

'You know he was trying to frame you? All that stuff with the menu, calling up Nielsen *and* Gardner to the café — he wanted everything to point to you.'

Wong merely sighed, shaking his head again.

'Well, I just hope all this hasn't hurt your business too much.'

'I'm not sure I want to stay in that business any more. It's not really my thing, to tell you the truth.'

'You're not going back to Malaysia?'

'No, no,' Wong said, waving a hand in disgust. 'There's nothing for me there anymore. I'm thinking of starting a pub.' A light came back into his eyes. 'An Irish pub. That's where all the money is.' He gave a cheeky grin. 'I think I'll call it O'Wong's.'

Epilogue

ANUBIS WAS POPULAR at the usual times, but for the past few nights they'd been in danger of breaching fire regulations. Everyone wanted a glimpse of the psychic who'd caught the killer. Tonight, being a Saturday, was even worse. Paxton put his head down and tried to blank it out.

'James! James! Have you seen this?' Mel flagged him down, shoving a piece of paper under his nose.

Paxton had to smile when he saw what it was — the cartoon that had appeared in that morning's *Herald*. He had to admit they'd really nailed Cristiana's features. She was portrayed as a crazy-haired fortune teller, sitting purse-lipped with arms folded at her desk, while the police stripped her room of everything from a box scrawled with OCCULT BOOKS: EVIDENCE to a squawking parrot in a cage. Leaning casually against her desk was an old-fashioned bobby in a helmet and a badge reading PC PAXTON, smirking and spinning a crystal ball on his finger. The caption was: *Didn't you see this coming?*

'I'm getting this blown up and framed,' he said, grinning.

'Oh my God, I can't believe I work with someone famous! Will you sign it for me?'

'*Sssssh!*' Paxton glanced round at the crowds, then stared at her, unsure whether to be amused or amazed. 'Not you too. Don't be stupid.'

'Do you think you could give me a reading sometime? I know you're busy, but . . .'

Paxton sighed. 'I don't know, Mel, I really don't know if I want to go down that path again. I've got so many letters at home I haven't even answered.'

'Oh come on, it's a gift. You should be proud of it.'

Adam passed them, carefully balancing yet another empty glass on his tray. He managed to nod in greeting without upsetting them. 'Don't go giving him an extra big head, eh, Mel? He's got nothing to fill it up with.'

'You should get yours done too, Adam,' Mel told him.

'Eh?'

'Don't you want to know if you'll finally get a decent woman in your life?'

'Ohhh, would you stop going on?' Adam took a good look at Paxton, and frowned. 'Nah,' he said eventually. 'I don't want to know my future. God'll sort it out.'

'Thank God for that.'

'Well, can't you at least tell me mine? *Please?*' Mel's expression was frighteningly sincere. Enough to make him hesitate.

Paxton looked at her for a long moment. Then he smiled.

'Waiting,' he said gently.

He reached over and tweaked the string of her apron. Then his eyes went inward, and he smiled wider. 'Sorry. But no tips.'

He walked back towards the bar, feeling Adam grin behind him.